KNITTING DEATH

Jean K. Tamer

KNITTING DEATH

JEAN K. TAMER

This is a work of fiction. Names, characters, places, and incidents either are the product of the author's imagination or are used fictitiously. Any resemblance to actual persons, living or dead, events, or locales is entirely coincidental.

Copyright © 2024 Aleksby Publishing

All right reserved. No part of this book may be reproduced or used in any manner without written permission of the copyright owner except for the use of quotations in a book review.

First eBook edition July 2024

First paperback edition July 2024

Book design by Aleksby Publishing

ISBN: 978-1-7381819-0-2

Published by Aleksby Publishing

Contact: admin@aleksby.com

KNITTING DEATH

Acknowledgment:

Copy editing by Janet Gyenes

JEAN K. TAMER

KNITTING DEATH

Contents

Prologue 9
1. Podcast & Herbal Tea 10
2. Ben & Jesse's Knits 15
3. After a Hard Day of Work 20
4. Wine & Knit 25
5. Drinks & Boys 32
6. Walk of Shame 36
7. Research@Cognit 39
8. Coucou & Sibling 48
9. Tea & Tensions 62
10. Inquiry & Chill 67
11. Out in LIC 74
12. Saturday Morning Road Trip 88
13. Dealing with the Real World 106
14. Last Day of Glory of an Office Princess 111
15. Upper West Side 126
16. Cognit After Dark 141
17. B&JKnits@Night 152
18. Anxiety & Chill 158
19. Apps & Data 178
20. Hacking & Chill 190
21. Brunchin' 200
22. Prying Open 232
23. Hudson Valley Ride 247
24. A Luxurious (but Comfy) Country House 252
25. Sheep & Wool (& Angry People) 255
26. Maze, Fire, Blood 258
27. Sabbath & Beyond 262
Epilogue 267

JEAN K. TAMER

Prologue

Blood ran fast through Arianna's head, over-pumped by her overexcited heart. She wanted to remain unheard, a challenging task when walking on a hardwood floor in high heels.

Someone was coming her way in the hall! She quickly fetched her iPhone from her purse and keyed her access code. If Arianna couldn't be discreet, she would at least try to show that she didn't care, that she belonged in the hall, that her presence there was legitimate.

"Hi, there!" said the stranger, a tall young man in a beige linen suit, as his path crossed hers.

Arianna lifted her eyes briefly, smiled a bit, and lowered her eyes back on her cell. Was the stranger suspicious? He looked more tipsy and flirtatious than suspicious—but what if he was putting on a show? What if he was onto her?

Arianna reached the end of the hall. Tall windows let the sunlight flood the house. To her right, the hall went toward one of the many staircases within the mansion; to her left was one of its multiple massive rooms.

Arianna glanced back; the strangers looked at her, waved, and disappeared toward the balcony where the guests chatted and laughed and drank mimosas.

Quickly, Arianna backed up and approached the second-to-last door to her right. She pushed down on the massive brass handle. It was unlocked. She glanced right and left: no one was in the hall.

Arianna pushed the door forward, just a tiny bit. "Hello? Hi?"

No answer.

She slipped inside and silently shut the door behind her.

Something caught her attention—something that moved. She looked right, froze, and held her breath. It was a young woman in her mid-twenties with auburn hair neatly pinned up on top of her head, wearing a silver necklace and a cream sweater dress, and holding a brown fabric bag: it was Arianna's own reflection. The mirror was so gigantic, it appeared that someone was standing at the other end of the room.

Arianna looked around. The bedroom was at least twice the size of her Brooklyn flat; searching through it would take some time, time she did not have. She tried to calm herself and look at the room methodically. Then she saw it: the laptop. The Spider Queen's laptop.

Arianna grabbed the computer and shoved it in her bag.

1. Podcast & Herbal Tea

Three weeks earlier

"I have two pairs of socks on my needles right now," said the woman on the screen. "For this one, I use a US size 2, or 2.75 millimeters. It has sweet, really nice details, as you can see. I wanted to stick to my one-pair-of-socks-at-a-time knit-way, but I couldn't help myself and began this new one. And now... for the first time in four weeks... Finished objects!"

KNITTING DEATH

Arianna watched the "The Yarny State" podcast as she knitted the Lizard Twins, a yellow and green striped socks pattern she had bought and downloaded the day before. Her right fingers pushed the bamboo needle through the wool rings that circled the other bamboo needle, the one her left hand manipulated. Each time the right needle went through between the wool and the left needle, Arianna's right hand looped the loose yarn around the needles' junction. And then she repeated the movement—she had made a new stitch. Arianna's bright green eyes moved between her MacBook's screen and her fingers as she worked.

"I bought the Zen triangular needles, which are really cool; I bought a set of US size one-and-a-half, or 2.5 millimeters. They really are triangular; they have three sides to them. They are mainly used to knit socks. So exciting!"

Arianna's pink nails moved around the lime green wool, against the background of her forest green Hitchhiker shawl (one of the first knitting projects she had completed, seven months before).

"I actually really like the look of this sock. All these things should equal a good finish for me. But I ended up stopping. The thing is, I have to prevent my hands for getting cramped—they don't hurt that much if I switch between small needles and large needles. So this is my third sock project; when I'm done with this one, I want to start the White Tigers socks. I have waaay more socks planned in my head. So... that's what's up next."

Arianna's dark-blondish, light-auburnish hair was disheveled. Hours one-before, it had been gloriously held just above the collar of her white cotton shirt, which rested above the dark gray jacket of her Nordstrom suit. Not anymore; the suit was suspended on a coat hanger inside the tiny wardrobe in her bedroom and the shirt lay at the bottom of the wardrobe, where it covered various types of shoes, along with other pieces of clothes that belong in a dirty laundry basket—something Arianna hadn't yet acquired.

The young woman whose voice came though the MacBook's speakers was Dorothy Lambert; she was twenty-seven years old (three years older than Arianna) and shot her weekly video from her knitting room on the second floor of her Pene, VA, home. Her podcast "The Yarny State," had broken the 1,000-viewer mark two weeks before.

Dorothy's head leaned forward when she finished a sentence. Her hair and dark brown eyes contrasted sharply against her pale white skin. Her lips were red and full and her nose angled out. She had on silver earrings that represented cat heads and wore a violet cotton shirt. That's all that was visible on the screen.

Arianna sat, crossed-legged, in her blue Ikea sofa bed (model "Balkarp") while her laptop rested on the coffee table, a model the Swedish multinational had named Lisabo. They were the only pieces of furniture in the living room, apart from an ancient wooden chair full of scratches and devoid of a brand name; it had been in the apartment when Arianna had moved in ten months before.

Not that there was much more space for anything else; the room was tiny. A futon, a coffee table, and a chair were enough to make the room full. The white walls were bare but for one large poster pinned on the wall above the futon. It was black-and-white except for the inscription "Grozny Pyknyc" on the top in bright red letters; below was the picture of two band members, one screaming in a microphone, the other one crouched forward, his long hair covering his guitar.

"Maybe, for a bit, I could add this... If you have any suggestion, please share; I would be grateful. Now... Dying! When I dyed this batch of bare wool with subtle colors last week, it looked grayish, not blue as intended. Clearly, I won't repeat this. They are sometimes more blue, sometimes more purple-ish... The camera doesn't really give the right color. But trust me: it looks gray, not blue! So... that's it for this week. As you know, I didn't have much time to knit and dye wool this week because this last weekend it was... my friend Kylie's wedding!"

Arianna stood up, put her knitting on the futon, and headed for the kitchen.

"For the venue, they chose this gorgeous chalet in the Adirondacks. The place is like a giant, three-story Swiss chalet, and her family had their own chalet right besides, and the groom's family had another chalet on the other side of the road. Me, I stayed in the 'friends' chalet,' which was located further away."

It took Arianna five steps to reach her destination, the countertop where her boiler and tea box sat. She put the boiler's electronic temperature selector at 175 degrees and pressed start. She then opened the tea box (originally the gift package for a bottle of wine whose name Arianna had forgotten; she found the wooden case very convenient to stash her tea) and grabbed the tiny brown bag of Kikuya, an organic Japanese sencha blended with rose petals, which she had picked at Bellocq in Greenpoint.

"Her robe was a-ma-zing!" Dorothy enthusiastically described, but Arianna had trouble hearing from the kitchen: the volume wasn't set very loud, so the podcast sound was drowned into the noise of the water heating in the boiler, as well as two cats having a very vocal argument in the alley behind the apartment block.

Arianna filled a tablespoon with the dry leaves and stuffed an empty tea bag in with it; she put the bag into her cup, a large blue coffee mug with "Cognit" written in bright green. The boiler hadn't reached 175 yet; she grabbed her iPhoneCc in her side pocket and glanced at her work emails: no news, good news. She switched to her Gmail account.

Nothing much, except a notice that her order for two 100% merino wool skeins had been processed by FleekDag, an online wool shop.

The boiler stopped upon reaching 175 degrees. Arianna poured the water in the mug and headed back to the living room. The podcast had just ended; YouTube was forty-six seconds away from starting another video, but Arianna pressed stop, went into her subscriptions page, and selected the latest episode of the "Lili Knits" podcast.

"Hi. Welcome to Lili Knits. This week I want to talk about this old sweater pattern my grandmother gave me. But... well, I... It's a bit hard..."

Something was odd. Lili was always energetic and happy and bubbly. But on this latest video she was not. She looked as if she was about to cry.

"I didn't really know Christina Bain, but... I've watched all of her podcast for the past two years or so, so..."

Lili was crying now. Arianna stared right at the screen. Her needles did not move; her hands, idle, just held the knitting project.

"So, I really want to send my sincere condolences to all of Christina's family and friends who are watching this podcast. I... We will miss her. It really is terrible what happened to her. This is not a... It really is hard to accept, to know this young woman died in such a way."

The video cut, most likely just before Lili broke down. It started back with Lili explaining, without much enthusiasm, a new mittens project she had begun for her niece, but Arianna wasn't listening anymore.

2. Ben & Jesse's Knits

The bright morning sun filled Ben & Jesse's Knits tea house through the two large front windows located on both sides of the store entrance.

KNITTING DEATH

The light bounced on the large mirror that hung on the left wall, which was made of unvarnished pine planks set vertically and painted white.

The walls were covered with sparse decoration: one abstract painting with lots of black and red (**Moreovert**, Ingrid Siage, 2010) and a collage (**Potted Porkupine**, Joshua Li, 1998) on the wall to the right of the door, each flanking a side of the mirror. On the left wall was the top of an old wood case with the words "The Gatling Furniture Co." written in washed-out ink and a pair of Japanese katana.

The shop's floor was divided in four quadrants: the two front ones, separated by the alley between the entrance door and the counter, were filled with small, circular bronze cast-iron conservatory tables with marble tops, all tiny and adorable, each surrounded with assorted chairs. The back-left quadrant was the service area, all enclosed behind display countertops; on the counter sat the cash register, three biscotti jars, and a massive, stainless steel Italian espresso machine topped with a large brass eagle. On the walls behind the counter were wooden shelves filled with one-gallon tins that held with all sorts of teas, each identified with handmade tags on the edge of the shelf planks below each tin.

The back-right quadrant's walls were built-in shelf cases filled with wool skeins of all colors, knitting needles, stitch markers, and other knitting accessories. The floor was furnished with two three-seat couches, a loveseat, and a single chair, all set in a circle around a large wooden coffee table.

Arianna sat cross-legged on one of the couches, knitting a purple leg warmer from a popular (and free) pattern by designer Jane Richmond. Beside her sat Diana, who took a sip from the white porcelain cup that held a large macchiato; on her knees was her knitting project, a simple scarf she made with yellow wool.

"It's three quarters done," Diana had remarked just a few minutes before, apropos the state of progress of her project. She wore dark blue fitted jeans, a black top, and a black jacket.

Melissa closed the circle. She had the second couch all to herself, and completed row after row of a Noro Stripped Scarf as she narrated to her friends her night out on the previous Thursday: "He rear-ended his Bugatti into the concrete pole that protected the gas intake beside the Prada store. He acted as if it didn't matter until he realized the car couldn't move anymore."

Melissa had long, silky black hair that she let loose; she was all smiles and giggles and never seemed to lose her tan. She was wearing a dark pink dress with a brown wool vest (the first non-sock project that she had completed, three weeks before); she had removed her boots and her pink socks rested on the horizontal bar under the coffee table.

She continued talking. "And then he went out of the car, looked at the damages, and came back to the driver's seat to make a call. As he waited for the answer, he looked at me and said: 'I think this is a rather expensive car.'"

Yuna, the new cafe employee, walked up beside Melissa, saluted the group, and began to remove the used dishes from the table, which was nearly entirely covered with project bags, wool skeins, spoons, cellphones (the latest iPhone, which belong to Melissa, Arianna's old iPhoneCC, and an antique BlackBerry that for some reason was provided by Diana's new employer), needles, plates, one tiny mint tin box used by Diana to store stitch markers, Arianna's chai latte, Melissa's large macchiato (made with 3.25% whole milk) and Diana's cafe au lait.

"Hi, guys!" said Yuna. "Are you done with these?" She pointed to the three superimposed plates that used to hold the organic Maine blueberry gluten-free muffins the girls had eaten before knitting. Diana confirmed the obvious; there wasn't much trace of any Maine blueberry gluten-free muffin on the plates anymore.

"So, how's the new job, Diana?" asked Yuna as she picked up the plates in her right hand.

"The new job is... great. How's your new job?"

"Oh, great! Well, I've been one of Audrey's martial arts students for over a year now, so I knew her already. Working in her cafe feels strange sometimes. This place is so cozy and warm when compared to our dojo!" Yuna left with the dirty plates.

"Where were we?" said Diana. "Oh—Melissa's date. Whose wealth is such that he struggles to evaluate whether a Bugatti is considered expensive or not?"

"Oh, I don't know about his wealth," said Melissa. "He works in a carpet store that belongs to his uncle."

Arianna dropped her knitting and massaged her right shoulder with her left hand; she had used that arm to prevent herself from falling when she had nearly lost her equilibrium while trying to perform the Dhanurasana position earlier in the morning at her yoga class. She reassured Melissa, who inquired about the gravity of the bruise, that it was minor, the pain would be gone by tomorrow, and dealing with a little shoulder ache was "much better than falling in front of the whole class, and also in front of the new teacher."

The attention of the group was diverted when Diana said, "Oh! Hi, Margaret," as a woman who had just entered the tea shop approached the sofa section.

"Hello, Margaret," echoed Melissa.

Arianna glanced to her right: the woman was probably in her mid-to-late fifties and had light-brown hair covered with a blue silk scarf. She wore elegant clothes: Arianna instantly noticed her Cinzia Rocca coat, Gianvito Rossi boots, and Tom Ford bag—all of them black. She had seen the woman before, most likely here in the shop, and had heard her name mentioned by her friends two or three times, but before that moment, she hadn't known that both belong to the same person.

"Will you join us?" asked Diana.

"I just came to grab one of those delicious mochas. I left my knitting attire at home this morning. Have a good day, everyone!"

Arianna lifted her arms and moved her shoulder left and right by rotating her waist. Alia, the nine-year-old daughter of their friend Heather, who sat at one of the tables not far from the couches, briefly lift her eyes from her homework to look at Arianna before plunging back into it, a pencil in her left hand, a tablet under the right, her eyes probably too close to the book opened below on the table. Alia was working on an assignment, or whatever nine-year-old kids were doing these days.

Heather was a much more advanced knitter than Arianna, Diana, and Melissa, who often asked for her help. She typically would sit with them, but right now she shared a latte with another acquaintance, an older woman who Arianna had never met.

"So, what about the British boy, then?" Diana asked Melissa.

"He's not British. He was visiting from Toronto."

"He told us he was British," said Diana.

"He said he was a subject of His Majesty."

"With a British accent! Well, with an accent that is not from Toronto. He's a fraud."

Melissa looked at her letter-sized pattern printout. "Guys? How do you do brioche?"

"It's rather complex. You should ask Heather to show you," said Arianna.

Diana dropped her knitting and grabbed her phone. After a few moments, still looking at the screen of her mobile, she said: "Poor girl. They found her dead in her bath; they say she killed herself. I watched her podcast. In the latest one, you could see that something was not right with her."

"Oh, I heard about her. I watched Lili's yesterday; she was very upset and shaken," said Arianna.

"I thought she had jumped out of the window," said Melissa.

"The article says they found her dead in her bath. No mention of jumping," said Diana.

Melissa picked up her phone and keyed its screen. "I was pretty sure the article mentioned a suicide by jumping, nothing about a bath... Here we go: 'Marianna Burrow, twenty-six, died Thursday morning after falling from one of the upper floors of the Manhattan apartment building where she lived.' Look at the picture... Do you recognize her? She does the 'Purrow' podcast. Well, she did the 'Purrow' podcast."

Diana abruptly grabbed Melissa's phone. "What... Marianna!?" she said. Her eyes opened wide and her fingers covered her mouth.

Arianna looked over Melissa's shoulder; she recognized the face on Melissa's phone. She had watched Marianna's podcast numerous times. And now she was dead. The second knitting podcaster who was dead.

3. After a Hard Day of Work

Arianna departed Bedford Avenue station. As she climbed the exit stairs, she opened her umbrella to shield herself from the cold September rain. She came out on North Seventh Street, walked a few steps on Bedford Avenue, and shut the umbrella just a few seconds later when she reached the door of Anna Maria Pizza. Arianna went in, ordered the hot eggplant hero sandwich, and answered emails on her phone as she waited for her food.

One email was problematic: she was supposed to design the corporate brochure for a farm equipment company, and Don, the project leader, asked for her first draft of the brochure for the next morning. Arianna, however, did not have the input required to even begin the work. The analyst tasked with supplying the necessary information had gone AWOL for the past two days—but the project leader wanted the draft anyway.

Arianna bit the nail of her left thumb as the right one typed words on the touchscreen, then erased them and then typed some more and then erased them again. Then her order was ready, so she picked up the white plastic bag that contained her dinner with the bill tacked to it and shoved her phone in her coat pocket. She paid, exited the restaurant, and again opened her umbrella above her head.

Arianna's boots hit the concrete sidewalk hard on each step she made. She was exhausted, angry (at Don, the farm equipment company brochure project leader), frustrated (because she would not be able to perform her task well), and cold. "You would've killed for this job," she muttered between her clenched teeth to calm herself.

KNITTING DEATH

She thought of the day the previous summer when she had answered her cellphone, and the lady from HR had told her that she had been selected for one of the six entry-level positions at the New York City office of Cognit, the super-cool new professional services firm that was all over the place in the business press. The scream of joy she had let out just after she had hung up, the celebratory BBQ in her parent's backyard, the congratulations from her friends, the excitement when she had prepared her luggage—how far away it all seemed now.

She turned right on North Eighth Street, walked past five doors, and stopped in front of a new building; behind its large store window, children dressed in white kimonos—karate outfits—practiced two by two, one child holding a blue pad with both hands, the other one hitting it with a front kick. Audrey, their teacher (and Ben & Jesse's Knits owner), also wore an outfit (a black one, in her case); she explained something to one of the student pairs. Among the children was Alia, who somehow realized that Arianna was watching her. Alia turned toward the window, joined her hands in front of her chest, and bowed toward Arianna. Her left foot then left the ground, went up in the air, and as it came back down the right one went up and then crashed into the blue pad held by Alia's partner, a boy who was a bit taller than her.

That scene made Arianna smile, pretty much for the first time of the day. She continued on her way home, a bit less angry and less stressed, but still tired and hungry. She turned right on Driggs Avenue and entered the second door to her right and climbed the stairs—at home, at last! And before nine o'clock!

She dropped her brown laptop bag and boots on the hardwood floor and threw her wet coat and umbrella on the blue patio chair, right beside the door. She moved just a few tiny steps, enough to reach the tiny wardrobe, and undressed, shoving all her clothes at the bottom of it—and then pulled her white shirt from the pile—a stain! A coffee stain! A large brown coffee stain right beside one of the lower front buttons, right where the shirt would come out of her suit skirt. How long had it been there?! Since her first coffee in the morning? Had everyone seen her hang around the Cognit offices with a coffee stain on her shirt?!

Arianna threw the shirt on the floor, disgusted, and grabbed her pajamas, her warm, comfortable, night-blue flannel pajamas printed with tiny yellow rubber ducks—she would feel good in them.

She heard her phone make the incoming message alert. It was still in her coat. She pulled the phone and entered her access code. It was a text message from Diana: "Come over; we're at Huckleberry!"

Huckleberry Bar was a fancy cocktail joint. Even if it had not been a mile away, even if it had not been located on the other side of the Brooklyn-Queens Expressway, even if the evening had not been cold and rainy, Arianna would probably have answered the same thing: "thnk you Diana but Ill skip for tonite."

So instead of joining Diana's booze-infused evening, Arianna finished putting on her flannel pajamas and turned on her laptop (her own personal laptop, not to be confused with the company's green iBook, which at the moment lay in its trendy brown bag with the green Cognit logo on it beside her damp raincoat) and selected her YouTube account. There were three new episodes of podcasts she subscribed to.

She clicked on "Knitting in Helsinki—episode 104." The familiar intro tune began, folksy, catchy, simple and joyful, for just ten seconds while gray water-colored patterns moved over the picture of a stack of yarns. The song made Arianna happy as her brain made the Pavlovian association between the melody and knitting and relaxing.

After the intro the familiar face of Mila, the show host, appeared. Mila smiled, opened her mouth, and as she said, "Hello, everyone!" with her

British accent, Arianna's phone rang again. So she clicked the "pause" button and checked her phone again. It was Melissa texting: "Watching Knitting in Helsinki ☐"

Arianna smiled and typed back: "Me too! I just started the podcast. You didn't want to go to Huckbry with Diana?"

Like Arianna, Melissa had recently scaled down the intensity of her nightlife.

Melissa: "Another time, not tonight. Tonite is knit nite. Ronnie and Fatima are gone; I have the whole apart for myself ☐"

Ronnie and Fatima were Melissa's roommates. Arianna knew their names and had vaguely caught a glimpse of Ronnie's silhouette when he crossed the hall from the bathroom to his room the one night she had picked up Melissa at her place. But that was it. Melissa shared an apartment with them, but they had no part in her social life.

Arianna's phone rang; it was Melissa. "I can't knit when I type," said Melissa's voice through the phone speakers. "Can you hear me? I've put you on the hands-free."

"Absolutely", said Arianna, "crystal clear. Are you still working on your vest?"

"It's more the vest that is working on me. I just realized that I made two mistakes in the shoulder pattern, so I have to frog seven rows."

"Don't give up, girl. Think about you wearing this vest when it will be finished, and how awesome and gorgeous you will look in it!"

"Diana just texted me. She's peer-pressuring me into going to Huckleberry. I'll try to text back without hanging up on you!"

Arianna also selected the speaker option and put the phone on the arm of the couch beside her. "Are you still there?" said Melissa's voice through the phone.

"I haven't moved an inch."

"Something weird happened yesterday. I had late dinner downtown with my colleague, and after we leave the restaurant, we walked toward the subway and then we passed in front of this place and guess who's inside? Diana. So I stop, look inside through the store window, and I'm about to knock on it to attract Diana's attention and then—bang! I freeze when I realize that Diana is with this old creepy dude. And it's not like a diner with a colleague or a client: she's flirting, and the guy is holding her hand over the table."

Arianna stopped knitting and moved her face close to the phone.

"I know it doesn't sound like that terrible when I explain it, but Arianna, I tell you, I literally froze out when I saw the guy and how Diana was behaving with him. He was creepy. Seeing him with Diana was creepier, and the situation just didn't make any sense. Why would Diana flirt with a creepy balding old guy with a dad bod?"

"I don't know, Melissa. You should ask her, not me!"

"I know but... I feel bad. I don't want to embarrass her."

"Okay... It's that bad?"

"It's worse! It didn't feel right, it didn't make sense, and I felt sick just watching the scene."

"There must be an explanation... I don't know what to say, Melissa. Diana is a close friend, but we don't know everything about her. I've been hanging out with you guys for what—a year? And back then Diana and you just had met."

"Yeah, I know. It feels as if I've known you guys for, like, forever but you're right. It was a few months before Phil and I broke up, which was in November, so... it's been less than a year actually!"

The signal for an incoming call appeared on Arianna's phone. It was Don, the manager responsible for the farm equipment brochure project.

"Damn! I got to take this!" said Arianna.

4. Wine & Knit

Arianna grabbed her wine cup and brought it to her lips while glancing at the 8.5-by-11 sheet onto which her leg warmer pattern was printed. A half-finished indigo alpaca leg warmer sat on the fabric of her skirt between her legs.

Knit four ... The thread rose slowly from the yarn ball, which sat on the chair right beside her right thigh toward the junction of the two needles. Knit fi, yarn over, knit two together, yarn over... A sip of Californian Chardonnay.

Come next winter, Arianna's legs would be warm.

Knit four, yarn over, knit two together, yarn over, knit five, knit two together.

Sitting beside Arianna, Diana connected the extremity of a size 4 carbon needle to a cable as she explained to Heather the virtues of bamboo needles; Heather listened while she focused on her winter hat project. Right next to her on the couch, Melissa held a blue skein close to her face, her eyes focused on a knot she desperately tried to untangle, a struggle that had raged for nearly ten minutes.

Behind the couch where Heather and Melissa sat was the old, tall, naked, glorious brick wall that made the western side of Heather's penthouse a relic of New York's industrial past that had survived the building's transition from manufacturing to luxury housing. It is way easier to tear down everything and build from scratch, but authenticity was a sought-after commodity—so the wall still stood.

"Take your right needle and insert this end through the front of the stitch... You have to make an X with the needles. Your working needle should be on top," said Heather, explaining to Diana how to fix a dropped stitch.

"Pinch the needles together... yes, like this... and wrap the yarn around your working needle... yep, like this."

Arianna felt good at the moment. Her back ached because of crunches she had done at the gym earlier, but her third glass of wine subdued the pain, as did the endorphins released by the exercise. And it was Thursday, the week was nearly over so, yes, Arianna did feel good.

"Go over the top... around the back... in between the needles, like this..."

Arianna stood up. She left the group and her leg warmer project behind to go to the bathroom, the most post-industrial room of it all: it had cooper pipes that flew from the granite-tiled floor straight under the sink, and also under the bath, an immaculately white quadruped beast that proudly stood on its four legs under the room's glass-block window.

After flushing, while she washed her hands, Arianna saw her reflection in the mirror. Oh, that look: "My IQ drops but my happiness soars."

She walked back to the living room. Diana and Heather's hands were no longer busied with their knitting; instead, they held their glasses.

"We never knit in your loft anymore," complained Melissa to Heather as she completed stitches on her vest (the tricky knot had been subdued), her legs crossed on the couch. "We always end up at B&JK" (Bee-and-jay-kay, as in Ben & Jesse's Knits).

"It's so true," said Diana, "we used to come over here aaaall the time!" (It was actually only the fourth time Diana had set foot inside the 7,000-square-foot loft, as far as Arianna knew).

"Having B&JK around is great," said Heather.

"Yeah, you're not stuck with us three crashing your place every Thursday," Melissa said before Heather could add anything else.

"Oh, I loooove having you guys here. Brian loves it, too; he can spend his Thursday night as he pleases."

Brian was Heather's husband; Arianna had seen him twice, and both times he was inside his car so she hadn't seen much.

"To Heather, our gracious host!" shouted Diana while raising her glass.

Melissa put her knitting aside on the couch and grabbed her cup to join the toast; Arianna gripped hers on the tiny table and walked toward the center to toast the others.

"Guys, you'll make me blush. Thank you!" said Heather as her glass clinked.

"You are right, though, Heather," said Melissa. "Ben & Jesse's Knits really is the most awesome coffee shop ever. Audrey is so helpful, nice, and impressive... and calm. And her calmness is... calming? Yet, when you look at her, while she's in her dojo, when she wears her karate outfit and gets into martial arts mode, it's as if she were another person; she performs those complicated moves and katas and acrobatics with such speed and strength and ease. She is so agile and athletic... and she must be a good teacher too; Alia's karate has progressed so fast! She's been there for what—a year? Right?"

"I can't argue with that," said Heather, "Alia is really into this karate thing. She is very dedicated and takes it very seriously. She definitely is performing. But to tell the truth... I worry."

Arianna (who had gone back to her knitting) lifted her eyes from her alpaca leg warmers and looked at Heather, puzzled about what she had just said.

"What do you worry about?" asked Melissa who, by the tone of her voice, was rather incredulous (like Arianna).

Alia was nice, polite, dedicated to her karate and schoolwork. It apparently was not the case before she took the karate classes; Heather had mentioned a few times that she had been getting into quite a lot of trouble in school and had been prone to throwing temper tantrums at home.

"These martial art classes are very demanding," said Heather, looking down at the coffee table in front of her. "Alia had some behavior issues before, it's true, but now she is... so serious."

"And you think she is too serious? That she stresses too much with her studies and martial arts?" asked Melissa.

"I don't know... Maybe. I can't really explain it; it's an impression that I get," said Heather. "She definitely improved her grades and general behavior. But at the same time, I feel like she becomes someone different. Sometimes I'm not sure I recognize my little girl anymore... She's growing up so fast. She tries to act like an adult and it scares me."

"She hides something," said Diana.

"Alia hides something?" asked Arianna.

"No. Audrey. Audrey hides something," replied Diana.

"Maybe she acts seriously," said Arianna, "but it's better than being an adult who tries to act like a little girl, like the new barista."

"Yuna? She has her style, but she gives good service," said Heather.

"She always asks questions about my work," said Diana. "What's the point of being a hippie if you bother yourself with law and boring business stuff?"

Arianna felt bad; she just had bitched about Yuna in front of everyone. But then, she had feared the conversation was heading into awkward territory.

"Yeah," said Melissa, "me too; I'd like to work in a knitting cafe in Williamsburg and spend the winter bartending in a ski station in Colorado, and then go to Australia pick fruit, and never ever would I ask a girl about her job once I knew she did corporate law like you, or—" Melissa turned toward Arianna, looked at her for a moment without saying anything, her index finger pointing ahead. Or whatever it is you are doing at this place where you work."

This made Diana laugh. "Oh! come on, Melissa!" she said. "Arianna works at Cognit; it's like the coolest professional service firm in the whole world!"

"Well, if I were a hippie like Yuna, I wouldn't ask questions about Arianna's... professional servicing." Melissa's four glasses of wine began to affect her speech.

"She doesn't, actually," corrected Arianna. "She only asks you guys, never me."

"She kinda asked me," said Melissa, "employment-related-wise... like once or twice. Nothing too insistent."

"She can be insistent, trust me," said Diana.

"In Yuna's defense, you guys have impressive careers," said Heather. "It's quite interesting to hear about what you do. Maybe she didn't have the chance to pursue higher studies. It's not that I regret the choice I made to be a full-time mom, but sometimes I wish I was doing something where I can challenge myself, develop myself..."

"You take my job, and I take Alia and the house," said Melissa. "You and Brian can move in my apartment with my roommates!"

"No! No! No!" shouted Arianna, "Heather and Brian move into my flat, and I move here with Alia. It's a much better deal; my apartment might be super-tiny, but there are no weird roommates, and no weird roommate's lizard!"

"It's not a lizard, it's an iguana!" protested Melissa, who now keyed her phone as she talked.

"Anyway, don't overemphasize the career thing," said Diana, "We don't do it because it's interesting. It's tedious and boring, most of it."

Arianna was slightly taken aback by Diana's affirmation. First, she feared Diana was edging on the condescending side as she painted an overly dark picture of the professional world; also, she looked straight ahead at no one in particular, a sad expression on her face.

Arianna: "Well, it still is better than cleaning rooms or nailing two-by-fours... but it's not better than knitting!"

Heather: "Nothing is! I'm so happy I met you guys! I didn't know anyone who knitted before."

Again, Arianna was relieved to have changed the subject of the conversation.

Diana: "Melissa, could you please tell me what is going on in your cell that is soooo much more important and interesting than us?"

Indeed, Melissa's phone hadn't been further than six inches from her nose for the past five minutes or so.

Melissa: "It's your friend, Mike. He wants us to join them."

Diana: "Mike? Josh's friend? Since when do you talk to him?"

Heather: "Mike and Josh? Those two are lovely. You still talk to them?"

Diana: "It's been a while, but it looks like Melissa made sure we wouldn't lose contact..."

Heather: "They're the one who invited us to this tech party, right?"

Diana: "Yes, we went to the release party for their app."

Heather: "Oh, the Minuit app; I remember. That was a fun evening!"

Diana: "It was. Actually, the launch party was much more successful than the app itself."

Melissa: "You mean the app that finds exclusive events and secret parties? That was them?"

Diana: "The app that was **supposed** to find exclusive events and secret parties. Yes, that was them. Anyway, this is knitting night, and I don't feel like going back downtown to meet them, as cute as those two are."

Arianna: "I am with Diana on this one. Tonight is knitting night."

"No one is talking about going to Manhattan. They're, like, just a few blocks away," said Melissa, still glued to the screen of her device. She then showed its screen to Arianna; on display was a picture of two young men. The girls had not exaggerated; both were exceptionally good-looking.

"They're so cute!" exclaimed Heather. "Where are they going?"

"Come on, guys!" protested Diana, "You're not seriously proposing that we go out, like, now?"

"Nobody said we'd have to move to meet them," said Heather, "Tell them we'll meet them at the pub downstairs!"

5. Drinks & Boys

Heather twisted the auburn curl of her hair with her the fingers on her right hand while the left ones were (still) busy holding her glass of wine. Her eyes, big and bright, focused on Mike (or was it Josh?), who gesticulated much as he enthusiastically narrated something to her. At the same moment, Diana detailed to Melissa a weekend she had planned when some of her old college friends would visit her (and benefit from free accommodations in NYC, even if the free accommodation in this case were an old Ikea futon) in a month or so.

The other boy (the one called Josh?) intervened and said something about a band that was playing on that very weekend: Green Life, or Grant Life, or maybe Greenlice was the name of the band. Diana nodded and looked back at Melissa and continued her story. Diana was playing distant, borderline uninterested. Yet Mike-or-Josh-or-whoever was, specifically, totally Diana's type and, generally speaking, just gorgeous: tall, lean, olive-tanned with an abundant light-brown afro and even lighter brown eyes. She would not have been surprised to learn that he was modeling, which would also be a logical explanation for his tight designer jeans jacket and pants and Baker Black shoes.

Arianna caught the other boy glancing at her while he took a sip from his Brooklyn Lager—and not for the first time tonight. His name was Nicolas, Arianna remembered, as he looked very much like her high-school friend Nick, a more laid-back, smiling and bubbly version of Nick, especially after this last one had turned into depression-and-drama-Nick just before college.

Arianna also took a sip and looked back at Heather, who laughed out loud with her new companion, the two of them facing each other on adjacent stools at the bar. Her hand wasn't twitching her curls anymore but rested on his torso; there was very little space left between them. Josh-or-Mike leaned down and whispered something in her ear; her mouth made a silent O for a moment before letting out loud laughs again.

Diana now chatted with The-Other-Guy-Who-Looks-Like-a-Model; she talked about a guy who had been found on the banks of the Hudson River, entirely naked but with a briefcase full of heroin cuffed to his left wrist.

Arianna had no idea what Diana was talking about, but the gruesome story reminded her of the dead podcasters. "Don't you think it's weird, all those knitters who died recently?" she asked the group.

"What?" Diana reacted as if Arianna had said something really funny. "What are you talking about?"

"She's talking about the two podcasters," said Melissa to Diana.

"Oh. Yeah, those. What about them?" Diana asked Arianna.

"Don't you think it's strange that two knitting podcasters died within, like, just a few days?"

Heather joined the main group as her boy headed toward the bar, followed by his two buddies. The four girls were now alone together.

"Yes, it is strange," said Diana. "Arianna, we're here to have fun. It would be nice not to creep out the guys. Well, I was telling a story about a dead guy, so I'm guiltier than you are... My bad! But if we keep on doing so, they might think we really are a bunch of creeps.

"A bunch of knitting creeps," added Melissa.

It was apparently so incredibly funny that Heather laughed and laughed and couldn't stop laughing, and when she finally did stop she said, "You guys are kinda scaring me!"

"You see! You're scaring Heather!" said Melissa while taking Heather in her arms and hugging her.

"I kinda understand why you worry, Arianna, but have so much on my plate, right now, that I... don't really care," slurred Melissa (Melissa was officially drunk).

The guys came back with a new round of drink for everyone; the girls cheered, except Arianna, who exited the bar and asked for a cigarette from the first smoker she saw outside.

Arianna was angry. That her friends had some incredulity about the deaths was one thing, but their reaction really made her feel stupid.

Nicolas had followed her outside. He also begged, successfully, a smoke and a light and came to stand in front of her. "You really are worried about those deaths," he said after exhaling the toxic smoke.

Arianna wondered how Nicolas had heard about the story. Wasn't he at the bar with his friends? Was she speaking that loud inside?

"I'm not worried. It is just a strange coincidence. Two knitting podcasters died within a very short period of time. I might be overreacting; it might just be a coincidence, but... I have a bad feeling about this," said Arianna before pulling on her cigarette. "So... you don't think I'm overreacting?"

Nicolas shrugged. "I don't know."

"Well, two young, healthy women are dead. Both are knitting podcasters. Don't you think it's weird?"

Nicolas smiled. "Out of a population of how many young, healthy, knitting women? There are tons of them online."

Arianna didn't say anything. This Nicolas hadn't chosen the right time to be a smartass. It would be easy to check up their online profiles and recent activity and that would most likely show that there was something unusual going on there. As if he'd read her mind, Nicolas said: "You should check their Ravelry accounts."

Arianna's eyes opened wide and she looked at Nicolas, speechless—not because he kinda had read her mind, but because the world "Ravelry" had just exited his mouth. The online social networking site was well known and widely used by knitters, but most people weren't aware of it.

He smiled and looked down toward the ground. He pulled the legs of his jeans to reveal blue-and-yellow wool socks: "My mom knits. She told me about that poor girl who died of an allergic reaction."

"One died by falling from the balcony of her apartment, the other one bled to death in her bath. None of them died following an allergic reaction."

"Well, my mother watches this podcast, and the host died after ingesting peanuts, to which she was very allergic. I think she lived in Manhattan."

6. Walk of Shame

It was 5 a.m. The sky was dark and the air was cold and humid. Arianna's steps reverberated on the sidewalk as she headed home, back from Nicolas's place where she had (more or less unexpectedly) spent the night.

As she neared her apartment, she passed in front of the dojo. The place was lit. There was a class actually going on inside. Startled, Arianna looked through the window; Audrey was there, sitting in the lotus position, wearing her black kimono. Six students, whose kimonos were white, sat in the same position, all adult women of varying ages. Among them was Yuna.

The scene made Arianna (once again) smile, and she shook her head right and left in disbelief. "New York Fucking City," she muttered aloud, before resuming on her path toward home.

As she reached her pocket to grab her apartment key, she felt her phone vibrate. Who the hell could be trying to reach her at this hour?

Melissa was the one who was trying to reach her by text at such an hour, 5:12 a.m. Eastern Daylight Time exactly: "I'm so hungover! I am terrible. And ashamed. Did you spend the night at that boy's place?"

Arianna unlocked her building's entrance and typed as she climbed the stairs: "Yep. I've just completed the walk of shame home from his place. Not hungover tho. Why aren't you sleeping if ur sick?"

Melissa: "Just finished puking. Well, it's not that bad. A few months ago, we'd both be hungover, both doing the walk of shame. Now instead of two hangover w-o-s, we each did one of both. That's a 50% progression."

"Yay progress?" replied Arianna just before she unlocked her apartment door.

Thinking about the night before didn't make Arianna feel ashamed; it made her worry. She had spent the end of the evening searching online with Nicolas for facts and information about the podcasters' deaths, and what they had found unsettled her.

The three victims were all knitters, all resided in or near New York City, all had a Ravelry account—and it looked as if they knew each other, or at least had a minimum of online interaction.

That was scary. Arianna felt there was a maniac loose in a small town, HER small town, and no one believed her, despite a mounting pile of corpses.

She had accepted Nicolas's offer to stay over. It was 2 a.m., she didn't feel like going home and, well, Nicolas was cute. He was also the only one who didn't treat her like a lunatic when she worried about those deaths. Maybe he had done so only to get Arianna in his bed. Well, that had worked, and anyway much worse schemes had achieved the same result. Good for him?

There was no way she would have walked back home after reading a blog post on Christina Bain's death: they had found her body, naked in the bathtub of the one-bedroom apartment she rented in New Jersey, her wrists cut, the tub filled with her coagulated blood.

Official reports and news article offered few details on the deaths, but Arianna had discovered a few social media posts and one message board that reported and discussed crimes. They, too, had picked up on the strange circumstances that surrounded the death of three knitters.

Arianna took a quick shower and put on clean clothes—a black Y.A.S. suit with a white top—and headed straight to the subway station. As she walked, she selected the browser on her phone; the message board had mentioned that an article on one of the victims would be published in today's news. Google News didn't have any results, and navigating the **New York Times'** mobile site proved annoying and frustrating— and dangerous.

"Yo! Be careful!" shouted a man she nearly ran into as she looked down, her device glued to her eyes.

Arianna stopped in her tracks and took a deep, long breath, and tried to calm down, annoyed and frustrated at her phone's inability to deliver what she needed.

She was about to throw her phone at the nearest wall (well, not really, but she vividly imagined the scene in her head) when something struck her in her field of vision: the **New York Times**, not the app but the paper version; it looked at her through the glass beside a Budweiser ad. Arianna stood in front of an actual newsstand (well, a convenience store that sold newspaper). She went inside, looked at the selection, and picked up the newspaper; it was the first time ever she had purchased an actual copy of an actual paper-and-ink daily.

The packed car on the L line didn't leave much room to spread open the **Time**'s pages, so she waited, again. When she emerged from the subway's entrails, some sun rays succeeded in hitting her directly as she walked between Manhattan's high-rises. It was a warm day, and holding the newspaper amused Arianna, as she imagined going to work into some **Mad Men**-esque office from the sixties.

7. Research@Cognit

But Arianna did not enter an office from the sixties, because Arianna worked at Cognit. Yes, that Cognit, the firm that offered an all-encompassing range of professional services that includes audit, tax, legal, risk management, business consulting, IT, software and data solutions, and also design and advertising—it has the tailor-made solution for your organization! Cognit, the rebel company that had taken the business world by storm with its surprise launch a bit more than three years before! Thirty-nine young partners and directors from Deloitte, Boston Consulting, CGI, E&Y, McKinsey, the Conference Board, and other established international firms had gathered to put together the first real twenty-first-century consultancy!

Within weeks of its inception, Cognit had been featured in the **Financial Times, Forbes**, the **Wall Street Journal, Bloomberg Businessweek**, the **Economist**, and in one viral YouTube clip that

showed Cognit's employees building a house with only reused waste—
the clip had reached the hundred-million-view mark within two months.

Arianna crossed the glass hall of the Western Chorus Tower, the brand-
new LEED Platinum-certified, 33-story office tower where Cognit was
headquartered.

It was early (6:30) so there weren't many people waiting for one of the
six elevators— just five, now that Arianna was among them. Someone
had already called an elevator for the fiftieth floor; the screen on the
wall indicated that elevator D would go there. The doors opened
silently. Arianna went in, following a tall, gray-haired, suit-clad,
briefcase-holding man inside.

She exited the elevator and followed the man into the small hall; the
floor was covered with gray carpet, the front and right walls all glass
panels through which she could see the cool, comfortable, creative!
open spaces Cognit offered to its associates. Like the man in front of
her, Arianna grabbed her phone, selected the Cognit app, and pressed
her device on the small screen beside the access door. CLICK! The door
unlocked, Arianna stepped in, and checked the app on her screen:
"Your WorkStation for today is P178" was displayed in green letters. At
Cognit, space is assigned on the basis of needs, not seniority!

Arianna dropped her handbag and newspaper on Workstation P178; it
was a good thing she had arrived early, because P178 was in an eight-
place aisle with no separators, located in the middle of a crowded
portion of the floor. It was an elegantly designed, aluminum-glass-and-
wood workstation with power, data, and phone sockets all in the right
places, along with an ergonomic chair, but by 10 a.m. it would be a
"very dynamic work environment!" indeed.

After her laptop finished loading, she brought up the Ravelry home
page on the browser. She wanted to follow up on the inquiries she had

begun the night before with Nicolas—but just a few seconds after she had logged on the site, something cast a shadow on her desk.

It was Bryan, who was standing between the window's light and Arianna. He was of medium height, with a receding line of short, light auburn hair, slightly overweight but not obese; Bryan was one of the most generic middle-aged white male Arianna had ever met. Everything about him was entirely proper. He looked clean, his suits were of good quality without being extravagant, he never swore, he was always clean-shaven, and Arianna had never caught him acting improperly, or even just looking improperly, at female co-workers (and Bryan being gay was not a credible hypothesis).

"Good morning, Arianna. We need to perform some research on a list of IT firms in Austin. It should be doable within an hour and a half. Is it something you could complete today before noon?"

Bryan was also a senior manager. He was not Arianna's senior manager—there was no such formal hierarchy at Cognit, where all work was project-based, and all employees were expected to manage their own workload. Also, his request did not follow the formal procedure for work assignments, which would have required for him to open a new file in the CRM (short for Cognit Resources Management) software. Which meant that Arianna had no obligation to accept Bryan's request, officially.

But a closer look at the situation revealed a much narrower range of options: Bryan was a rising star, rumored to be on the fast track to partnership, who worked on interesting contracts, and thus gave interesting assignments (notwithstanding the current boring internet research one). So Arianna could say no, and there was nothing Bryan could do about it.

KNITTING DEATH

What Bryan could do, however, is never ask for Arianna's involvement in one of his projects ever again, or give her a bad review, or just hint negatively about her to other managers and partners. That would result in Arianna receiving fewer assignments, and her billable hours would tank, and she'd be in trouble, and Cognit would replace her with one of the thousands of graduates who flooded to the company's servers with application emails.

"I'll take care of it," said Arianna with a warm smile.

Bryan left after thanking Arianna and letting her know she'd receive the assignment by email soon.

Arianna opened her Google account and selected a text document on her online drive. "Inquiry," she had named the file, last night:

> Marianna Burrow: 26; investment banker; lives and works in Manhattan
>
> Cause of death: Fall from her apartment window
>
> Podcast: "Purrow"; Ravelry ID: Purrow908
>
> Christina Bain: 29; bar server/singer; lives in Jersey City
>
> Cause of death: hemorrhage (wrist cut); found dead in her apartment bathtub by her mother (her roommate wasn't there)
>
> Podcast: "StarKnit"; Ravelry ID: StarKnitsBD

Now she would look on the third deceased person, Marie-Louise Thompson, the one who had died of complications following an anaphylactic shock. But first, she had to take care of her work assignment.

Arianna stood up and looked around. She found what she wanted. He had short, brown hair and the reflection of blue screen light in tiny glasses. Edwin was his name; he had started at Cognit at the same time as Arianna and they had attended the training week together with the same small group of new employees.

"Edwin! What are you doing at the office this early in the morning?"

"Oh, hi, Arianna! Well, I have three meetings today, so I figured that if I wanted to do any work I'd start early. What about you?"

Edwin looked quite pleased to see Arianna. Edwin also looked as if he was nineteen, and his suit was too big for his skinny frame.

"Edwin, I just screwed up! I have this deliverable to complete by ten, but Bryan just came over my workstation and asked me to do this assignment, and I just said yes—like, I just couldn't say no! So I just accepted, and now I will screw up both assignments. Can you believe it? I feel so dumb!"

The smile was now gone from Edwin's face. "Oh! I understand. It's hard to say no when they don't go through the CRM. What is he asking, exactly?"

"Simple research. Bryan told me it would take an hour, max. He needs info on those Austin IT firms."

"Oh, it's for the Brome project?"

"Yes, this one." Arianna had no idea if the assignment was for the Brome project—she hadn't even opened Bryan's email. "So, you can do it?"

"Yeah, no problem. Send me the email," said Edwin, with much nonchalance.

KNITTING DEATH

"Thank youuuuuu!" said Arianna while leaning forward and putting both her hands on Ewin's shoulder, before turning back and departing quickly toward her place.

"Back to the serious stuff," she muttered under her breath as she selected her "Inquiry" text document on her machine.

The only thing she knew about the second deceased person was her name (Marie-Louise Thompson) and the title of her podcast ("Pic Knit").

Arianna plugged her earphones into her laptop and selected Marie-Louise's page on YouTube. The last (last ever) episode of the podcast was dated August 19, so slightly over two weeks old. She clicked on it; the short intro song was followed by a close-up on Marie-Louise. She had short light brown hair, large dark brown eyes, some very light makeup, and she was wearing a dark pink wool sweater she probably had knitted herself. Behind her was a shelf with skeins, needles, books, and various project bags.

"Hello, everyone! Welcome to Episode 23 of Pic Knit! This week, I have three finished objects to share with you—by far my personal record!"

There was nothing in Marie-Louise's demeanor that hinted at fear or suicidal thoughts.

Arianna stopped the video; people were getting in and she didn't feel at ease looking at knitting clips with her co-workers around. She dragged the page down to the information section under the video and found exactly what she was looking for: Marie-Louise's Ravelry ID ("MaLouTh"). She typed the ID in Ravelry's search box and pressed the Search button; a link toward the profile page appeared. Arianna clicked it.

There wasn't much on her profile page: forty-three projects, thirty stashed, one queued, eight faves, sixteen patterns in her library, 301 friends, 226 posts... Profile: "Attorney by day, crafter by night, exotic bird enthusiast—Peru here I come!"

Arianna clicked on all MaLouTh's pictures and read every post she had written. Nothing. Projects, yarns, giveaways—normal, everyday knitting stuff.

An idea crossed Arianna's mind: she copied and pasted "MaLouTh"; "Purrow"; and "StarKnit" together in the Google search bar. A good idea it was; the links in the result page were all from the same website, a message board called Coven Craft. She clicked on the first link; the layout of the page was rather ancient, an old pre-social-media common message board template, this one formatted with white letters on a black background. There were two sections on the main page: Coven Bat Wing and General. Arianna clicked on the Coven Bat Wing link, but it led to a login page. She expected the same thing to happen when she clicked the General link, but no login was asked this time: she accessed the message board.

There were only ten threads; three of them hadn't been updated during the past five years, but the three at the top of the list had seen activity during the last hour. Arianna clicked the most recently updated link: The Witty Workout. The original post was the description of a series of exercises to "perform in the morning to get a firm round butt and killer abs." Arianna came back to the posts list. She clicked the second one: "Taking advantage of the falling euro." There was some sort of technical chart in the original post, which to Arianna meant there wasn't anything interesting to read there.

Arianna used the board's search engine to look up for "MaLouTh"; "StarKnit"; and "Purrow." MaLouTh and Purrow were indeed the ID of two members, but there was no trace of a StarKnit. She clicked on

MaLouTh and Purrow; she couldn't access their profile pages, but she could browse the many posts they'd left on the public section of the message board.

Both seemed mostly preoccupied with investment and high-end shopping. Exchange rates and real estate were the subject on which MaLouth was the most opinionated; Purrow discussed mostly private investment in unlisted companies.

As for shopping, it was borderline painful for Arianna to read both girls describe their latest acquisition: Prada, Yves St. Laurent, Motubi, and other shoes, clothes, and accessories she couldn't afford.

Arianna turned her head toward Edwin. From her spot, she could only see the top of his head—and there was not much interest in seeing the rest of him anyway. She had second thoughts about letting the opportunity to work on a tech project; it was only an internet search, but an internet search was what she was doing anyway, and for no benefit to her whatsoever. Working on a tech project for Bryan was the kind of thing that, at Cognit, could lead to advancement, and advancement led to a salary that enabled her to afford Prada, Yves St. Laurent, Motubi, and other awesome brands.

Well, she probably would be able to bill the hours for this project anyway. She would just have to intervene soon—before Edwin sent his research directly to Bryan.

Arianna turned her head back toward her screen. The posts left by Marie-Louise and Marianna were interesting, much more interesting than this Houston tech thing.

"Farmingdale Private Jet is much more recommendable than Concord"; "Guys, where should we go for the Post-Davos Ski?"; "NYC-South-Beach by Yacht!"; and one thread where board members planned a week in a rented house in the Hamptons.

Something caught Arianna's attention: both MaLouTh and Purrow often mentioned a certain "SQueen."

"I have a meeting with SQueen"; "SQueen said I should focus on this pattern"; "SQueen says we are meeting at the Bowfries at 8"; "SQueen disapproves of contracting this firm."

Well, these Coven Craft people were a weird bunch, maybe even more so than the anime-loving recluse teens who populated regular image boards.

There was an IP number under the board member's name above the text section of any post. Arianna checked the two IP numbers that appeared under MaLouTh's posts: one was in Lower Manhattan, the other in the West End—most likely Marie-Louise's workplace and home. The same pattern applied for Purrow: one location in Midtown, the other one near Central Park, both in Manhattan.

Arianna typed "SQueen" in the search box; it matched the name of one of the board's members, who had only two posts. "So this is your message board you are talking about nonstop?" and "Carrie, please call me on my mobile, ASAP."

Arianna performed the search on SQueen's IP number, the only number that shown beside her posts. The IP linked to Williamsburg.

Arianna recoiled from her desk deep inside her chair. There was something fishy going on with those dead podcasters. But there was something else she was certain of: she had no evidence. Nothing that was likely to alert the police.

Arianna would have to find the evidence herself.

She might be able to uncover some more information online, but at some point, she would have to meet the people who knew the dead podcasters. This should not be too difficult; Arianna's personal experience within the knitting community would make it easy to invent reasons to meet with people close to the deceased.

One thing, however, would be more challenging: finding the time. There was no way Arianna would be able to meet people in Long Island or New Jersey after work. It would have to be done during the weekend (that is, the next day; it was Friday). Arianna, however, was pretty sure she had something else planned, something that was relatively important. She looked at the calendar on her phone for the current week. One thing was written under both Saturday and Sunday: "Stacey."

"Oh God! You must be fucking kidding me!" said Arianna out loud.

8. Coucou & Sibling

"Can you believe she faked being sick to avoid attending Cindy's wedding? She even posted pics online to make her excuse more believable. She switched from being the overenthusiastic bridesmaid to making up an illness so she could avoid her best friend's wedding—that just doesn't make any sense. I was afraid Dona would be sooo upset that Cindy would miss her wedding, but she took it well. She was really mature about it, you know. Well, it's true that the wedding was woooonderful! We had a great time—you should have been there with us!"

There was no question mark in Stacey's last sentence, but Arianna knew a question lay behind the seemingly casual affirmation: "Why didn't you accept Cindy's wedding invitation?"

So instead of shoving the piece of the fried-egg croissant sandwich that was impaled on her fork into her mouth, Arianna took a sip of her double espresso and said: "I worked during that weekend. Attending the wedding of a non-relative would not have cut it with the partner in charge. It sucks because it would have been nice to see everyone in their beautiful dresses."

Delivered at the right moment, with the right tone. Too much professed sadness would have seemed hypocritical, not seeming to care would have been rude; also, there were no lies for Stacey to find because Arianna had told none.

Arianna could now shove the fork into her mouth. She worried, again, about the fried-egg croissant sandwich. Not that there was anything wrong with it. **Au contraire**: it was delicious. The problem was that the menu had no prices. Menus with no prices usually meant expensive menus. Especially in Lower Manhattan.

"Olivia! Drop your phone!"

Olivia, Arianna's nine-year-old niece, raised her eyes toward the sky, shoved her iPhone in her bag beside her chair, and grabbed her glass of orange juice.

"We'll take the bills, please," shouted Stacey to a waiter or waitress somewhere behind Arianna. "You're done, right?" she added, looking at her little sister.

Arianna was tense. She didn't look at her bill when the waiter put it on the table; she just pulled her debit card from her phone case.

"Mylene was right! This is awesome," said Stacey. "How come you didn't know about this place before?"

"I, like, never come to this part of town," said Arianna. And *it's most likely way too expensive*, she didn't say.

"You never come around here? But we're downtown; how is it possible? Isn't your office in this area?"

KNITTING DEATH

The waiter arrived at their table with the card processor; he took Stacey's bill first. Stacey looked at Arianna: she expected an answer to her question.

"I work in Midtown and live in Williamsburg, so I'm never in this area. Sometimes I go to this pub near the office with my co-workers, after work, but that's about it... Manhattan-wise."

The waiter took Arianna's card. He handled her the processor, she typed her pin, and waited, eagerly, as the machine made its mind: did Arianna have, or not have, enough funds to pay for the brunch?

"Don't tell me that you are spending all your time in this microscopic apartment of yours!?" asked Stacey. "I would actually be worried if I learned that you don't get out of that dark, damp, and cramped place."

DECLINED.

Such was the machine's verdict. Arianna was guilty of trying to purchase goods and services without having the adequate funds or credit. It made her red with embarrassment. She reached nervously for her phone case to fetch her credit card, but her sister interrupted: "I'll take it!"

Arianna protested, but was relieved; she doubted her Visa had more spare space than her checking account.

"Have you seen celebrities since you arrived here?" asked Olivia, as her mom processed the (second) payment. "There are tons of celebrities in New York."

Arianna was grateful for the diversion. "I'm afraid not. Well, I've seen Don Prince, but I'm not sure you know him..."

"Don Prince? What does he do?" asked Olivia.

"He plays Beaumont in Conqueror. It's a Netflix series. "I did cocaine tracks with him at Melissa's manager place in the Upper West Side after a night out, but I ended up too wasted to fuck him, so he finished the night with Diana... and this is why I don't go out in Manhattan anymore, my dear niece.

"Conqueror? Hmmm..." Olivia put her finger on her mouth and raised her eyes toward the sky. "Nah, I don't know this series."

"It's about William the Conqueror. He was a French king or an English king or something like that. "

Arianna had gone through the first episode with Diana and Melissa, while knitting, and chatting, and actually not paying too much attention to the show, until Melissa let a loud, high-pitched "IT's HIM!" which had nearly made Arianna drop her glass of wine (because while they knitted and chatted and more or less watched Conqueror's pilot episode, they also shared a bottle of Italian rosé).

"So, should we go shopping now?" asked Stacey.

Arianna looked at Stacey. "Today is the opening of the Brooklyn Craftfest. I know you didn't come to New York to look up for knitting stuff, but—"

"A craft fair!" shouted Olivia. "Let's go to the craft fair!"

"A craft fair? In Brooklyn? But that's awesome! Let's go!"

So Stacey agreed to the fair. The day would not be wasted.

The sisters and Olivia exited the restaurant and stepped onto the sidewalk: the taller (Stacey) wearing a beige trench coat that nearly matched her hair; the other a black raincoat that stopped exactly at the length of her skirt, with purple legwarmers covering her checkered socks right above her brown leather boots. The child was the most colorful of the lot, with her bright red glittery autumn coat with two vertical rows of buttons, and rubber boots, all yellow and green and blue. It was obvious to all they were related; all three had the same bright auburn hair, same slightly rising pointy nose, same bright green eyes.

"Do you have a boyfriend? Do you go to many parties?"

Olivia was in full interrogation mode. Her mother smiled, her ears waiting eagerly for the answers to her daughter's questions.

"Nope, no boyfriend." New York is awful for single girls. A colleague at work had characterized the Big Apple as a "guys' market," meaning men had more choices. The colleague was a male, the kind who doesn't get any, which is also, usually, the type who use expressions like "guys' market."

"I used to go out a lot when I arrived here. Now I mostly hang out with my friends Dianna and Melissa, and most of the time we just knit together and chat." And drink wine.

"When I go to college, I'll come live with you," said Olivia, matter-of-factly. Arianna didn't have the time to comment before her sister interjected.

"By the time you're in college, Arianna will be married and will live in a house. Maybe even back home!"

Arianna didn't add anything. Anyway, they had reached their subway station. Neither Stacey nor Olivia said much during the ride; Olivia looked fascinated; Stacey worried by the train's colorful crowd. That suited Arianna quite well, as she could look at her investigation notes on her phone. There were three crafters at the fair she had to talk to: Aline Li, Jane Desmond, and Linda Rossi.

They exited at Greenpoint on the G line, not far from Arianna's apartment, and headed toward the Brooklyn Expo Center. It was only 10:10; there were visitors but it was not crowded yet. Arianna had been slightly irritated when she had to wake up at seven on a Saturday morning, but now she was glad they were early; getting the attention of the fair's vendors would be easier than during the afternoon rush.

Olivia went to look at a stand that sold cacti planted in dinosaur-shaped pots, and her mother followed. "I'll be at this stand, right next to the big green rug," said Arianna, pointing to her left. She walked toward the green rug; according to the Craftfest plan, this is where Aline Li's booth was located.

As she approached, she realized the green rug was not a rug but grass held in containers fixed vertically to a pallet. She immediately recognized Aline, who stood alone in her booth, surrounded by her hand-crafted project bags.

"Good morning," said a smiling Aline as she made eye contact with Arianna, obviously glad that someone had come toward her.

"Hello, Aline. I'm so glad to meet you! I'm a big fan of your podcast."

"Thank you!" Aline was obviously surprised that Arianna actually knew who she was.

Arianna grabbed one of the larger bags, which was about two feet in length by one foot in height; instead of a zipper, a fabric flap attached to the side with one large blue plastic button. The flap was burgundy, the navy-blue button fixed on light gray fabric and the other side of the bag was bright yellow tissue with tiny orange flowers. "Having this bag would be so practical right now; the ones I own are too small for my current project. You made this one around Christmas, right?"

"I did—well, just after Thanksgiving. What is your name?"

KNITTING DEATH

"I'm Arianna. I just moved to New York last year and I got back at knitting a few weeks after arriving here. I find it's a good activity to deal with the stress."

"Absolutely; I couldn't agree more. You have to be careful, though; if you're careless you can hurt your hands, your shoulders, your back... I began sewing when my doctor told me to lay down the needles for a bit," said Aline, while pointing at the bags that surrounded her.

"Yeah, having to stop knitting would be a tragedy. Speaking of tragic... it's so sad what happened to Christina. Were you still close to her?"

Arianna wasn't too proud her herself; she had brought up an actual death to the conversation in an abrupt way. Aline might think, at best, that she was a little off. At worst, a creep. But she was here to find information; there was no point in beating around the bush eternally, not with her sister who could drag her away from her inquiry at any moment.

Aline looked taken aback. She stood silent for a few seconds, then answered, "Yes, it is sad. It had been a while since I'd seen her; she had pretty much ceased to knit. She had serious issues, you know. What happened to her is sad, but I'm not that surprised."

"True. But what surprised me," said Arianna, "are the two other knitters who died so soon after Christina." Again, Arianna was not very satisfied with the way she drove the conversation.

"There are others?" asked Aline, her eyes wide open, her head jerking backward. She didn't know about them.

Arianna gave a very brief description of Marie-Louise's and Marianna's deaths; Aline stared at her with fright, obviously learning about those deaths for the first time. Arianna left Aline's stand—again, abruptly.

The next crafter on Arianna's list was Jane Desmond, and her stand happened to be close by, only eight places away. Arianna looked around for Stacey: she was chatting with an older woman whose stand featured some sort of woodwork; they were laughing and having fun. Good, the inquiry could go on.

Jane Desmond's stand was enclosed between weathered wood planks that looked as if they had been pulled away from an old barn. The display tables were packed with baskets filled with innumerable socks; they were made of diverse types of wool, where earthy tones of green, brown, burgundy, and sable dominated specks of lighter colors: blue, pink, white, a bit of yellow. On the stand's wall hung shawls, vests, and hats in the same tones. Again, Arianna was lucky: as she approached, the lone customer in the stand concluded a purchase and left.

"Hello, Jane. I'm so glad to meet you! I'm a big fan of your podcast." (This opening had worked with Aline, so Arianna didn't bother thinking of something new).

"Glad to hear it."

Arianna pointed to a beige shawl with two dark red maple leaves hanging on the wall: "You completed this one last month, right?"

"That's right. What are you looking for today, young lady? Anything I can help you with?"

Despite the rustic look of her stand, Jane spoke quite Newyorkishly: accent, tone, and attitude. Arianna felt she would be a tougher nut to crack than sweet and nice Aline.

"I just got in the convention center. I start by touring the stands I know; I mean, the ones for which I watch the podcasts. I was just with Aline before... do you know her?"

KNITTING DEATH

Arianna's mouth was on automatic pilot; she felt she was babbling nonsense, letting out random sentences to avoid hitting awkward silence. She realized her pronunciation getting heavier with Midwestern undertones. First it triggered an alarm signal in her head (you work in NYC; speak properly!), but then she realized she was not at the office or in a party with Brooklyn hipsters—she was hunting for clues in a craft show: Midwestern was okay.

"Oh, I know Aline."

Someone else came into Jane's stand: a woman, tiny and very old. Jane greeted her; Arianna went to look at the socks in a basket, sorting through its content as she tried to find a way to discuss the murders with Jane. Jane looked nice and warm and welcoming in her podcast; she struck Arianna as rather cold and abrasive in person.

Arianna tilted her head in her direction: Jane spoke to the old lady, and she looked just like in her podcast, nice and warm and welcoming and not difficult of approach. I must be doing something wrong, thought Arianna.

The lady bought a pair of beige socks and left. Arianna was alone again with Jane. She looked her straight in the eye with the most pitiful expression she could muster: "It's sad what happened to Christina. Were you still close to her?"

To Arianna's surprise, Jane provided a complete answer.

"Yes, we were good friends, but before her death we had drifted away. She sent me a couple of messages a few weeks ago about brioche and merino wool, and after that, nothing. I think she was going through a rough patch. I was very sad when I learned that she died, but I was not surprised. She seemed distressed. I think she was using drugs. I've seen other people hit that downward spiral, so as I said, I was not surprised by her death. The two others, however…"

"Marianna and Marie-Louise?"

"Yes, those two. They were serious girls, they had good backgrounds, promising careers... These two... it really upset me when I learned they had died."

"Did you know them?"

"Not at all. I just watched their podcasts. Did you?"

"No, same thing. I didn't know any of them. I learned about Christina in the 'StarKnit' podcast, about Marianna in 'Purrow,' and then my friend told me about Marie-Louise. It really, really bugs me; I don't know what to make of all of this."

Jane looked at Arianna with a puzzled expression, her large light brown eyes fixing her with intensity, her full lips shut tightly. Jane looked at something behind Arianna and a small hand grabbed Arianna's left middle finger: it was Olivia. Her presence made Jane's face lit up with a bright smile. Then, two women who looked as if they were Arianna's age entered the stand. Before going to greet them, Jane grabbed Arianna's shoulder and whispered: "You be careful, hon."

Olivia, still holding Arianna's middle finger, dragged her along the alley toward a stand that displayed bright and colorful winter hats with animal ears. Some were just beanies with cats' ears; others were much more elaborate, such as one with a long green dinosaur tail with spikes in the back and two yellow eyes and white fangs that hung under the rim on the front.

"Look at this one!" said Olivia, pointing to a brown and green hat that represented a turtle. "Isn't it awesome?"

The hat was quite nice indeed: a tiny head, four paws, and a tail hung under the brim, while above it hexagonal patterns that made the hat look like a turtle shell. "It is very nice, Olivia. But are you sure you want to be associated with a turtle?"

If you wear that in school, the other kids will call you turtle-head, crossed Arianna's mind.

"No one associates California with bears, and they have a huge bear on their flag."

"I'm not sure that it's a valid argument, but if you want a turtle hat, I'll knit you one myself," said Arianna.

Arianna still doubted the turtle would last one day in school, but she knew she could knit one with some leftover wool, and she knew Olivia's birthday was two months away, which meant she just found a way to offer her beloved niece a nice gift she wanted for zero dollars.

Olivia was quite happy with Arianna's answer and went away running in the alley— toward Stacey, most likely. And if she got lost, she had a cell. Yay, technology.

Arianna looked at the plan of the fair she had fetched at the entry. Linda Rossi's stall was located at the other end of the floor, so she accelerated her pace. It took her nearly five minutes to reach it; she looked at her phone to make sure Stacey wasn't looking for her. Nope, she was good to go.

Linda Rossi was the most promising one: she had participated in an episode of "StarKnit" with Christina Bain herself. Also, she lived in the Upper West Side, really close to Marianna Purrow, the second victim. She was also the most intimidating one: she was tall, gorgeous, and her perfect yoga body was adorned in Lolë gear.

Linda's stall was bare: a few handmade jewelry pieces, four alpaca scarves, and a dozen project bags. Obviously more of a photo op than a mercantile endeavor. Linda had arranged the jewelry on the tiny display table, an old coffee table freshly painted white. She didn't seem to notice that there was someone in her stall, because she continued to move the chains and earrings around without looking at Arianna.

"Hi!" said Arianna.

"Hi!" answered Linda, who threw a quick glance at her visitor before going back to her jewelry table.

Arianna went to look at the handbags, which rested on a narrow table with tiny drawers, also painted in white. She looked at the items on display, trying to find questions about them to ask Linda, but they gave Arianna no inspiration: they were not especially well made and the fabric, for all its shine and glitter, seemed cheap from up close.

The scarves were better. They were made of bright blue alpaca wool and had no obvious knitting flaws. They hung on wooden hooks fixed to the raw pine planks that made the sides of the stand. Along with the white furniture, the untreated wood, as well as a stack of birch branches that rested on a glass vase, it gave a Scandinavian deco look to the place, which was probably the whole point, if not the sole point of the stand.

Linda had left her jewelry and was now in the process of swiping vigorously at something on the screen of her phone. She still gave no impression of realizing that she hosted a stand in a trade show, and that, as such, visitors were bound to visit, and that it was more or less her duty to welcome, or, at the very least, acknowledge them.

"It's so sad what happened to Christina Bain, right?"

Well, that made Linda Rossi acknowledge Arianna. Her head turned sharply toward Arianna, her eyes big, her lips, for an instant, tightly sealed.

KNITTING DEATH

"What did you say? I... I have nothing to do with her. Do you work for the police?"

"Me?" Now it was Arianna who looked at Linda with big eyes full of shock. The fact that someone could entertain the idea that she was a police officer was beyond her. "Of course not!" she said, her arms spread, her eyes looking left and right. "Do I look like a cop to you?"

"Look," said Linda, "I don't want to be bothered with this. I have a very busy day; you should go now."

Arianna left without saying a word.

"Just stay away from this," she heard behind as she went away.

Arianna looked at her phone: no message, no missed calls. Her sister wasn't looking for her, so she wouldn't be accused of abandoning her alone with her daughter in the middle of New York City. There was, however, a message from Melissa: she was coming to the Craftfest. It was good news. Stacey liked Melissa, and Stacey was better behaved toward her little sister when there were strangers around.

As she paced the convention halls, her eyes scanned for knitting-related stands while she replayed the scene at Linda's stand in her head. On one hand, she hadn't learned anything new; on the other, Linda's behavior had been odd and rude. Maybe the oddness was only due to grief and sadness; maybe the rudeness was only due to her being a total bitch. But would a grieving bitch really say something like, "Just stay away from this"? Maybe. But then again, maybe not.

Arianna had come for answers, but the way things were going, she would leave the convention center only with more questions.

Stacey and Olivia appeared just behind a tall, pumpkin-headed scarecrow man that held a pyro-engraved sign that said: "Emily's

Blankets & Drapes." Stacey looked grumpy and Olivia was pouty; they'd had a fight or maybe were in the middle of one.

Arianna attacked right away with a diversion: "Melissa will soon be with us."

"Is Diana coming, too?" asked Olivia.

"I saw Diana yesterday when going to your place," added Stacey. "She was with her boyfriend."

"Boyfriend?"

"An old man. Well, not old, but not young. Like, middle-aged. Older than—"

"He was older than my dad," Olivia cut in.

"Olivia, please!" shouted Stacey, "It's not nice—"

"He must have a lot of money."

"Olivia!"

9. Tea & Tensions

Arianna didn't feel like going to Ben & Jesse's Knits, but Stacey did. She wanted to go to there because Arianna had talked so much about it. The sisters did not have many things in common, but knitting was one, so Arianna had talked extensively about the place—and now they sat at Ben & Jesse's Knits.

Alia, who was also in the cafe with her mother, Heather, had pulled Olivia to another table. Arianna didn't know what they were doing, but it involved looking at their own phones, and looking at each other's phones, and communicating with a mix of whispers and interjections.

KNITTING DEATH

Melissa stood on the sidewalk outside the coffee shop, talking on the phone with her mother; Stacey chatted with Heather on one of the couches; Arianna sat on a single chair across the coffee table while keying her phone. It was not very polite, but no one needed her attention at the moment, and she wanted to update her notes while the encounters at Craftfest were fresh in her memory.

Aline Li: Only knew about Christina Bain (Dead No. 1). Reaction to questions seemed normal.

Jane Desmond: Knew Christina Bain; was not surprised by her death; said Christina was "distressed" and "might have been consuming (drugs)." Didn't personally know Mariana and Marie-Louise; was surprised by their death because they were "successful."

Linda Rossi: Total bitch. Very upset when interrogated.

As Arianna stared at the screen of her device, she realized that her sister was talking about this very subject: "It's terrible what happened to those poor girls."

No! thought, Arianna. Not here! Shut up! Oh please, Stacey, keep your mouth shut!

"I know," said Heather, while looking at the floor, her café au lait bowl held under her chin between her hands. "It's really sad. It really bothers me, actually."

"Me too!" said Stacey, "I must have seen over a hundred podcasts of the three of them. I just can't wrap my mind around it!"

As far as Arianna was concerned, Stacey sounded more excited than bothered by the whole ordeal. Heather, however, really looked affected.

"Arianna, you don't have anything to say?" asked Stacey, before looking back at Heather. "Arianna is obsessed with these deaths. While we were at the craft fair, this morning, she played the detective! She interrogated the participants who knew the victims."

Arianna froze. She stood still on her seat, motionless, a deer caught in the headlights of an approaching car at night. She should play it cool, say a just a few casual sentences to show that it was not a big deal, but no: here she was, paralyzed by fear.

She never really had much success hiding anything from her sister. And her sister wanted to remind her that she still could read her game, even now, even when they spent most of their time apart, three states away.

Heather looked at Arianna with big, surprised eyes; Stacey with a bright, proud smile and tiny, vicious eyes; even Alia looked at them, having caught up on what was happening with the grown-ups.

Arianna stood up and stormed to the bathroom: a tiny, single place, unisex, well-decorated, squeaky-clean bathroom where she could cut herself off from her friends (and sister, especially) for a few moments, take the time to catch her breath and think straight. There was only one problem: Arianna couldn't think straight. Her breath was short, her belly was tied into a knot, and her heart pounded hard and fast.

Anxiety crisis.

Arianna tried to reason with herself: she was preoccupied by the death of three young women who were her age and shared the same hobby; there was nothing wrong with that per se. Her friends didn't share her preoccupation, which could also be considered "normal." So, nothing to worry about; the anxiety probably was also caused by her sister being mean... in NYC, in front of her friends. The anxiety probably was also caused by her sister importing a pattern (Stacey embarrassing Arianna) from home to NYC.

Arianna flushed the nonexistent contents of the toilet and exited the bathroom, ready to face her sister and her friends. Instead, on the other side of the door was Audrey, who stood straight in the tiny hall, unsmiling and severe. The white apron she wore gave her the look of an angry housewife. Only the rolling pin in her hand was missing.

"What you are doing could be very dangerous, Arianna," she said. "We don't know what happened to these young women; they might have been murdered."

Arianna was taken aback. Audrey looked preoccupied, borderline angry...

"I... I know. That's why I—"

"Arianna. Inquiring into suspicious death in a large city is unwise; inquiring into suspicious death in a large city when you have a similar profile as the victim is dangerous."

"But... but... but why is the police—"

"You are not the police, Arianna." Audrey gently shook Arianna's shoulder and left her there, returning to help customers at the counter.

Arianna walked back toward her seat. Stacey and Heather didn't pay attention to her, and neither did Melissa who was back inside; they all vividly discussed about what sounded like a TV series that Arianna didn't know about.

Arianna grabbed her project bag; there was no way she would be updating her notes now. She grabbed her Lizard Twins socks project and its pattern sheet. As she ended a second row, she realized she had made two mistakes, so she unraveled her work. It made her angry, but she didn't want flaws to show.

Stacey looked at Arianna. She opened her mouth, but before she could say anything, Heather shouted, "Margaret! Diana!"

Arianna was safe—for now. The little group would have other businesses to chat about than Arianna's newfound passion for amateur investigations.

The two were dressed rather seriously for a Saturday morning: gray skirt and white shirt for Diana, and a long black dress for Margaret. Margaret smiled and walked toward the group, while Diana headed straight toward the bathroom, a serious expression on her face.

"Margaret!" said Heather, "please meet Stacey, Arianna's sister."

Stacey rose up from her chair and shook Margaret's hand. "Stacey? As in Stace-lace?"

"That... would be me!" answered Stacey, visibly very pleased to be greeted by her Ravelry name by a stranger in a knitting cafe in New York City.

"Oh, I just love your new Froggy Jumpsuit! I know it's a popular pattern, but the buttons you choose and the front pouch you added just made such a cute piece out of it!"

"Thanks! I don't know what to say!"

"Stacey, this is Margaret," continued Heather. "She works with my husband."

Margaret put her handbag on the center table and waved to Alia, who looked at her but said nothing, turning her attention back to Olivia's phone.

"Alia! It is quite impolite not to answer when someone greets you," said Heather, with a hushed yet angered tone.

"Oh, it's nothing," said Margaret. "She thinks I keep her father away and I'm afraid there is some truth to it. Well, at least I brought back Diana."

Yuna walked to Margaret, who was not even seated: "Hi. What can I bring you?" she asked, with much coldness in her voice, which was rather at odds compared to her usual enthusiast demeanor.

"I think I'll go for an herbal tea. Would you please bring me a belladonna infusion?"

"We don't have that here!" replied Yuna.

"Then I'll take a Russian Caravan tea, my dear Yaga. I mean, Yuna."

Margaret sat on the corner of the couch while Heather and Stacey took back their place, which pleased Arianna, as this likely would keep her sister busy, thus preventing any more venomous remarks aimed in her direction for the time being.

As Arianna resumed the unraveling of her faulty Lizard Twin, she realized Alia and Olivia were standing right next to her.

"They hold the auditions at the place where you work," said Alia.

Arianna had no idea what Alia was talking about.

"Marianna passed the auditions," added Alia.

"Marianna Burrow?" asked Arianna.

"ALIA!" shouted Heather, sounding quite displeased with her daughter.

"Yes," answered Alia, ignoring her mother who shouted again: "ALIA!"

Arianna was lost.

10. Inquiry & Chill

Drinks and cars and boats and shoes shoesshoesshoes more shoes, all luxurious and expensive and beautiful. In all pictures, the best brands money can buy, with backgrounds of beaches, posh hotel rooms, and five-star restaurants.

And Nicolas, after going through their social media, had said, "Their parents are not even wealthy."

Arianna struggled to concentrate. She scrolled Marianna Burrow's Instagram account for clues, but all her eyes saw was bling, glam, and glitter.

She sat on the couch in Nicolas's living room, a pillow squeezed between her laptop and her lap. It was Sunday night. Her sister was (finally) gone (too bad she had to bring Olivia back with her). Arianna needed to concentrate and relax and feel safe and not be alone, so she had answered to a text message Nicolas had sent the day before—an invitation to come over to his place. And the invitation still stood after 24 hours, apparently.

So she was in Nicolas's living room.

She unglued her eyes from the dreamlike photo feed and looked at her notes:

> Marianna and Marie-Louise appear in each other's pics and traveled together; their pics feature luxury travel and shopping.

"It doesn't look like they were whoring themselves," Nicolas had said about half an hour before.

Arianna thought the comment lacked compassion and class and was rather offensive. Arianna also thought the observation was irrelevant: she knew they were not having sex with rich guys in order to generate those pictures, which were full of cute boys with bright grins and tanned six-packs who obviously didn't need to pay to get some. But Nicolas's remark brought up the important question:

Where did the money come from?

An obvious, yet overlooked question up to this point.

Arianna continued through her notes to the section devoted to Christina Bain:

> Christina Bain doesn't appear in Marianna and Marie-Louise's feed; her pictures feature

Feature what exactly? Christina's photographs were mostly generic social media material: drinks with friends, restaurant plates, weddings, cats, dogs and social commentary of some sort (but mostly the self-righteous kind). There were also pictures of her singing with musicians on the scene in small venues. So nothing, really.

And again:

> All 3s parents are not wealthy

Four of the three girls' six parents were prolific Facebook posters, and their pictures painted a middle-classish portrait—in Arianna's mind. Nicolas thought the middle-class designation was overly generous (as far as Arianna was concerned, not living in a trailer park or ghetto 'hood qualified someone for middle-class nowadays). The two other parents, Christina and Marianna's fathers, were absent from social media and had probably been absent from their daughters' lives as well.

Arianna was annoyed by the meagerness of her notes.

She looked at her inbox to see if some of the girls' relatives she had contacted had written back. Nothing. There was no new message, only the one reply she had received ten minutes ago: "I'm not interested," coming from Martine Cunning, who had been a close friend of Christina Bain.

She selected back the browser with Marie-Louise's Instagram. Arianna didn't lie to herself: she was envious. Marie-Louise and Marianna were the real deal. They were living the life; maybe now they were dead, but at least they'd had a blast, a bright and shinning and glorious blast, before they left.

Dammit, Arianna! You made it to Cognit's New York office. On your own, without any contact to push for your candidacy.

That was the worst part: these girls made the joy and pride she felt about her own achievement look silly. She was bright, she worked hard, she presented herself well, she had made it to a prestigious place, but...

But what was next for her? She was a junior associate with a junior associate pay. Her junior associate colleagues were bright and hard-working and presented themselves well and were ambitious and not everyone would make it to senior, let alone manager. And the competition had skills in high demand like coding, while others had good contacts...

Enough Instagram!

She selected Google's My Maps, on which she and Nicolas entered the addresses of people close to the girls they could find: family, friends, colleagues, roommates, classmates, ex-boyfriends. Most of them were clustered in New York City, Long Island, and New Jersey.

There is no way Arianna would have been able to collect all of this info only using Google and social networks, but Nicolas had, for some reason, access to databases that could identify the location and contact info for many of the people they looked up. He had explained he used them at work for something related to real estate and consumer info. Arianna didn't care much how it worked as long as it helped the inquiry.

"How should I contact them? Message or phone call?" Arianna asked Nicolas.

"What?" Nicolas was now in the kitchen, serving wine. Arianna didn't usually drink wine on Sunday night. But Arianna didn't usually spend a whole weekend with her sister, either.

"Those people, who know the victims—"

"We don't know if they're victims yet," said Nicolas as he came back from the kitchen, a glass of red in each hand.

Arianna took the one he handled her; "Thank you for the precious insight, Mr. Smart-Ass."

Arianna took a sip. The wine was good—tasted good and felt good, which was somehow unusual for a Sunday night, a time when she was most likely to be fed up with drinking. But this time it was different: the sensation was similar to what she felt when sipping her first glass on a Thursday night at the end of a rough week at the office. Which apparently had a similar effect on her as a weekend with her sister.

Arianna looked back at her screen. There was a new message! From Karina Mendez, a friend of both Marianna and Marie-Louise! It read:

"Please leave us alone."

Dammit!

"I should meet with them in person," said Arianna.

"That's too dangerous."

"Face-to-face meetings would be more efficient; I have a lot in common with these girls. I would not strike most people as suspicious. Messaging them is not working."

Nicolas's eyes left his screen and looked directly at Arianna beside him. "Yes, but meeting them would be dangerous."

"One-on-one meetings would... yield more data." Arianna wanted to convince Nicolas that she was right. Using expressions like "yield more data" with guys who were enamored with computer stuff was, in her experience, convincing.

"I'll come with you then." Nicolas's eyes reverted to his screen. "I can't narrow down the locations of the posters on the weird message board, the one you found at your office the other day, "SQueen." I'm still waiting for news from a friend who's good with that kind of thing... he might have been luckier than me."

This mysterious message board bothered Arianna. She shared her feelings with Nicolas. "I feel this whole thing is closing on me."

"Hey, YOU are the one who wants to get involved in this, whatever is it," he said. "Now, all we know so far is that one poster is from Brooklyn. There are 2.6 million people in Brooklyn."

"I know. But I still feel it getting near."

It was the main reason why Arianna was currently at Nicolas's place: she felt increasingly involved in this whole story of knitters dying prematurely and it scared her. Of course, he was right about the part where she was the one who had peered into that story in the first place. But when her sister had revealed Arianna's interest in this at Ben & Jesse's Knits, Alia immediately understood what they were talking about. Alia, the nine-year-old daughter of a friend, knew about Marie-Louise.

"So, have you figured out what is this Bat Wing thing is about?" asked Nicolas; "I have run into this expression on three different occasions tonight. It's all over the place on the message board, and Burrow mentioned it in one of her tweets, and now it's on Pinterest. But there are only pictures of the hashtag itself, #BatWing, written in stylized letters, with no mention or illustration of what it is exactly."

Arianna had no idea either. She felt tired of wrapping her head around unsolvable riddles.

"Holy shit!" said Nicolas, which prompted Arianna to turn her head toward him. "This article says that people who wear those Bat Wing shawls are involved in drug trafficking, fraud, and kidnapping."

"Nothing about murder?" asked Arianna.

"Not exactly," Nicolas said slowly while still reading, "but with the tone of the article, it's kind of implicit that murder would figure on the menu."

"That would explain the luxury and the bling in those pictures," said Arianna. "It's just that..."

Nicolas looked at her. "It's just that cute, twenty-something, one-hundred-pound chicks would not actually be involved in drug trafficking, fraud, and kidnapping."

"You are so wrong."

Arianna knew girls back home who dealt drugs. And although Arianna didn't know Irina Berg in person, she vividly remembered the mug shot of the woman who had landed in a state penitentiary after kidnapping the thirteen-year-old nephew of an acolyte over a drug debt. Yet, she had to admit that Nicolas was partially right. For one, whatever cuteness these girls back home had, the drugs were eating at it quite fast. Also, criminals who bragged openly about their wealth tend to have a very short career.

"You are mostly wrong," conceded Arianna before Nicolas said anything. "Where did you get this information about the Bat Wing?"

"On an alternative news site: 'Pleyades Vault.' They are not always serious or credible, but I find they are often insightful."

Arianna looked at Nicolas, a frown on her face. "Are you telling me that you are checking conspiracy websites?"

"I'm telling you that this Bat Wing thing is big enough to catch the attention of conspiracy websites, yes."

"Big enough? Like alien abductions and Men in Black and the Mothman?"

"Exactly," said Nicolas.

"So what you are telling me is that the Bat Wing doesn't exist?"

Arianna went back to her laptop, suddenly having doubts about Nicolas being involved in her ordeal. Things were already complicated enough as they were in the real world without adding a layer of delusions made of aliens and ghosts and werewolves and government conspiracy to the picture. Nicolas had struck her as someone serious and well balanced, enough to share her fears with him, enough to trust him, enough to have sex with him.

Now she had doubts; doubts that Nicolas was helping her only to fulfill his desire to play in his own mystery/science fiction/horror movie/video game. Nicolas was cute, nerdy without coming off as geekish, but maybe the nerd part of his personality was more important than Arianna had first perceived. Maybe he was one of those guys heavily involved in fantasy games and role-playing; maybe if she opened the closet door across the room, it would reveal a full set of medieval armor that he wore every first weekend of the month for live re-enactments...

Despair filled Arianna. She had no one to talk to, not her knitting friends, not her sister, not Nicolas... And then she noticed there was a new message in her inbox.

It was from Martine Cunning again: "Arianna, I think I understand why you contacted me. Stay away. Stay away from Bat Wing. It killed me."

11. Out in LIC

"...You see, this guy is using these stupid spreadsheets. Don't get me wrong, I love Excel, I really do, but for this project? This is sooo time-consuming? So I'm like, I'll do it in R, it will be muuuch faster, and much easier, and we'll save a lot of time. So what does this guy do? He refuses. He says we have to stick with Excel."

Arianna was usually not in the mood after a long workday to listen to someone rant about spreadsheet-related issues.

"I'm like, 'OK, the guy doesn't know about the R programming language, his client probably doesn't know about it either—let's do it with Access then. 'But NO! The guy still doesn't want to. Like, OK, I get it, you don't want to use R, which you don't know, but Access? Dude, it's on the fucking Office suite, and you can transfer anything in Excel anyway—"

But Arianna was in a good mood today.

"Like, we work for Cognit, right? THE Cognit? Which is supposed to be the digital, paperless, twenty-first-century firm? But somehow uses Excel for database work?"

Arianna was in a good mood because she had a great client meeting. Great, as in the-partner-in-charge-was-impressed-and-told-her-great.

"Like, I get it: this old fart got to be a founding partner of Cognit because he brought all these cool clients and contacts. That's, like, basic business."

She had been assigned to a project with Nicky Page, a partner who specialized in tax, which was, on one hand, strange, as the mandate didn't seem to involve any kind of tax work, but on the other, better off this way, as Arianna's knowledge of tax sat somewhere between extremely limited and quasi-nonexistent.

"But if you want to update spreadsheets, ask an intern, not an associate—even a junior one, you know what I mean?"

The client was Silvia Prescott, chief operating officer of Traphistry, a producer and distributor of elementary-school-level learning software. Nicky Page had warned Arianna that the relationship with her was "cold" and "a bit tense at moments."

"This guy should take Bryan as an example. Everyone says that Bryan is calculating and severe, but you know what? Bryan doesn't micromanage you; Bryan just wants results, and he doesn't care how you reach your objective if you can justify your methodology."

The beginning of the meeting with Silvia Prescott and Nicky Page had, indeed, been cold and a bit tense at moments. But as Silvia spoke, Arianna realized she was from Ohio, her home state, and at this very moment also realized she knew exactly where the Traphistry office was located.

"Your office is on Vine Street, right?" Arianna had said to Silva, cutting off Nicky, her superior, mid-sentence.

Silva had been surprised by the interruption—and delighted that a young lady she'd met in a Manhattan office knew about her business and hometown.

Arianna's intervention had been a true icebreaker, and from there the conversation had flown freely, first about Traphistry and software business in Cincinnati, and then about how Cognit could help Traphistry reach its goals. At some point during the meeting, Silvia was looking more often at Arianna than Nicky Page, which worried Arianna.

Would the partner resent being upstaged by her underling? But no: Nicky had looked relieved to see Silvia's mood improve, and had thanked and praised Arianna warmly after it. So Nicky, too, was focused solely on the bottom line, just like Bryan...

"I'm so glad I can work with Bryan now. All thanks you, Arianna!"

The person who ranted about data analysis practices at Cognit as he rode the M train to Astoria with Arianna was Edwin. Edwin now worked with Bryan because Arianna had involved him in the Brome project. After Arianna asked Edwin to perform the research instead of her, he had billed the hours in the system.

And somehow, Bryan had ended up entirely satisfied by the whole ordeal. Both Arianna and Edwin were now fully involved in the file. And Edwin had just thanked Arianna for stealing hours from him. While they were going for an evening out in Astoria, to which Arianna had invited him because she felt bad for having stolen his hours.

Her guilty feelings aside, it was true that their work on the Brome project was going well: Edwin handled the data and analysis while Arianna dealt with most human interactions, design and marketing. They had applied the comparative advantages theory, had said Edwin. Bryan seemed quite pleased with their work and had even taken both of them out for lunch. Nothing fancy, but the fact that Bryan and not Arianna had paid the bill at Palace Restaurant genuinely had made that gluten-free corned beef sandwich she ate there tastier in her mouth.

Now co-workers noticed Arianna becoming a fixture in Bryan's crew, and people she had never talked to started to say, "Hi, Arianna!" to her. This morning, a new employee she didn't even know had asked for her opinion on some assignment, even though Arianna was still just a junior with nine months of experience.

"I tell you, if we continue this way, you and I, we'll make it to senior within two years!"

Edwin looked straight at Arianna. His rant was over and he expected an answer from her.

So Arianna said, "If we don't make it to senior within two years, they'll fire us anyway."

Here was another reason Arianna invited Edwin to go out with her friends: she suspected he was developing feelings for her, feelings that, if they existed, were not reciprocal, not at all, not in a thousand years. Arianna really wanted to maintain a good relationship with Edwin. She needed him. And she knew she needed him more than he needed her—professionally speaking.

So, tonight, Edwin would be on the town in Astoria with three girls out of his league, something Arianna doubted would happen often if he stopped being friends with her. She felt bad about playing games like this, but she was even more afraid of the consequences of not playing them.

They exited the M train at 46th Street Station and walked toward their destination, a wine bar called DiWine. Astoria felt strange to Arianna: it was less dense than Williamsburg, let alone Manhattan. Most buildings had three stories max, and they even walked pass detached houses. Still, the traffic, motorized and pedestrian alike, made it hard to forget that they hadn't left New York City.

KNITTING DEATH

The two co-workers entered DiWine; Arianna saw Diana wave at her from a booth, which was made of two brown couches facing each other, with two tiny coffee tables in between. There was a guy with her: Josh, the hottie who was there the other night at the bar. He warmly greeted Arianna with a kiss on each cheek before shaking Edwin's hand. Arianna sat beside Diana; Edwin sat with Josh on the other couch across.

"Melissa should be here any moment," said Diana to Arianna. "So... don't you have something to tell me?"

For a fraction of a second, Arianna experienced panic. Diana's question made her think of her inquiry on the three dead knitting girls. But no. Diana's demeanor was not one of accusation, but of fun girls gossiping... Still?

"Such as...?"

Diana rolled her eyes before adding, "Oh, come on, Arianna. Josh here is a good friend of Nicolas, who you are... dating? Seeing? Just fucking?"

"Oooh! Nicolas!"

Yes, Nicolas. So Nicolas had told his buddies about her. And Arianna had not told her friends about him. And her friends had the right to know, for all purpose and intent. But to know what?

"Yes. Nicolas. You, apparently, spend some time, including whole nights, at his place. Are you denying it?" asked Diana with a mocking smile.

"No! I spent the night at his place last Thursday after we met the guys at the pub, and I went back Sunday."

Arianna wanted to tell Diana that one of the main reasons that had motivated her to go to Nicolas's place was he had been supportive of her desire to look into these three suspicious deaths. But Diana had not been too keen to explore the subject, and Arianna had no desire to antagonize her.

Nicolas had come close to ruining the whole thing when he started to link the three deaths to stories on conspiracy websites... but he made it up afterward, when he found the contact info for Judi Di Fiori, Christina Bain's former roommate and, generally, just by being serious and helpful about this whole thing that started to obsess Arianna.

Diana looked straight at Arianna; she expected more details. Arianna was saved by the waiter, who came to take their orders. She asked for a glass of Laurent Miquel, the same thing as Diana (Diana was a safe bet in terms of choosing white wine on Thursday night). After ordering, Diana's attention was kept busy by something on her phone; across from them, Edwin and Josh looked like they already were in the middle of a conversation, despite having met each other only five minutes ago.

They made quite the contrast: Josh with his tall and slim frame, calm, big brown eyes and large grin, silky black locks falling around his head, looking sweet but manly, dressed like a magazine model with a checkered shirt and jeans perfectly fitted to his body and, although she couldn't see them from her seat, Arianna had noticed the Martin Dingman loafers he wore upon entering the place.

Edwin played yin to Josh's yang, with his demeanor all unharmonious in gestures, tone, tempo, choice of words and timing; he obviously tried to dress up for the occasion, but his blue shirt was too large, his khakis too short, his shoes too black, and his socks too white.

And then there was Nicolas, absent in person, present in mind—present in Diana's mind, at least. While nowhere a hunk like his friend,

Josh, or even the other one, the mixed-race-American with the gorgeous afro who had been at the other end of Heather's heavy flirt the other night, Nicolas was officially cute. And funny. And he always stopped being an obnoxious smart-ass just before Arianna seriously considered leaving his apartment and deleting his contact from her phone.

So... what about him? It struck Arianna that she hadn't even thought about it. That realization scared her a bit—was she already entirely jaded by boys at her young age? Had she lost all hope of finding someone to share her life? But her train of thought stopped there: thinking about Nicolas made her think about Christina, Marie-Louise, and Marianna, may God rest their souls.

A waiter arrived with four glasses of wine. The quartet lifted them above the tables to toast and cheered. The liquid felt good in Arianna's mouth, throat, and belly.

Josh and Edwin went back to their conversation. "They really look like they hit it off," remarked Diana, speaking softly to Arianna so the guys couldn't hear her. "I would initially have qualified this turn of events as... unlikely. What do you think they talk about?"

"Must be video games or something," guessed Arianna. "Boys, right."

"Melissa!" shouted Diana.

Their friend had arrived, along with Fred, a colleague of Melissa who Arianna had met previously. More greetings and kisses and handshakes; their seating area was a bit tight for six, but everyone squeezed in.

Arianna's phone vibrated: there was a new message in her personal web account from some Marvin Wilmar. He was someone she had contacted for the inquiry. And if she remembered well, he was actually... Marie-Louse's ex-boyfriend!

She had to read that email. Now. But she didn't want to do it while the others were around.

Time for a bathroom break, where Arianna had to go anyway.

The restroom was unoccupied. Arianna read as she peed: "I'll be at my place Saturday; text me before you arrive."

"Yes!" Arianna shouted a little too loud; if someone was waiting on the other side of that door, that someone would wonder what was happening in this washroom.

She went back to the group. "Arianna! So apparently, you're the new corporate star at Cognit!" shouted Mellissa. Everyone looked at Arianna.

"What are you talking about, Melissa?"

"Your colleague here was telling us how you're getting the both of you all these cool assignments and how the partners bring you along for clients' meetings!" she said, pointing at Edwin.

"Oh, Edwin does the hard part; I mostly just package it all nicely. You know I'm right, Edwin!" Arianna didn't really mind being put on the spot, but was curious to see how Edwin would react to the attention.

"You saved a client meeting with Nicky Page; I definitely had nothing to do with that," protested Edwin.

"Well, that was funny," said Arianna, addressing the whole group. "You know how in movies, the girl from the countryside who comes to the Big City is made fun of because she's not sophisticated enough? Well, the exact opposite just happened to me: I just scored big with this partner, simply by realizing that the client was from Cincinnati, my hometown, and exchanging generalities about home with her. Like, at the beginning of the meeting, she was cold and distant, but then I shouted, "Oh my God! Your business is on Vine Street!" literally cutting off the partner mid-sentence, but then that woman was soooo happy, her face literally lit up! So we chatted about random Cincinnati stuff for fifteen minutes, and then real business and it went well so the partner was soooo happy. And... that's about it. I was lucky, really."

Arianna concluded by taking a sip (the last one) from her glass.

"Ohio is recognized as a place with no accent; how could you know she was from there?" Edwin asked the question as if it was a really serious one (and maybe it was for him).

"Redneck sixth sense," said Arianna.

"Redneck my ass; have you ever seen a redneck who knits?" said Josh, pretending to put an icing of aggressiveness and abrasiveness over his charm and niceness and beautifulness and hotness.

"THE REDNECK KNITTERS"!! shouted Melissa, much too loud considering they were in a public place that, even if it were a bar, was rather small and quiet. "Girls, we have the name of our podcast: 'the Redneck Knitters.'"

"Well, it does sound good..." said Diana. "But it... doesn't sound good."

"Why doesn't it sound good?" asked Melissa.

"The name sounds good..." said Josh. "It's too bad you can't use it for a YouTube channel with video of you in it."

"Why not?" protested Melissa.

Arianna realized Melissa really thought it was a good name, while Josh and Diana's faces said they were absolutely sure it was inappropriate.

Arianna was entirely agnostic on the question but wondered why everyone suddenly was so tense about it.

"Come on," said Josh, "you cannot film the three of you guys knitting and chatting about yarn and needles and then call this stuff "The Redneck Knitters."

"But why? ReD-NeCk-NKitTers! It sounds sooo good."

"Because that would be condescending," Edwin cut in.

"Condescending—exactly!" Josh added enthusiastically. "That would sound super condescending and you could be in trouble. Thank you, Edwin!"

"That's not condescending! It's just a play of words!" said Melissa.

Arianna didn't know whether she didn't understand or didn't want to understand.

"Melissa," Edwin calmly explained, "three young professional women from New York City who use the word 'redneck' are fishing for trouble. You just told me you worked in market access at Pharmathrice, which isn't that bad as no one knows what you or your employer do, but Diana practices corporate law at Burkett Gurewitz; that hits the imagination. As for Arianna, like you, no one knows what she does, but it's not hard to find out she works in big business firm in NYC. You'll get hate comments, hate videos, whole posts dedicated to how condescending you are."

"Look, Edward," said Melissa, "this is just a knitting podcast; how can it be more innocent than that?"

Edwin didn't correct Melissa calling him Edward and just answered her question. "It's even worse: a political show would just pass as provocation and attention whoring and would mostly be ignored, but an innocent knitting show would look totally insensitive. You live in Williamsburg, you're educated, you're all young and pretty ("Ah, thank you!" said Diana before taking a sip from her glass), and for you, Melissa, it's even worse—"

"WHAT? Why is it worse for me?"

"Well, our friend Arianna, right here, basically admitted that she's a flyover-state-white-trash-transplant, so she might manage to get away with the redneck part, but from you, an Asian, it would just look like provocation."

"OH! You mean that would be, like... racist?" Melissa looked as if she was suddenly realizing something.

Edwin smiled. "Some people would perceive it as something akin to racism, but maybe with more emphasis on class than race."

Melissa looked down; it seemed as if she was concentrating hard on something. Diana and Josh looked at each other with a complicit smile—the kind of complicit smile of two people who have seen each other naked? Maybe? Edwin and Fred discussed, facing each other, crouched above the coffee table.

Arianna took her phone: another email! From someone named Judi Di Fiori. Who was Judi Di Fiori? ...Christina Bain's last roommate!? Arianna refrained herself from cheering out loud at the good news. All her efforts were finally paying off! She was making progress!

Arianna grabbed her glass of wine—her new glass of wine, which had appeared in front of her just like magic. She was happy: the job was going well, the inquiry was going well and... and Josh was hot. She would not do anything that could be interpreted as flirty with him as long as she had doubts about Diana's status with him. Diana's friendship was precious (and so was Melissa's), so she would avoid provoking unnecessary strain on their relationship. As close as they felt, they had known each other for less than a year. And once you feel too much at ease with a new friend, you run into the danger of not being careful enough.

Familiarity breeds contempt... you attract people who are like you, and things you don't like about yourself will annoy you when displayed by people you are close to, and you will notice it even more so because it's so much easier to criticize others than to change oneself...

On the other hand, Arianna had felt she was underachieving compared to her two friends. As Edwin had just pointed out, Diana was a corporate lawyer, Melissa a microbiologist, but Arianna... Well, Arianna was, apparently, the rising star at the New York office of Cognit. So maybe, after all, she really was an achiever like her friends.

Melissa and Diana stood up from their seats. Diana looked at Arianna; her stare meant "follow us," so Arianna followed. They all went inside the tiny bathroom.

"Talk!" said Diana as she fetched the eyelash brush from her purse while Melissa positioned herself on the toilet seat.

"About Nicolas?"

"Yes, about Nicolas!" answered Melissa.

"Unless you have more interesting stories to share about your friend, Edwin?" said Diana, her nose nearly touching the mirror as she did her left eyelashes."

"He's all yours!" said Arianna. "But as I was just telling you before Melissa arrived, I've seen Nicolas twice aaaand... that's it. So, what about you and Josh?

"You're changing the subject!" protested Diana.

"Yeah, what about you and Josh?" said Melissa. "It doesn't matter if she's changing the subject."

Diana was done with her eyelashes, so she turned around and seated herself on the counter besides the sink. "Nothing," she said. "I'm not interested."

"What?"

"How come?"

"But why?"

Arianna and Melissa didn't understand Diana's answer.

"He's not my type... well, he's my type, he's pretty much everyone's type, but he reminds me sooooo much of my cousin Steve that it's a turnoff."

"You don't like your cousin?" asked Melissa.

"You're not supposed to like your cousin," said Diana, "unless you're a redneck like Arianna."

Arianna raised her glass (which she realized she had brought in the bathroom)."Ah nevah did anythang with none cousins of mine' y'all should know! There's that on time in the barn, but it don't count, 'cause it was raght before my cousin Jimbo he left fo his deploymint in the Middle East! Aye did nowthang wrong; ah was jawst baing aye pay-triot!"

Diana and Melissa's laughs were interrupted by three knocks on the bathroom's door. The three girls exited their ad hoc meeting room under the judging eyes of a large woman, the three of them barely able to contain their laugh.

Diana said, "Nicolas isn't here... aren't you worried?"

Arianna came closer to her and whispered. "I don't mind if he fucks other girls; all I want is that he thinks about me when he does."

As they reached their table, the three guys were looking at them. There was something new on the table: shot glasses filled with a transparent liquid, each of them with lime placed on their rims.

Melissa turned toward her two friends and said, "Guys, it's all downhill from here…"

12. Saturday Morning Road Trip

Arianna carefully took a sip from her venti soy Cinnamon Dolce Latte as she engaged the eastbound lane of the Garden State Parkway. She realized she actually had missed Starbucks. She never drank Starbucks in New York City; her caffeine fix came from Gregory's and Blue Bottle around the office and sometimes Oslo, Grade, or Gimme, in Williamsburg, when she cheated on Ben & Jesse's Knits. Arianna preferred Starbucks to Gregory's, Blue Bottle, Oslo, Grade, Gimme and, yes, even Ben & Jesse's Knits if she was honest with herself.

Now, there were plenty of Starbucks around in Midtown and Williamsburg, so nothing, in theory, prevented her from drinking Starbucks. In theory. In practice, she would not have been caught dead holding something as corporate, generic, and basic as a disposable cup branded with the Seattle company's green mermaid.

Caffeine was in order. Even after sleeping more than eleven hours on the night from Friday to Saturday, Arianna still felt the effects of her lack of sleep and excessive alcohol consumption from Thursday. The glass of white at DiWine and the shooters had been followed by more wine and more shooters, and at some point everyone went dancing to a place whose name Arianna could not recall, which was followed by a cab ride to Nicolas's place. For the first time, her visit there did not include any inquiry, just sex and sleep—drunken sex and inadequate sleep.

There was some traffic, but driving on a car-friendly New Jersey road felt like a piece of cake after she had to navigate the mean streets of New York City in the morning. The drive between the rental car dealership and the Elizabeth, NJ, apartment where Christina Bain used to live had been a nerve-racking experience: narrow streets, yellow cabs, pedestrians, Manhattan Bridge, Canal Street, Holland Tunnel, all of them filled with aggressive drivers, and she would have to do it all over again in the other direction later.

At least getting through all this trouble had paid off, relatively speaking. Arianna had met with both Judi Di Fiori, who was Christina Bain's ex-roommate, and Casey Carson, her ex-best friend; both had been generous enough to answer all her questions.

Both agreed that Christina had become insufferable about six months before her death; the girl they would previously have described as generous, kind, and sincere had morphed into a shallow, self-centered, egocentric wannabe star who only thought and talked about her upcoming singing career.

Their description did fit with Christina's social media history, which had taken a turn from generic cat pictures to glamorous scene shots (or tentative glamorous scene shots).

"My sweet Christina turned into a mean Instagram bitch," Casey had complained, sad, but also angry.

Casey had mentioned that Christina talked nonstop about Bat Wing, which most likely referred to the #BatWing hashtag found on the Coven Craft message board. They also shared that Christina ranted endlessly about some Reverend Mother who had promised her a successful career; the nature of the rants oscillated between praise and curse, depending on Christina's violent mood swings.

No smoking gun or even any new clues that could help explain the three deaths, but Arianna felt she was digging at the right spot, which gave her satisfaction (enough satisfaction to justify the car rental and gas cost).

Something else brought some satisfaction to Arianna—not being Judi or Casey. She was like them enough to be able to get them to talk to her, a perfect stranger, about the loss of a loved one. And Arianna had made sure to be like them as much as possible—by wearing tight off-the-shelf jeans and white top and a sports jacket and just a bit too much makeup.

It was frightening how easy it was for Arianna to get accepted by those suburban girls as one of them. She didn't even have to look at Stacey's friends' Instagram pictures for inspiration. But it was also satisfying knowing she was not like them, that she had dodged the bullet of a dead-end suburban life in Nowhere, USA.

Arianna turned the radio on and selected 100.3 FM. If she could drink Starbucks in peace, it meant she could also indulge into commercial Top 40 music. She immediately recognized the bass line that came through the car speakers, vividly remembering having danced on that tune with Melissa and Diana in a club in Manhattan a few months ago:

> Girl forget the other men I'll blow up like St. Helen
>
> In HD your nudes I saw them in HD blow my mind
>
> I'm no messed-up boy I make up my mind
>
> I've been through the grind what don't kill you
>
> Make me stronger when I'm with you

KNITTING DEATH

> I've been through the grind I'm chiseled a Grecian statue
>
> In HD your nudes right on cue
>
> Like blowin' Yellowstone
>
> I'm blowin' Yellowstone

Arianna had no idea who the artist was, or what was the tune's title, but it was a popular hit of the moment, so at some point she would know. It was catchy; she pumped up the volume and enjoyed the song, slightly moving to the beat in the car seat.

> He say let up steam I say beware the geyser
>
> I say grab the dough my mind focused like a laser
>
> High-hanging fruits they're the one that taste better
>
> Cherry-picking you the tastier
>
> In HD the explosion
>
> Like blowin' Yellowstone
>
> I'm blowin' Yellowstone

Had the tune played, at some point, on Thursday night, at the club? Maybe. That part of the evening was rather blurry in her mind. She also worried that it was not healthy to have partial blackouts.

Well, at least she remembered going to Nicolas's place; the cab ride probably had been long enough for her to sober up. She remembered what he had said the second time she'd met him—that he wanted to come along with her when she would go meet people who knew the girls before they died. For security. Well... no. Arianna was old enough to take care of her own. And also, she feared his presence might be counterproductive. Arianna had one major asset: she had a profile that was very similar to the deceased girls; it would make her questioning less suspicious. With Nicolas, however, they'd look like... Well, Nicolas didn't fit in the picture.

Arianna took the exit for New Jersey Route 3, as suggested by Google Maps through the car's screen. She was now in the city of Clifton, home of Marvin Wilmar, Marie-Louise Thompson's ex-boyfriend.

Arianna left Route 3 onto a series of residential streets lined with old but mostly well-maintained detached houses. She parked her car in front of a two-story house covered with wood cladding painted in light blue. In the driveway was an immaculate black late-model Dodge Ram pickup. On the yard besides the house was a young man crouched over a kayak; he vigorously washed the yellow fiberglass watercraft with a sponge. Tall, athletic, short curly black hair: Marvin it was.

Arianna exited her rental vehicle and waved toward the man. He did not wave back and continued his kayak-washing business, although Arianna was quite sure she was within his sight. She also was quite sure he had noticed that a car had parked in the quiet street in front of his home.

She walked toward him, stepping onto the green lawn.

"Are you with them?" he said in lieu of greeting, without looking at her.

"Am I with whom?"

"Are you with THEM?" he repeated, louder and with more aggression in his voice.

"I'm not a member of the message board. And I don't participate in the Bat Wing knit-along."

"How did you meet Marie-Louise, then?"

Marvin scrubbed his boat harder has he spoke.

KNITTING DEATH

"I've never met her." Arianna nearly added, "I told you over the phone" but refrained. The guy was obviously, and understandably, distressed.

Marvin (finally) lifted his chin and looked at Arianna. "Why are you here then?"

"Three girls are dead, all within a few days. All three are about my age, and all three enjoyed knitting, just like me. Maybe I'm overreacting, but I can't help it: it's scaring the fuck out of me."

"Three... there are two more?" said Marvin. This time, he stopped sponging his kayak.

"Marianna Burrow; she apparently jumped out of the window of her apartment in the city. Christina Bain; died in her bath, not far from here in Jersey City."

Marvin sat on the front end of the kayak. He fiddled the blue sponge he still held with his fingers, looking at the ground in front of him.

"I've heard those names. Marianna... Do you have a picture of her?"

Arianna took her phone, accessed the folder dedicated to the inquiry on her Google Drive, and selected a profile picture of Marianna she had saved there. Marvin's lips contracted when she put the screen in front of his face.

"Yeah, I've seen her. Just about when it hit the fan with Marie-Louise."

"So Marianna and Marie-Louise had been friends just for a few months before they both died?"

"I guess."

Arianna selected a picture of Christina Bain.

"I know this one," said Marvin. "The singer. Well, I don't know her, but I had to endure two of her shows at this crappy place in Newark."

"Why did you go the second time if you didn't enjoy it the first?"

"Marie-Louise insisted. She said it was important for us to be there. Don't ask me why; I know she didn't enjoy it more than I did, even if I was never able to have her admit it."

"So, she wanted to be there to support Christina's promoters, the people who are behind her?"

"I don't know about that. She would talk to all those people who were also present at the show. It was just about the time when she started that big job..." Marvin then looked straight at Arianna. "You do know a lot for a total stranger. Are you sure you're now with them? I don't think you're telling me the whole truth here."

Arianna somewhat expected to be put on the spot. Marvin looked as if he was the suspicious type, and she did know a lot for a total stranger.

"I wish!" exclaimed Arianna. "She lived the life."

As expected, Marvin was surprised by Arianna's answer. She went on. "I don't do grocery shopping with Valentino sneakers on. Marie-Louise did. So... you were telling me about that big job of hers... Where did she work?"

"She did corporate law at this firm in the city since June of last year. The name of that place never stuck in my memory; she just called it 'BeeJee' or something. I can give you one of her business cards; she left a lot behind when... I tell you, the day she started there is the day when everything begun to spiral down. It's not that I wasn't happy for her; she had worked hard to get there, she deserved it. I was super supportive when she was in law school... but when she started working, she began to change... and not for the best."

Marvin stood up from the ground and sat on the front end of the kayak. "She worked all the time, went out all the time, complained about stuff all the time... I was not good enough for her anymore. It all got up to her head: this new job, these new cool friends, this new lifestyle. But it killed her. I was not perfect, but I know that if she had stayed with me, she'd still be alive."

It was mostly anger and frustration that oozed from Marvin, but underneath it all, Arianna felt genuine sadness. It was hard for him to talk about her, yet she had to press on. "How did Marie-Louise pay for all her trips and all her shopping?"

"What do you mean?" he answered, rather aggressively.

"She did work at a reputable law firm, but unless I am mistaken, she had not made it to partner during the few months she had worked there. Top firms pay their associates well, but not that well."

"She told me she was invited to these things." Marvin sounded upset now. "Why was she invited to these events? Well, since you know Marie-Louise so well, maybe you can tell me? Because I've been asking this question for a long time. To myself, but also to Marie-Louise herself, when we were still together. Which, apparently, I had no business asking. But you, you're a girl, you're her age, and you're also asking that question. So just to be clear, right now, you and I are agreeing that me asking her asking particular question was totally legitimate?"

"Well..." Arianna was taken short by the new direction the conversation was going.

"Oh, come on. Don't you tell me it's not all tied in together: her expensive lifestyle, her so-called new friends, and her death? That it's the same son of a bitch responsible for all three? And you are here right now because that son of a bitch is at large?"

"Oh! No! Well... I really don't think so..." Arianna suddenly realized what Marvin had in mind. "Look, we don't think there's one... like one creepy rich dude behind these three deaths. Actually, the other day, I was talking about the situation with this guy I know, and he told me, well, he said..."

"What did he say!" screamed Marvin.

"It doesn't look like they were whoring themselves. It doesn't look like there was an evil sugar daddy involved there."

Marvin burst in tears. He put his hand on his mouth, he sobbed, he closed his eyes, and told Arianna, "Come with me inside."

Arianna followed the total stranger in his house—into his garage, actually. Marvin opened the white fridge located there beside a shelf filled with gardening accessories. He pulled out two bottles and popped their caps with an opener. He rapidly swallowed about ten sips before handling the other bottle to Arianna. The label read: "H-Town Helles."

"So if it's not some old pervert who killed her then... who is it?"

Arianna took a tiny sip from the bottle—not bad. She was not much of beer drinker, but at the moment it felt quite good.

"Well, Marvin, before we go further... let's go back to the beginning. Specifically, the way you talk, you take for granted that Marie-Louise was killed."

"So do you!"

There was much less anger in his replies to her. What Arianna had said, about Marie-Louise's lavish lifestyle not being supplied by a rich lover seemed to have removed a weight on his chest, despite Arianna producing no evidence or even argument in that direction.

KNITTING DEATH

"The deaths are suspicious, but not enough to take for granted they were murders... Look, I don't know what killed her, but this whole thing smells fishy, and people around me think I'm being paranoid, but you... well, obviously you have your suspicions—"

"You bet I have my suspicions. This job made her batshit crazy, but it didn't make her suicidal. You know what I mean?"

"Yes, I—"

"Yes, you know what I mean; this is why you are here."

"So, you will help me finding who is behind all of this?"

"Well, this is where you and I are different... Miss Arianna. As much as I miss Marie, I knew she was getting involved with dirty people. And so did she. I mean, she denied it—vehemently, aggressively, with much anger, actually—but she knew. I am sure that deep inside she knew that she was dealing with some shady shit."

Arianna was taking aback by Marvin's comment. "So because she was somehow aware that her new surroundings hid malevolent characters, she deserved what happened to her?!" As Arianna finished the sentence, she realized she verbally attacked a complete stranger who was kind enough to let her in his home and answer her questions about the death of the girl he loved. *Don't let your raw emotions screw up with your inquiry!* she thought, angry at herself. But Marvin did not take offense.

"Look, I perfectly understand why this whole thing keeps you up at night and why you probably think of asking your doctor for a higher dosage for your anxiety prescription; it looks like the bad guys went after chicks like you. But here's the thing. Nothing would have happened to Marie-Louise if she hadn't gotten involved with the bad guys in the first place."

Arianna felt like screaming insults at Marvin. Was he insinuating that it was Marie-Louise's fault if she was dead? But she did not scream insults, as she had just told herself to "not let your raw emotions screw up with your inquiry" just a few seconds before. So Arianna said nothing, and Marvin went on.

"It's like the drug trade. If you get involved in the drug trade, bad things are likely to happen to you. Bad things can happen to you in any trade, but if bad things happen to you in the landscaping trade or plumbing trade, you can call a lawyer or the cops. Not if you work in the drug trade. So because you can't call the cops in the drug trades, more bad things tend to—"

"So you think Marie-Louise was involved in illegal activities?" Arianna interrupted. She was about to ask which activities exactly, but instead said, "Let me guess. You did ask, and she denied, and was quite angry about you asking, and said, 'You don't understand!' a lot..."

"Pretty much." Marvin stared at the ground, holding his bottle between his hands.

"And these criminal elements you suspected, there is nothing that Marie-Louise said or did that gave any clue about their nature?"

"She was a lawyer, wasn't she? She would know what to do to cover her tracks. And she would know when her tracks were not covered well enough, which is what I suspect drove her insane."

Arianna had the strong feeling she had harvested every bit of useful information from this particular person—at this moment. She might need him in the near future, like to check if he had seen a particular person in the company of Marie-Louise. There was no point in staying longer and running the chance of antagonizing him. "Thank you, Marvin. I will go now. I appreciate the time to share all this with me, even if it brought back painful memories."

She exited the garage and hoped back in her rental car. She drove back toward NJ Route 3, slightly angry, upset at Marvin. He had been, under the circumstances, rather welcoming and generous, but she resented something about the way he talked about Marie-Louise.

How super-supportive had he really been of Marie-Louise's studies and early career? Was he really happy she had found a job in a prestigious firm? He said so, but something in him said otherwise. Something non-verbal, something about the way he expressed it and verbalized it... something that reminded Arianna of the way some people back home had reacted when she had announced she would move to NYC. "I'm happy for you, but..."

As unsympathetic as he was to Arianna, Marvin, at least, agreed that there was something highly suspicious in the death of the three young women. She was not alone anymore in this, just in bad company.

The next meeting was the most promising one: Martine Cunning. She was an actual participant in the Bat Wing knit-along and also the host of a podcast Arianna watched—used to watch, as Martine hadn't posted any new videos on her feed for the past six months. She had, however, replied to Arianna's message through Ravelry and accepted her request to meet.

Arianna was eager to know what this Bat Wing was really about; whatever it was, it constituted the main theme the three dead girls had in common. But before she could ask any question, Arianna would have to drive the fifty miles between her current location and Huntingdon, the Long Island town where Martine resided.

Arianna's mind suddenly dropped all matters related to her inquiry, as signals of hunger rang from her belly. She was ready, having planned for this moment while preparing her trip the evening before. Arianna kept on rolling for a bit, but instead of continuing on Road 3 toward

New York City, she took the exit to NJ Road 17, and then the first exit for Meadow Road, and then entered the parking of the Popeyes Louisiana Kitchen.

Arianna reasoned that if she were to skip her Saturday morning yoga and Saturday afternoon gym and eat on the road, she might as well go all the way toward full self-indulgence. It was not the first time, and her body would soon let her know if it were the last one without consequences, as it always had been, so far. **Let's touch wood.**

She parked, went inside, and ordered a Loaded Chicken Wrap and sat in the restaurant, the sandwich in her left hand, her phone in the right one.

She stopped chewing. Someone had contacted her through Facebook Messenger; someone she had added just a week ago. Denise... If Arianna remembered well, Denise had been close to Marie-Louise. She continued reading: "Marie-Louise brought the case to the SEC. This is why she died."

"Holy shit!"

A woman who sat on a table nearby with her two kids was looking straight at her. Arianna wondered why for a few seconds until she realized she just had cursed aloud in a family restaurant. She then looked back at her phone, trying to put her thoughts in order.

"The SEC, the... SECond most dangerous guys, after the IRS. "So IRS is for taxes, and SEC for financial stuff. Or so Edwin had said the other day at the office.

Arianna mechanically ate her Loaded Chicken Wrap as she processed the message and its meaning. There was a third person who thought Marie-Louise had been murdered. And, as opposed to Marvin and herself, this person had put forward a motive for the murder.

KNITTING DEATH

Arianna shoved the last piece of the wrap in her mouth and slipped her cell in her pocket. She desperately wanted to reply and ask question after question, but she opted to wait and think about it all first.

Thinking about it all was not easy as she drove through New York City, an operation that required a fair amount of attention. Denise's Facebook message was always in the back of her mind, but by the time she could relax behind the wheel without fearing for her life, she was nearing Martine Cunning's house.

Huntingdon was rather nice: well-kept lawns, picket fences, many trees, and large houses that were opulent, sober, and always well maintained. "We're not in Jersey anymore," said Arianna aloud as she parked in front of Martine's house—Martine's parents' house, to be exact. The first thing she noticed was the pretty yellow wooden garden shed, which actually was not a garden shed but Martine's craft room—craft cabin? The gorgeous, tiny cabin was featured in Martine's podcast opening. The interior was even better, with shelves full of yarns and accessories.

Still, Arianna rang the bell at the house's main entrance. The door opened. Arianna froze. She was shocked. It was Martine. The same person she saw in the podcasts. But she wore an old night gown and was disheveled and her eyes... her eyes were like death.

"Hi, Arianna. You want to come in?" said Martine with an empty expression.

The Martine in the podcast was smiling and laughing and had nice light brown hair and just enough makeup and wore the nicest knitted vests, sweater, shawls or lighter, non-wool stuff when it was warm. The Martine in front of Arianna was all the opposite. She looked like a terminal patient.

Arianna shook herself out of her torpor. "Yes, thank you," she said as she followed Martine inside.

Martine sat in a rocking chair in the living room; Arianna sat in a couch beside her. The living room had been featured in footage that Martine sometimes put at the end of her podcast episodes, which somehow reassured Arianna. The orderly and sunny room contrasted with Martine's gloomy aura.

"Thank you for receiving me in your home, Martine. I really appreciate it," said Arianna.

"Oh, it's nothing," answered Martine. "It's nice to have a visitor."

"I was a big fan of your podcast. I've seen all episodes!"

"It was a lot of work," said Martine. "The filming, the editing, focusing the camera on tiny details... but it was fun. A lot of work..." Martine somehow warmed up a bit as she talked about her podcast.

"So in the message I sent you, I was saying—"

"Stay away! These people are dangerous. Stay away from them. Stay away from anything they touch," shouted Martine, staring straight at nothing in front of her, her eyes wide opened.

The warm-up was over.

Arianna pressed on. "But who exactly..."

Martine's head turned straight at Arianna, her wide, dead eyes peering right into her: "This is why you are here!"

"Yes! But I don't even know—"

"You think about joining! You think about joining them!"

"I haven't been invited, Martine!" shouted Arianna, hoping to shock Martine out of her trance-like bout.

"It will come." Martine looked like a tired old lady. "They will come for you, too. They will bring you to nice events in beautiful places with impressive people, with delicious food, they will offer you well-paying jobs, you will meet pretty boys... rich women... rich, gorgeous men..."

"Who are they?" asked Arianna with much insistence.

"...ski trips, houses on the beach, exclusive clubs... they will bring you to paradise..." Martine continued her rant without answering Arianna. "...but at some point you will look around and realize they have dragged you to the bottom of hell."

Arianna was annoyed at Martine's cryptic answers. And creeped out; the only reason she could refrain from running away from this madness was that it was happening during the daytime in the middle of a well-off residential area. Her curiosity was still stronger than her fear—for now.

"What about Bat Wing, Martine. What is it? What is Bat Wing?"

Martine stopped talking for a bit. "The knit-along. The Bat Wingknit-along. This is how it all started, this project. At first..." Tears started to drop under Martine's eyes. "At first you think it's just another knit-along, another shawl... just more complex. You are amused at all the secrecy they put around it, you feel like you are part of something secret, something cool... And you realize that you are, indeed, part of a group..."

"So Bat Wing is the name of the pattern? And it's the pattern for a shawl?"

"It's a pattern to destroy you. It takes all your strengths and store them in the shawl... The pattern is made so the various stitches send you a message..."

"A message. Okaaaay." Arianna wanted to know if her contemptuous remark would shake Martine out of her current state—but no, she went on.

"Each stitch is like a letter of the alphabet, and together they make sentences that are printed inside your head—"

A car just parked in the driveway; it was probably one of Martine's parents. Arianna decided to try to speedup things. "Christina Bain, Marianna Burrow, and Marie-Louise Thompson. All three were members of the Bat Wing knit-along."

"I did bad things. Very bad things. I am not proud of what I did."

"Did you do anything that is related to their deaths?" Arianna looked outside as a silhouette neared the main entrance—Martine's mother, most likely.

"I lied. I stole. I intimidated other girls. I..." Martine was sobbing now; her mouth was shaking and abundant tears fell on her cheeks.

Martine's mother walked straight to her daughter. "Help me bring her to her room," she said to Arianna.

There was not much help to give; Marine followed her mother. Arianna followed them; they climbed toward her bedroom, and the mother put the daughter to bed, after which she shut the shades, turned off the light, and closed her door behind her.

"Martine has health issues. It's very nice of you to visit, but you have to try to steer the conversation away when she starts to get into her delusions. We are actually making good progress; her situation has really improved since she started her new medication."

"Can I use the bathroom?" asked Arianna.

KNITTING DEATH

The bathroom was as the end of the hall, and in the hall Arianna had seen, in a porcelain bowl on a tiny lamp table, the key set, which she had seen hanging to the craft shed's door in one of the podcasts. Coming back from the bathroom, she picked it up and shoved it into her purse while Martine's mom stared at her phone. Arianna saluted her, exited the house, and went straight toward the shed.

It was unlocked—she had taken the keys in vain.

A vile smell hit Arianna when she opened the door. Old garbage? Some light came through the tiny windows. Arianna immediately recognized the place: the thread wheel, the white dyeing vats, the jigsaw drying pad set, the soap bottles, and the skeins, hundreds of them packed into the shelves. There was something, however, that she had never seen, something that hung from the ceiling by many threads: a large black shawl, with holes in it and concave arcs—the Bat Wing, at last, had revealed itself.

Arianna approached. There were... things hanging from the shawl. It was darker in this corner of the shed, so Arianna used her phone's light. The thing that had attracted her attention looked like a chicken thigh bone; three threads attached it to the rest of the shawl. As she moved the light across the shawl she came across two similar bones, and then a series of teeth, all pierced in the middle, a thread holding them together through these holes. And then her phone lit up four more teeth, but these teeth were not tied to the shawl; they were in the mouth of a rat, a dead rat in an advanced state of putrefaction, its four legs spread apart on the shawl, its rotting body melting and drying in the wool.

Arianna was about to scream, but the flow of air in her throat was interrupted as she violently unloaded her Loaded Chicken Wrap onto the floor.

13. Dealing with the Real World

Arianna stared at the screen of her computer, which displayed her Fifth Third Bank online account details. Her checking account was empty, her saving account was empty (as it always had been), and her credit card account had a few dollars to go before reaching its limit. The rent would be due in eight days, but her next paycheck would be deposited the day after.

Her previous day's road trip was an expedition she couldn't afford. The rental car, the gas, and the snacks had made a massive red hole into her finances, and so had the lengthy, and thus expensive, taxi ride to Nick's place on the previous Thursday. And while on the subject of transportation budget, her MTA monthly pass would also need to be renewed soon.

Hunger suddenly distracted Arianna from her financial woes. She hadn't eaten anything since her stop at Popeyes the day before in Jersey, still sickened by the haunting sight of the dead rodent who had greeted her inside Martine Cunning's knit shed. She felt nauseated the moment she thought about eating. Still, she had work to do, and grinding through the various Brome-project-related-tasks that awaited her on an empty stomach wouldn't bring her far.

She opened the pantry and grabbed a pack of instant ramen noodles, which had been there since she had moved in, thirteen months before. She filled her boiler, turned it on, and stood still in front of it, fixing it as it slowly heated the water inside, her lack of activity being the result of one question for which she tried to find a potential answer but found none.

Who the hell sews a fucking rat onto a shawl?

KNITTING DEATH

Yes, Martine was obviously deranged, but she also looked sick and weak. The act of putting stitches around the rodent's paws as its carcass rested on the shawl needed a minimum of presence, energy, determination—and planning.

What kind of deranged mind could entertain a thought process that can even begin to consider that, maybe, it could be a good idea to sew a rat onto a shawl? Why didn't Martine's parents check inside her craft cabin? What if they did check, but left that awful thing there, and that actually they're as insane as she is?

The boiler clicked off, which pulled Arianna out of her daydreaming. She looked at her cell: 1:52. Still eight minutes before the conference call.

Why did Arianna have to get on a conference call on a Sunday afternoon? Because Arianna, as a Cognit associate, was expected to provide tailor-made solutions adapted to each and every client. And the Milwaukee Wiring Corporation, the organization that had hired Cognit to perform the Brome project, needed deliverables on Tuesday morning, which involved working on Sunday afternoon for a number of Cognit employees, among which Arianna was included.

Arianna looked at her phone to see if there was a new email on Brome—Sunday afternoon conference calls tended to get canceled. Nothing on her job email account, but she had a new text message from an unknown number in the 212 area code: Manhattan.

"Hello, Arianna. This is Charlotte. You contacted me regarding the Bat Wing project. We can meet this week if you wish."

"What?!" shouted Arianna out loud. There was a Coven Craft message board user whose online ID was "ch@rL00Te" and who had a history of exchanges with Marie-Louise Thompson. One of their subjects of predilection was mergers and acquisitions— M&As. Arianna did a simple Google search: "Charlotte M&A New York City." Among the results was the profile page of young investment banker named Charlotte Braun on the team section of the website of a small boutique firm called Gaba Investment.

So, in essence, a long shot, but which apparently had hit the target right in the middle. Arianna texted back: "Thank you, Charlotte. When and where?"

There was one thing that did not, however, make much sense: Arianna had not written her phone number in the email she had sent Charlotte. And she has not programmed any automatic signature in her personal Gmail account, which she had used to contact her.

"Sept 18 at 4 p.m., Midtown. I will txt you the exact location later."

Arianna texted the "thumbs up" emoji as a sign of understanding and gratitude with her right hand as she poured the water from the boiler onto the noodles with the left one. She then selected the "Brome catch-up" item in her Outlook account and clicked on the videoconference hyperlink, which in turn started Microsoft Teams. She set both the camera and microphone to the off position. She was not expected to intervene, so there was no need to show her face or the dirty blank wall behind it on the camera feed.

"...so yeah, Hartford and back, and Manmohan is in the loop and so is his team. This is great. This is great. I'll wait for Jerry to get on to go in the details, but the meeting went well and we're all on schedule."

Pre-meeting chit-chat. Why were the people on the conference call so early?

"That's great to hear, Bryan. I've had the chance to work with Manmohan before and was genuinely impressed by his work and knowledge of the industry. Still, considering the major impact that this project will have on his employer, you made the wise choice by undertaking this preliminary meet-up."

Arianna suspected that many of those late night and weekend calls provided these white, middle-aged men an excuse to avoid the company of their families.

The guy called Jerry joined the call; the official meeting could begin. The first item on the agenda concerned Arianna only indirectly. "Brome transfer pricing optimization" was mostly out of her scope, as far as she understood what Brome was about and what she was supposed to contribute.

As the laptop's speakers amplified Jerry and Bryan's chit-chat across Arianna's living room, Arianna grabbed her Lizard Twins socks knitting project; her afternoon wouldn't be entirely wasted, after all. Hopefully, the knitting would prevent her from entirely losing focus on the conversation. Her mind could only wander so much as she handled the needles.

Her respite was short-lived.

"Tom and Arianna, who are on the line with us, can take care of the carbon footprint section. Once you send them the raw data, they will liaise with our Green Economy practice and add the benchmark section," said Bryan.

"Okay, I'll share the data as soon as possible," said Jerry, and they concluded the phone call. Arianna held her needles above her knees while looking at her computer screen with a blank expression on her face. She was supposed to do something, but she didn't know what. She had only the vaguest idea what a carbon footprint was and had not a clue about what a benchmark section was supposed to look like.

Well, Tom, the senior analyst, would likely know more and was, as his title indicated, the senior one among the two of them; she'd let him figure it all and come back to her.

Arianna's cell buzzed. It was a text message from Nick.

"I thought you should know I met your colleague Edwin yesterday. Josh told him about you and me, and I don't think he was too happy about it."

"Ah, damn it!" shouted Arianna. She had one ally in the whole office and this Josh dude had probably ruined it all.

She threw her Lizard Twins project on the couch and grabbed her laptop. Knitting angry was likely to produce mistakes, and knitting mistakes would only make her angrier. She opened her personal email account. And there it was: the email promised by Denise, Marie-Louise's friend who had texted her while she was inquiring in New Jersey. Arianna forgot about all her job woes; this email was likely to contain crucial info about the circumstances that surrounded the suspicious death of Marie-Louise. Her pupils dilated in anticipation as she clicked on the message:

> Hello, Arianna:
>
> As promised, here are some details I picked on during the last few months before Marie-Louise died.
>
> I think you've figured out a lot by yourself already, but in case what you have come across already has not made it clear: please don't think for a minute that this coven is a game for them. Neither is it a fashion statement nor a creative enterprise. There are elements of both in their activities, but you'll notice that they are actually rather discreet about this witchcraft business. Because a business it is. They are involved in high-

stakes financial dealings, some of which I suspect are rather dishonest and at odds with the law.

At least one of the transactions in which they are involved has attracted the scrutiny of the Securities and Exchange Commission, the agency responsible for applying some key federal laws and financial regulations. My knowledge of finance in general, and of this particular file in particular, are rather limited. What I can tell you, however, is that both the coven and the SEC refer to this particular file as the Pharmathrice M&A and that the coven is involved through the law firm Burkett Gurewitz LLP.

Arianna recoiled from the screen and her left hand rose instinctively to cover her mouth. Pharmathrice and Burkett Gurewitz. Those were respectively Melissa's and Diana's employers.

14. Last Day of Glory of an Office Princess

Risk management, regulatory compliance, digital strategy, forensic investigation, capital management, insurance. All major consultancies have dedicated professionals within their financial advisory group with in-depth expertise who can help you with these individual issues.

Cognit has the expertise for your situation.

Arsenal, Cognit's unique AI-driven analysis system, performs the preliminary assessment of your issue and submits a roadmap to the relevant financial experts, taking into account all the relevant numbers and applicable laws and regulations.

More data, more attention to details, more scope.

Less billing.

At the moment, the U.S. Securities and Exchange Commission's (SEC) EDGAR (Electronic Data Gathering, Analysis, and Retrieval system) processed nine data requests from Cognit. Five of them were from Arsenal and four from human employees. Four searches were for merger and acquisition (M&A) projects, two for conformity, two for the creation of a new investment portfolio, and one for an amateur investigation into the suspicious deaths of the three young women in and around New York City.

This last one had not yielded any results yet, since the user stared at the screen without clicking or typing anything. Because as much as she desired to focus on the new financial element of her inquiry, there was one question that really, really bothered her and often made her mind derail when she tried to focus on something else:

Does Melissa know? Does Diana know? Are they in on the murders?

Staring at the SEC home page did not do much to help her inquiry, but at least it did look like legitimate work, if someone looked at her, not for too long hopefully.

"Arianna, did you finish the editing I asked you to do for the Brome project?"

A job-related interruption. From Tom. Arianna turned to her left and looked up. "Yes," she said before turning back to her screens.

"When?"

"Monday," she said without looking up.

"I'm not talking about those edits; I'm talking about the ones I asked for this morning."

KNITTING DEATH

The fuck you talking about, Tom? You didn't ask me for shit, was the reply that Arianna's brain formulated. That, however, would most likely have been interpreted as workplace harassment, and workplace harassment was not only strictly forbidden by the CCC (Cognit Code of Conduct) but, even more importantly, was entirely at odds with The Cognit Values. Now, Arianna's brain had to answer one question: had Tom actually sent a request for edits this morning? If he was asking, the answer was most likely yes. However, Arianna did not remember such occurrence. She looked at him this time when she said, "Which ones exactly?"

"The carbon emission graph. You said you would do it today."

Ah. That edit. Arianna did not think this request was an edit, as it was entirely new content, for an entirely new section. Which the client had not requested.

"No, I haven't done that one yet."

"Will it be done by five, as you said it would?"

"As I said in my answer, it will be done by the end of the day." Arianna put a tiny emphasis on the end of the day part of her answer.

Tom departed. Arianna looked at the guy who sat to her right (and whom she didn't recall having ever seen before) and said, "How can you interpret end of the day as five? Where does he think he is, the South Dakota Bureau of Motor Vehicles?"

The guy, a short and pudgy young man with round glasses, looked at Arianna for a second before answering. "I guess he meant today before the end of regular business hours."

Well, a sympathetic ear Arianna would not find there. She looked at the clock at the left bottom corner of the left screen: 3:20. It was time to leave. She stood up, picked up her purse and phone, and headed for the elevators. Tom's retarded carbon graph would have to wait; there was no way she would cancel this meeting, where she would meet Charlotte, an actual and active member of the Bat Wing knit-along. Not for a dumb Excel graph that no one at the client's place would ever look at.

Still, she felt uneasy about the whole ordeal with Tom. He was a senior analyst. He often worked with Bryan, thus the reason why she was stuck with him today. She had to be careful... But then again, she had to stand up for herself; if she let mere seniors bully her, she wouldn't last long in this place.

She passed besides the desk where Edwin sat at the moment. He actually had improved his appearance. He had nicer clothes... Clothes that fit him well and that coordinated. Overall, he was... less unattractive. Arianna was pretty sure she had heard someone say, or read a text, that said that he had done some shopping with Josh.

Also, Edwin had barely acknowledged Arianna's presence and entirely avoided looking into her eyes ever since he had learned that she was seeing Nicolas, four days before. This state of affairs was both annoying and impractical, as Arianna worked on the same project as Edwin.

Arianna reached the elevator and went to the ground floor. As she exited into the building's hall, she saw a familiar figure: five feet, dark hair, school uniform. Alia. Arianna smiled and was about to greet the girl with a loud "Alia!" full of joy and surprise when she suddenly realized, with much horror, that: 1. It was school day and that 2. Alia's school was in Brooklyn.

"Alia! What are you doing here?!"

KNITTING DEATH

Alia walked fast toward Arianna, a serious expression on her face. She held something between her hands. "Take this!" she said when she reached Arianna.

Arianna's hands instinctively closed on the book, but her eyes didn't leave the girl. "What are you doing here?!"

But Alia didn't answer. She left toward the exit and said, "I have to go!"

There was not a chance Arianna would leave Alia alone in Manhattan—so she followed her. "What are you doing here, Alia!?" she said, as they exited the building.

"Read this book; it explains everything."

"Alia, you cannot skip school and come over downtown just to give me a book! This is insane! Your school must have noticed you are not in class... they probably have called your mother! She must be worried to death!"

Alia stopped in her tracks, turned toward Arianna, shoved her hand in her coat, and pulled an iPhone encased into a glittery pinkish cover. She unlocked the device and looked at the screen and said, "No message, no missed calls. No one has noticed, no one is worried."

Arianna was about to protest again, but Alia did not let her. "My class is visiting the Museum of Modern Art. Actually... you see, there? That's my class. I gotta run." Alia bolted, indeed toward of a large group of girls who all wore the same uniform as hers. She then stopped, turned around, and shouted: "Read the book!" before resuming her sprint toward her classmates.

Arianna was annoyed by the situation. What was she supposed to do? If she told Heather, she betrayed Alia; if she didn't tell Heather, she betrayed Heather. Had she been a young mother or a schoolgirl, the choice would have been obvious—she would have stuck with her peer.

In theory, Arianna was an adult and was supposed to do the adult thing: report the situation to the responsible adult. But the truth was, although Arianna enjoyed seeing Heather socially, she was not close to her. She knew she would not betray Alia, who was now in safety anyway. But doing so would be stressful; if she got caught, there would be consequences.

Still, Alia was safe, and Arianna had a meeting. She would have to think about it all later. As her heels hit the concrete sidewalk, she was again aware that something burdened her right hand. The book. She looked at it: old, dusty, dark gray with dull beige lettering: VVITCHES. Like WITCHES, but with two Vs instead of one W. It looked like a Victorian steampunk novella that had spent too much time in a humid garage after its owner had found a new cosplay fad. Or, maybe, it was a real old book on witches.

Arianna's phone rang. The screen said it was Tom. It was 3:28. In less than two minutes, she'd be late.

"Fuck Tom," said Arianna aloud. She was nearly there: 119 Fifth Avenue. The building was in sight, a building that would have been exceptional in any other American city, tall and classic and reeking of wealth but, in this particular Fifth Avenue setting, absolutely nondescript. Arianna got in, went into the elevator and pressed 2; seconds later she exited into a gray, badly lit, dull, and undecorated hall with dull brown doors. Unidentified doors, which both struck her as odd, and made her realize she most likely was in the wrong place and would be late.

She motioned to hop back in the elevator when she heard a voice behind her: "Miss Arianna?"

KNITTING DEATH

Arianna turned around. A man with a classic waiter's outfit—black pants, white shirt, black apron, serviette—looked at her from the frame of one of the doors. "Please."

He stood there, obviously waiting for her to get in first. She walked up to him and was about to put her foot through the door but froze there, shocked by what was on the other side of it: a vast dining room, with maybe twenty large tables in the center, and smaller ones around, near the walls. The room was not as large as it was high, at least three stories. Four massive chandeliers hung from the ceiling far above, all of which held hundreds of real, lit candles, which bathed the room with a dim glow. In the middle of the room was a circular bar, behind which were circular mirrored shelves filled with bottles up to and beyond the chandeliers. The floor was black marble and each large table had a burgundy rug underneath it.

Only about a quarter of the larger tables had people sitting at them, most of whom looked like they were finishing lunch. The smaller tables, however, were mostly full, with one, two, or three people around sipping on a coffee or drink.

"This way, please," said the maître d'.

"Where am I? What is this place?" asked Arianna as she followed.

No answer. She stopped in front of a woman: Charlotte, the Bat Wing insider. She had long, silky, dark-brown hair, slightly tanned skin, a tiny nose and bright gray-blue eyes. Her dark suit and white blouse were obviously high-end items, although Arianna hadn't identified which specific brand it was. On the table where she sat was a silver plate with five pitch-black cupcakes with bright red icing.

"Hello Arianna," said Charlotte, smiling. "Please sit."

Arianna sat. "Thank you for agreeing to meet me; this is very nice of you."

"My pleasure." She turned to the waiter. André, I think Arianna here would enjoy tasting your coffee. Could you please bring the bean selection?"

Arianna had already had five coffees since the morning; she feared a sixth one so late in the day would complicate her sleep. Still, she did not contradict Charlotte. A coffee would very most likely be quite enjoyable with the chocolaty cupcakes that looked and smelled delicious.

Arianna was quite intrigued. Where was she? What was this place? Why was it accessible only from an incognito elevator?

"So, what is it that bothers you?" asked Charlotte.

Charlotte and Arianna had agreed to a half-hour meeting; as much as Arianna wanted to ask questions about the premises, she wanted to know more about what this Bat Wing was about.

"Christina, Marianna, Marie-Louise: aren't they bothering you?"

No, a sixth coffee wasn't ideal. Arianna was tense and stressed and adrenalized and did struggle, again, to not come across as too aggressive.

"They do. I knew Marianna. I am quite sad that she died this way."

At this moment André came back, a rectangular basket in his hands. In the basket were many compartments filled with green coffee beans. A tag identified the different varieties: Harrar, Molokai, Los Planes, Mi Esperanza, Fazenda, and La Esmeralda.

"Los Planes is back! I strongly suggest this one," said Charlotte.

Arianna did not feel like asking questions about green coffee beans. She told André she would get a long espresso with the Los Planes beans.

"Madam will have a Los Planes as well?" André asked Charlotte.

"Maybe later... for now I'll have a kopiluwak, filter, please."

André departed. Arianna resumed: "Don't you find it strange that three girls who participated in the same knit-along and lived in the same area all died within a few weeks? Doesn't it bother you?"

"Yes. As I told you, I knew Marianne. I had also met Marie-Louise a few times and she was quite nice. But to be honest, I'm a bit too overwhelmed by Marianne's suicide to pay much attention to Marie-Louise. As for Christina, it didn't even cross my mind to put her in there with the two others, although you are... technically right; she did participate, at some point, in the knit-along."

"How did you meet Marianne?"

"Both of us were twenty-four, investment bankers, knitters, New Yorkers... who spent way too much time on the Bat Wing knit-along message board. Actually, most of our exchanges happened there."

"The knit-along message board is much more than a knit-along message board, isn't it?"

"It is. It began as a forum dedicated to the knit-along, but over time grew into something much bigger."

The conversation was going in all directions. Arianna had so many questions to ask; having a notebook would have made the task easier. It would also have been weird, so the exercise was going notebook-less, with the added confusion, and most likely frustration over missed questions later.

"So, Charlotte, you were telling me... it didn't cross your mind to put Christina Bain along Marie-Louise and Marianne, even though—"

"She used the board to promote her shows. I doubt she ever completed two rows of the Bat Wing."

"What about Martine Cunning?"

"Who is this?"

"A girl who worked on the Bat Wing. And who did more than two rows, if the unfortunate encounter I had at her place was, as I suspect, the Bat Wing."

Charlotte looked Arianna straight in the eyes: "I don't know who Martine Cunning is. Do you know her Bat Wing forum username? I knew Marie-Louise IRL and was aware of Christina's existence through her shameless self-promotion, but most users I know only through their nicknames. As for the Bat Wing ... I am not sure what you are talking about, exactly."

Anger rose inside Arianna. She felt like Charlotte was lying in her face, which, in itself, wasn't the problem—people lie to each other all the time. The problem was that her arguments were unconvincing, weak, and lacking in logic. But still, she sat there as if she thought Arianna would gobble them all.

"I am not too sure what I am talking about, either," said Arianna, "because it all revolves around a so-called knit-along that somehow needs to be hidden into a member-restricted section, out of sight for the common mortals."

Charlotte took a sip from her coffee and slid her hands under the table; from there, she pulled out a black Balenciaga gym bag. She undid the zipper and drew something from it: all black, with silver and white pieces of jewelry tied to it that chimed together as she unfolded it with both hands. It was the blackest wool Arianna had ever seen, yet it did shine a bit, as if there was silk fiber mixed in with the wool.

Charlotte wrapped the shawl on her shoulders: knits, purls, dips, garters, brioche, cable stitches, all filled with decorative jewelry, as if she had forgotten to remove stitch markers as she completed what was... a giant shawl. There was also lace in it. So much lace, including one giant pattern that represented a spider web, in the middle of which was another spider made of what looked like solid silver, except for its two ivory fangs.

"It really is a big shawl," said Charlotte. "A special big shawl, for sure, but a big shawl nonetheless.

It was a big shawl. The size and complexity of it all awed Arianna; it must have taken months, maybe years, to complete, considering that Charlotte did, actually, work full time.

Arianna grabbed a cupcake and took a bite out of it. It tasted rich and chocolaty and sweet and perfect; its texture was fluffy and unctuous. The thing melted in her mouth. André approached, a silver platter in his hands, two white and blue porcelain cups with the matching creamer and sugar set on it.

Charlotte's cell vibrated from somewhere under her shawl; she grabbed it and typed on it as André served the coffee.

Arianna didn't mind the interruption, as she could enjoy the last bites of the cupcake without having to talk. Still, what dominated her mind was the urge to confront Charlotte, who sat there as if everything was normal, yet was so very oblivious with her coven and Bat Wing and spiders and secret gatherings (even of the electronic kind) that even a nine-year-old like Alia had caught on about the act: those girls were playing witches. But instead of dressing up as actual witches, taking pictures, and just posting them on Instagram, they acted as if they were members of some secret society.

"You are right. It is strange. It is scary."

Either Charlotte had caught on to Arianna's annoyance, or something had finally lit up inside her head and... and the coffee was absolutely delicious. Arianna barely ever drank her coffee black, but this time she had tried, just to make sure she could get over all the fuss they made about those damn green beans. But she had to admit: they were right. It was the most delicious coffee that ever touched her taste buds, even more so as it dissolved the residual cupcake inside her mouth.

Charlotte went on: "When all these tragedies happened, I looked at them as separate events. But you are right that the overall picture is rather odd."

Yet three of them were now six feet underground and while a fourth one sat across Arianna, obnoxiously sharing some of her luxuries with Arianna, her mouth saying she didn't understand, her behavior, demeanor, her whole body was screaming, "Yeah they're dead. So what are you gonna do about it?" Yet...

Yet, behind the bullshit that was behind the surface politeness, she stayed respectful. A girl like her could have sent a loud, yet entirely silent "fuck you" had she wanted to. But she did not.

Sigh. There was not much Arianna would get out of this one. Which meant there was no point in staying (delicious coffee and cupcakes notwithstanding). "Well, thank you for your time, Charlotte, I really appreciate you took the—"

"You're not leaving now?" Charlotte interjected as her eyes left her device to look straight at Arianna. "I can't finish these cupcakes alone! You want to kill me?"

Arianna had not expected Charlotte would try to hold her; when they had agreed on the meeting she insisted that she had only little time for it.

"Why such a hurry?" said Charlotte.

"I need to go back to work."

"Oh please, Arianna; you're the new rising star at Cognit. Everyone will assume you're out meeting clients or prospects."

Arianna was taken aback. That Charlotte knew her employer was unremarkable, but that she was aware of her situation at the company left her speechless.

"Of course I know," said Charlotte, as if she could read her thoughts. "I know many people there. It's part of my job. So tell me: will you try to make it to partner?"

Charlotte looked straight at Arianna; after a few seconds Arianna realized that she was waiting for an actual answer and that, therefore, the question was not rhetorical.

"I don't know! I've been there for less than a year."

"Cognit is not known for its tergiversations. I'm sure you've heard, 'Go for the top or go for the door.'"

"Of course, but—"

"But you thought it was just something people said to reflect the intense competition among the many junior employees for the few top spots? Well, it's not; the expression is an actual description of what any new Cognit employee should seriously think about."

Arianna grabbed the last piece of cupcake on her plate and shoved it in her mouth. It was slightly larger than what a proper bite would be under the circumstances. It didn't matter: her mouth was full, so she couldn't answer right away, so Charlotte would continue taking and maybe bring the conversation elsewhere (and also, the deliciously chocolaty cupcake's chocolaty deliciousness calmed down Arianna).

Charlotte went on: "Oh, I'm sure other firms are after you. These days, you have HR staff doing nothing during their day but hunting for new Cognit hires."

Charlotte's eyes were all lit up; her mouth was switching between flirty and inviting and pouty, her hips moved slightly on the chair as she talked. The whole thing was probably quite efficient to seduce a boy (was without any doubt quite efficient on boys; Arianna had seduced some with half the pouting and staring and flirting), but just succeeded in annoying the hell out of Arianna (which was obviously Charlotte's goal). "Cognit has offices everywhere in the country; why did you choose New York?"

"I did not choose; I was hired for a position here."

"But you could move. How is it, living in Williamsburg on a Cognit associate salary?"

Charlotte's act was getting tiresome. "Living in Williamsburg on a Cognit associate salary is like being poor anywhere else in America, but without access to a Walmart."

Charlotte smiled. "Well, you're the rising star of a rising firm in the Big Apple. Needless to say, this situation is not likely to last, but you will likely enjoy recalling the... material constraints of moving to NYC for an entry-level position."

"You speak of experience?" asked Arianna, with hints of sarcasm in her voice.

"Oh, I did make my mind quite fast. Not so long ago, the rule was: you join a big firm out of college, do your two years, then decide if you try to make it there, or use the name on your resume to find a decent position elsewhere. Not anymore; it's either coding or slaving and I'm not into either of those."

Charlotte's cell vibrated; she grabbed the device, unlocked it, and after staring at it for less than three seconds, put it back on the table. She grabbed her purse, which was hanging on the back of her chair, opened it, and fetched a business card, which she handled to Arianna.

Charlotte Braun

Investment Banker

RedBroom LLC

"Look," Charlotte said, "I think you are right; this is all rather strange. Text me if you think something else is up or makes you worry."

Arianna shoved the card in the inner pocket of her jacket. She and Charlotte rose from their chairs at the same moment and shook hands. Arianna thanked her for her time and the snack and departed. André, who had appeared besides her, as if by magic, walked her to the exit/anonymous hall. As she waited for the elevator, she looked at her phone, and let a sigh of exasperation when she saw that Tom had tried to call her THREE times. She opened her work inbox: Tom, Tom, some generic HR message, Tom, Cognit social club, Tom.

Alone in the hall, Arianna closed her eyes, raised her face toward the ceiling and said: "God! What have I done!?"

15. Upper West Side

Now she had to bolt toward another inquiry-related meeting: Marie-Louise's landlord (former landlord) had agreed to meet her at her former Upper West Side residence. It was an occasion she couldn't miss, one that allowed her to advance her searches during a weekday evening, without having to rent a car, without having to drive in New Jersey, without having to peek into knit sheds decorated with sewn-up rats (hopefully).

She already had planned and registered the trip on her Google account; she remembered she had to get the R train at 23 Street Station, just a few yards north of her current position. She walked fast, doubled slow walkers, pestered interiorly against people who blocked her path until she realized she was slightly in advance. Her pace slowed, but still she kept a good walking speed (why take more chances than needed with the New York City Transit Authority?).

Many commuters filled the cars, making a crowd too dense even for browsing her phone. She exited the train at Times Square–42nd Street/Port Authority Bus Terminal station to transfer on the 3 line, again among a compact mass of people, most of them leaving Manhattan toward the outer boroughs and suburbs. The 3 line train was also packed to capacity, but somehow Arianna ended up facing someone seated on a bench, so she had enough room to operate her phone without poking anyone.

The new mail indicator on the Cognit mailbox icon had reached eighteen unread messages. "I sooo fucked up," she whispered. There was no way she would go through those emails; at this point she might as well declare she'd had a medical emergency.

She opened the Google Drive folder with her inquiry note and re-read the section with the addresses of the buildings, the landlord's name and phone numbers, and the questions she wanted to remember to ask him.

KNITTING DEATH

The questions list was scarce; what was she supposed to ask him? "I think your tenant Marie-Louise was killed. Would you, by any chance, have an idea who the killer is?"

Marie-Louise's and Marianna's apartments were located a few blocks apart on Columbus Avenue. Arianna could imagine the two of them running in Central Park early in the morning, dressed in Lolë from head to toe, cute millionaire boys smiling to them as they passed while jogging in the opposite direction, the two girls sharing a complicit smile as they ran...

Arianna exited the subway at the 72nd Street station and walked south on Broadway toward Marie-Louise's apartment. As she walked, Arianna contemplated the high-rises/castle hybrids that dominated the skyline. As gut-wrenching and nauseating this amateur inquiry endeavor of her was, Arianna had to admit if made her discover her new city.

She reached into The Raven, the luxury apartment tower where Marie-Louise had lived the last few months of her life. The spacious entry hall, all in metallic gray–polished granite, only had two stainless steel benches and one palm tree for furniture, which stood between the benches in a black pot. Across the hall, the three sets of elevator doors did not seem to be fitted with any button to call for a lift, which meant they probably were controlled by a mobile application.

As Arianna crossed the entry door, a large screen lit up to her left: THE RAVEN, it read in a large black art-deco-style font onto a light gray background. "Please say out loud which tenant you wish to contact, or press the screen to use a keyboard," said a female voice. Recorded? Synthetic? Arianna couldn't tell.

"Mario Russo," said Arianna to the machine, pronouncing the name as clearly as she could.

"Please wait," answered the machine. Less than a minute later, the machine spoke again; "Mr. Russo is on its way to the lobby; please wait."

A man exited the central elevator door. He was old, short, portly, and sported a tiny white mustache. "Ms. Arianna? You are the one who called me for Marie-Louise, right?"

"Right."

"You want to see the apartment for yourself?" he asked.

That had not been Arianna's initial intention; just having the opportunity to ask questions of Mr. Russo was enough to motivate her trip. But visiting the apartment was even better, so she agreed. She went into the building and followed him toward the elevators.

Mr. Russo typed something on his phone. "It's terrible, dying so young. She was a nice young woman. She was kind; she brought me tickets for the Knicks for Christmas." The elevator signal chimed; one of the three doors slid open, and she followed him inside. "So, this Miss Thompson, she was a friend of yours?"

"Well... I know her from the internet." Arianna's answer did not make much sense, but was not factually wrong. Starting with the hypothesis that a New York City superintendent must have, on average, some higher-than-normal bullshit detector, she opted to dispense with bullshit (and instead go on with vague statements).

They got out at the sixth floor, where Mr. Russo opened one of the doors. The interior was all white and bright and luminous, the smell indicating it was freshly repainted. It was also large—NYC large—with maybe four times the square footage of Arianna's flat.

"The tenant below her, he called me," said Mr. Russo. "He said, 'There is something leaking from the ceiling. So, I went up to Ms. Marianna's apartment to ask her if somethin' was wrong. But when I got to the door, right at this moment, I knew something was not right. It was the smell; it's always the smell. So I opened the door... and there she was, lying on the floor of the living room. It was not the first time I had to deal with a dead tenant; it's part of the job. Many of them, they're old, so sometimes we find them dead in their apartment. But her, she was not old. She was a beautiful, bright young woman. It ain't right to die so young, all alone in your apartment."

"Was there any sign of a struggle in the apartment when you found her?" asked Arianna.

"Nothing that I noticed. I didn't stay long; I closed the door and called the police. As I said, the smell said she was dead; there was no point going to see if I could reanimate her."

"Do you know what the cause of death?"

"The news article said it was peanut allergy."

"Are you the one who cleaned up afterward?"

"I'm not the one doing the cleaning; I have two guys I contract for that. But what I do is that, before my two guys they do the clean-up, I inspect the apartment. So, I guess your next question is: was there anything unusual in the apartment when I did the inspection? Well, my answer is: no. Nothing stood out. She kept the place clean. Everything was what you would expect to find in the apartment of a young woman who is doing well. She had made her luggage—I think Ms. Marie-Louise really liked to travel, which is quite common with people your age. Do you travel a lot, Ms. Arianna?"

"I don't, actually."

Arianna's lack of travel experience weighed on her. Mr. Russo was right; many people her age had traveled in numerous countries, often to exotic locations, far from tourist itineraries and modern amenities. Not Arianna. She had been outside the States only twice: once to Kitchener, Ontario, when her family had visited her dad's friend who lived there, and once in Dortmund, Germany, during a student exchange in college. Kitchener was closer to home than New York City (and was much more of a normal place, as far as Arianna remembered); as for Germany, Arianna had yet to hear of an ancestor of hers who did not trace their lineage to that country, which meant she probably was more related to the people in Dortmund than New Yorkers.

"Good for you. It's crazy expensive all this traveling. Young people, they complain everything is too expensive. Of course everything is too expensive when you have no money because you spent it all in Thailand or Peru or whatever place is fashionable this year."

Arianna did think everything was too expensive, even though she did not travel. She kept this thought for herself, however.

"The news article said she died of an allergic reaction. Has this been confirmed by anyone?"

"Confirmed? Why would anyone confirm anything to me? I'm not a cop or a prosecutor. I only know what the media said, for what it's worth. And what I saw with my own eyes: when I found her, she laid besides the dining table, a chair tipped over, a single plate of stale pasta collecting mold on the table…"

Mr. Russo stared emptily at nothing as his voice trailed. Finding Marie-Louise's body had obviously shaken him—which probably a very human way to react. And also one that made him share info with Arianna.

"What was on the plate?"

"Pasta."

KNITTING DEATH

"What kind of pasta?"

"What do you mean, what kind of pasta? You think I took the time to check what kind of pasta was on the plate? The girl was lying dead, right there on the floor!"

"So... it was Asian pasta?"

"What do you mean, Asian pasta?"

"Asian pasta... like rice noodles... Ramen, pad Thai, stir-fry..."

"No! No Asian food; she was having regular pasta..."

"Like Italian pasta? With tomato sauce?"

"Yes! That's what I meant. Since when does pasta means rice noodles in Asian food?

"Mr. Russo, Marie-Louise was allergic to fucking peanuts, which go on pad Thai and ramen but not Italian pasta meals... unless there is a new food trend that I am not aware of."

"I did not see any peanuts in there. I threw the brand-new Locatelli Pecorino Romano that was on the counter in the trash. Like, if it was my brother I had found dead, I would have kept that cheese, because he wouldn't have wanted me to waste it."

"There was another girl our age who died recently. She fell—apparently—from her apartment, not far from here."

"I have heard of it..."

"She was a friend of Marie-Louise's."

"Was she?"

Mr. Russo looked at Arianna with wide eyes full of disbelief; his mouth was open. Arianna could see the many fillings that covered his teeth.

She thought about showing him a picture of Marianna, but there was no point; whether he had seen her or not made any difference at this stage.

They took the elevator to the ground floor in silence, him shaken and sad, her processing the new information she had learned during her short visit.

Arianna walked the three blocks that separated Marie-Louise's apartment from Marianna's on Columbus Avenue. It was a nice, warm sunny evening and Central Park, which she had visited only twice so far, was only one block east. Still, Columbus was the fastest way to Marianna's former place, she had no time to waste, and maybe the superintendent would make her wait and she'd have to go kill time in the park anyway.

But the superintendent did open the door. Once again, a portly Mediterranean-American; Tony was his name. He looked, and sounded, abrasive and businessy; yet he was, obviously, nice enough to agree to the unbusinesslike endeavor of receiving Arianna.

He let her in the lobby, again luxurious and spacious. She thanked him for taking the time to receive her and was about to start questioning him, but Tony was the one who began the questions first.

"Why do you think your friend got defenestrated?" He looked straight at her, his hands on his tights.

"This is what I hope to find out. I see that you have cameras in here. Do you still have the footage of the day that she died?"

"Who are you?"

That was not the answer that Arianna desired. "Arianna Sarringhaus. I'm an associate at Cognit, a professional service firm. I moved in here a less than a year ago, when I got this job after college. "

KNITTING DEATH

"Is she family?"

"No, we're not related."

"So she's your friend? Business partner?"

"No, I didn't know her. I heard of her when she died. One of her friends also died around the same time. She lived not far from here, at The Raven, and probably came here a few times. I was with Mr. Russo, the superintendent of her apartment, just a few minutes ago."

"Who sends you?"

"No one. I'm here on my own initiative. Those two girls, Marianna, your former tenant, and Marie-Louise, her friend, they were knitters, just like me. They went on the same social forums, watched the same videos, and probably bought from the same online stores. I've never met them, but it freaked me out when I heard about their tragic and, especially, mysterious death." Again, Arianna felt that candor and straightforwardness gave her the best chances to get some useful info out of the super.

"So you really are on your own? What are you gonna do?"

Arianna wasn't sure whether Tony's last question was rhetorical or not, so she didn't answer.

"What are you gonna do if you find the killer?" he repeated.

The question was not rhetorical, it appeared. Arianna still had no answer to it.

"So, you're wasting your time?"

Arianna expected to be kicked out of the building any second now. Instead, Tony indicated with his hand to follow him inside.

"Come with me. I'll show you what the cameras caught on that day."

They went through a white utility door on the side of the hall, which he unlocked from a key that hung on an overloaded keychain he pulled from his right pocket. Stairs went down toward a dimly lit hallway that led to an underground garage. Also, behind another commercial door, which Tony opened, again with a key from his heavy key set, was an office.

The decor and furniture showed its age, but the room was well maintained and clean. Besides an old desktop PC, three screens showed security camera feeds from different parts of the building: the license plate of a Mercedes SUV that reflected some light in the garage; an empty hall; a garbage container in an alley; an old woman in yoga gear who exited the main hall holding a Yorkshire terrier on a leach.

Tony sat behind the desk and grabbed the computer's mouse. After a minute, he turned the screen toward Arianna, who went to sit on the chair facing the desk. "She fell from her apartment on Thursday, September 28th. I've checked all the ins and outs on that day. Most of the people are just doing their usual thing, like here Ms. Langburt getting out at 10:00 a.m., and like here this guy with the gray rain jacket: he gives yoga lessons at the gym on the top floor."

He continued recalling the events of the day. "Now, the first unusual thing I noticed, it is not something that is on camera, but something that is not: Ms. Marianna did not go for her morning run at the park. She usually gets out around 6:00; we often run into each other, because this is the time I tour the facilities to see if everything is okay, that nothing has been broken or spray-painted during the night, that no bum is sleeping beside the garage door, that kind of thing. Now, I don't see Marianna every morning, but I see her often enough to know that she goes running pretty much every morning, at least during weekdays. Also, I know that she gets out to work between 7:00 and 7:30, because at that time I'm here at my desk dealing with stuff and I often see her on this screen."

Tony continued detailing Marianna's movements. "Again, I don't run into her every day, and I don't see her on the camera feed every day, but often enough to know her morning routine, you know what I mean? So there was nothing unusual with the fact that I did not see her on this morning, on the day that she died. But she did fall from the seventh floor, so I did watch camera captures from the previous days: she does go for a run around 6:00, gets back at 6:30, 6:40, and then gets out again about twenty minutes later, always wearing a nice business suit. But while she did not get out, she did have visitors. First, this guy."

Tony selected a folder on Windows Explorer (from a Windows version that must have been released before Arianna had hit kindergarten) and clicked on a picture file. The pic was a still from the camera footage, taken from a camera in the lobby: a young man, who looked well-built and well dressed; his face remained a mystery until Tony opened another pic, this time taken from the elevator, in which he looked straight at the camera. Well-defined jaw, light-colored curly locks, tanned; the guy looked like an Australian beach bum, or a Californian beach bum from the '80s.

"So this guy, he came in at 10:47, and got out at 11:05. He spent his whole elevator ride fidgeting on his phone, on the way up as on the way down. And no, it was not a romantic encounter, unless they did it elsewhere than in her bed, or on top of her bed without ruffling the sheets, or Ms. Marianna made the bed during the two hours and thirty-four minutes between his departure and the moment when she fell from her apartment onto the pavement.

"And then, there's this woman—I assume it's a woman, but it could be a guy; there's no real way to tell with this big red hat that she's wearin'.

Like, no one wears a hat like that except for to the Kentucky Derby, but this person, she wore an outfit like this to commit a murder."

"Wait—how do you know that person is the murderer?" said Arianna, pointing at the screen.

"Only footage I got from her is when she enters the seventh floor elevator at 9:34, two minutes after poor Marianna hit the concrete below. There is no trace of her anywhere else. Then she gets out, not through the lobby, but in the garage—where she disappears."

"How is this possible? Did they hack into your camera system?"

"Hacking? This thing is too old to be hackable. Also, it's closed-circuit. My security system is not online; there is no way to access it from the internet. No, you see, that red-hatted killer, she knew the building well. She just used the dead angles."

"Dead angles?"

"Hey, I'm no Big Brother, okay? We don't monitor every inch of this place. We got cameras for basic security; like, if a lunatic or a bum or an ex-boyfriend tries to get you, we'll catch him. If someone cold and calculated is out to get you, well, you have some security work to do on your own. We provide luxury amenities and services, not 24-hour protection against well-organized hit jobs."

Tony's tone was now much more aggressive. Or, to be more precise, defensive. Arianna realized that he resented that a tenant had been killed in his building (Arianna doubted Tony was among the owners of the building, which was probably worth in the hundred million, yet obviously he was quite possessive about it) and felt like she was judging him for letting that happened.

"Oh, Mr. Tony, for what I know they are quite resourceful and organized and Marianna... well, Marianna was in too deep with them all. If not here... I mean, it looks like this is all work-related, if we can say so. They probably got into the trouble of organizing the murder in your facilities in order to deflect the attention from the job-related... aspects of... this thing. I think they wanted to make it look like a suicide, you know...."

"That's what you believe?"

Tony sounded like he suspected Arianna of letting him off the hook too easy, as if she had made a diversion.

"That's what it looks like after three weeks spending way too much time looking into this. Into these three deaths."

"Three? You told me about this other girl who lives near, now you tellin' me about a third one?"

"Well... there is a third girl who died about the same time as Marianna and Marie-Louise. She knitted; she posted on the same websites... But she didn't live in the Upper West Side in a fancy luxury high-rise. She did not jog at 6:00 a.m., covered in Prana, in Central Park. She was an aspiring singer who lived in Jersey; they found her bathing in her own blood inside her crappy flat, two or three days past the time of her death."

Tony looked straight at Arianna, his half-closed eyes focused on her, his large forearms crossed on his large belly. She felt his gaze pry on her soul. That could have been scary, except that she had nothing to hide and nothing to gain, as he had himself previously explained.

"That's the thing that I never got my head around with Marianna: the money. She worked for good company, but at her age she still was in an entry-level position, with an entry-level salary. Her family, they have no money—no Upper-West-Side money. I've met her dad, once. A nice, decent man, but he was not the one paying for this, I know that."

"Just because he was not weaning expensive clothes and driving a luxury car doesn't mean he has—"

"Luxury? Who's talking about luxury? I'm talking about money, not about luxury. They're not the same. Like, you have this girl who lives here, she also came with her dad, and her dad he wears white socks in his sandals and he drives a Volvo SUV—but he has money. And he's the one paying all of this for his daughter, I'm sure about it. Marianna's father... he was not the one paying."

Tony did not explain why he knew Marianna's dad did not bankroll his daughter and why he also knew the socks-and-sandal guy did. Arianna felt that if she asked, he would just answer, "I just know." Also, she believed he very likely was right. So she did not interrupt him, since he was getting quite vocal on the subject that had brought her in this building.

He continued, "Also, Marianna, she was not whore—"

"Here we go again!" interrupted Arianna, looking at the ceiling, her arms in the air. "Of course, she was not whoring herself."

"Here we go... again? Miss, me and you, this is the first time ever we talk. There can be no 'again' between us."

"That's exactly what my boy... m... my boyfriend said: she is not whoring herself. And then, Marie-Louise... the other girl... her boyfriend: he was afraid she was seeing older men for money. When I told her she was not, he started crying, he was so relieved."

"And? What's your point?"

"My point is: how is it relevant?"

"Whores get whacked more than girls who are not whores. And you are here because you want to know why Miss Marianna got whacked, so it is relevant. But you got a lot in common with those girls, you relate to them, so you don't like when we point out that we actually took the time to think about if they were whores or not—I get it. But if you really are serious about what it is that you think you are doing, you got to look at all the angles, even those where there are things that make you uncomfortable."

Arianna shrugged. There are poor girls who have been used and abused, most often than not betrayed by the ones who were supposed to care for them, and now they have substance abuse problems and they sell their bodies—so those girls, they fall into the "whore" category. Arianna spent most of her days being nice to people she didn't like at a job she most likely would not have had she not been pretty and where her closer colleague was (had been...) a guy who had a crush on her and that she kept around only because he was professionally useful. But she only fucked guys she found attractive, so she was not a whore.

Also, had she just called Nick her boyfriend?

"Now, what really should get you more uncomfortable is—"

Arianna interrupted Tony and finished his sentence. "Is that if that red-hatted killer can whack Marianna, they can whack me, too. Thank you for your concern, Mr. Tony, but I already figured this one out by myself. I'm not suicidal and I'm not in the habit of taking unnecessary risks. But this thing, I'm not yet ready to let it go."

"You must be getting nervous sometime. Don't you feel like looking over your shoulder to see if someone is following you?"

"Yes, but every time it happens, I look around and there are people everywhere, and all these people they have cellphones with cameras. The fear might, however, have made me spend more time than I had planned with... my boyfriend."

Tony looked at the screen, at the camera capture of the woman with the big red hat (the person with a big red woman's hat and a red coat). He pointed the screen with his open hand. "Who dresses in bright red to commit a murder? No one does that. And you tellin' me it's about knitting?"

"I would not say it's about knitting, but so far everyone involved is a knitter."

"Who are these people? Are you one of them?"

"Someone I know thinks these women are witches." Arianna didn't mention that the someone in question was a nine-year-old girl.

"Witches?"

"Women who think of themselves as witches. Something like that."

"They told me you would come here."

A shiver rippled down Arianna's spine. She froze, all her muscle contracted, her eyes opened wide. Was she in danger? They? Who were they? Would the witches come through the door and seize her? Was Tony in with them since the beginning, chatting her up just to know how much she knew?

"Who told you I would come here?" said Arianna, her voice barely audible.

"A girl, about your age, but her style was very different. Some sort of hippie. I don't know how you call 'em nowadays, but to me she looked like a hippie."

"That girl—she had dreads?"

"Dreads?"

"Her hair. Dread locks. Like a Jamaican Rasta."

"Yes, dreads. That's right. She had those. It's a shame, really; if she arranged herself well she—"

"Piercing on the right eyebrow, raven tattoo on the neck, many earring holes…"

"That was her. That was the girl."

"And she told you I'd come over here?"

"Yesterday. She was right there in this chair you currently sit on when she told me that you would come here."

16. Cognit After Dark

Arianna wanted to talk about all the stuff she had learned (and been through) throughout the day and her misadventures in New Jersey and Long Island over the previous weekend. And she was horny. And she had a clean outfit in her bag for tomorrow morning. So, yeah, Nicolas's it would be. She was nearly done typing "I'm coming ov—" when she stopped and erased the text. "Hey, when you have a moment there is some stuff I would like to discuss with you" is what she sent to his number instead.

No need the scare the boy away by appearing possessive and clingy; she really, really did not feel like having an, "I'm not ready for this; it's going too fast" talk with Nicolas tonight.

Ironically, the text she just had sent, "Hey when you have a moment there is some stuff I would like to discuss with you," would have been, in most contexts, even worse to all the frisky, uncommitted fuckboys. Nicolas, however, would understand "Hey I want your opinion on this and after we're done discussing and researching we can have sex."

On one hand, Nicolas was, by far, the longest "relationship" Arianna had had since arriving in NYC, and even since quite a bit before that. He also was the only guy she had slept with sober since arriving in NYC. And the only one she had called a boyfriend while discussing the murder of a girl with the superintendent of her apartment.

All it took to reach this level of commitment were three young women dying, in strange circumstances, all of them probably assassinated in cold blood. Yay, progress?

"Hey, gorgeous. I'll be at my place at 10; see you there."

Then again, frisky uncommitted fuckboys did not include compliments in their text replies. Although, it was true, many such boys had the habit of signaling interest for something serious, until the girl expressed or demonstrated a reciprocal level of attachment, at which point the boy would back away with much drama, shrieking off like a vampire caught in the first rays of the rising sun, looking for a place to hide from the clingy broad who wanted to take their freedom away.

Was Nicolas one such vampire, or not?

If she was honest with herself, Arianna had to ask: did it really matter?

What mattered what that it was not even 7 p.m., so she had three hours to kill before going to Nick's.

She grabbed diner (lamb kofta kebab at an Afghan kebab house, on Ninth Ave.) and headed to the Cognit building. Rays from the setting sun, reflected by adjacent buildings, lit her table with an orange glow. There were many people still there, much fewer than during business hours, but the place was far from being deserted. She finally could have a shot at that fucking carbon graph that Tom was so anal about.

She went onto the intranet and selected the Brome project folder: "Access denied. You don't have permission to access the content of this folder."

KNITTING DEATH

She grabbed her cell and began keying the Cognit 24-hour International Tech Help number, suspecting technical problems. But a second thought made her stop dialing: her access might also have been removed by the project leader, Bryan in his case.

So she did nothing. She didn't feel like hearing some dude in India telling her that there was no technical problem and that the access denial was voluntary.

"Excuse me. Would you mind eating somewhere else; the odor of your meal is distracting."

Arianna raised her head. A girl, who sat across from her station to her diagonal left, was looking at her.

"I know company policy is less enforced for evening meals, but right now I just can't work."

Arianna stood up. "No problem. The spice mix makes it quite... odorous, indeed."

"Oh, I don't mind spices," said the girl. "It's meat that I can't stand."

Arianna locked her computer, grabbed her purse, her bag, and her cell, and stabbed the largest piece of lamb that lay within the Styrofoam plate. She shoved the piece inside her mouth while looking the girl straight in the eyes, after which she shut the plate cover, grabbed it with her free hand, and departed toward the cafeteria.

Between her workstation and the cafeteria sat Tom. She could have taken another path, one that avoided Tom, to reach the cafeteria, but she was too irritated, and also busy trying to say "fucking vegan bitch" with her mouth full of kebab, to think about Tom.

Tom ignored her as she passed a few inches from him, which more or less confirmed that she had been expelled from the Brome project.

There was no way Tom was too concentrated on what his screens displayed at the moment to not notice her, not when she carried such an odorous meal, made from dead animals, so close to him.

Arianna should have been nervous, not to say panicking at the moment: being expelled from a project was probably not something that was well considered within Cognit's Peer Talent Development Appraisal process. But she was too angry to be afraid. Angry at Tom for wrecking everything she had built with Bryan. Angry at the vegan girl. Angry at the killer who had distracted her from her job.

She reached the cafeteria; the room, which could accommodate more than a hundred people, was empty. She sat and felt her anger dissipate. The situation had an interesting upside: she did not have to do the fucking carbon graph. Also, she had a delicious kebab to eat.

Her phone vibrated: "Are u coming to the brunch on Saturday morning?" Diana had texted.

She took another bite of kebab. "What brunch?" she texted back, dropping a bead of odorous kebab sauce on the screen of her device. She then selected her inquiry folder, opened her notes, and started typing:

- Marie-Louise's former landlord had been warned of Arianna's visit by Yuna, the Ben & Jesse's Knits barista.
- Marianna had packed her luggage on the day of her death (but then again, she traveled all the time).
- The main suspect ("Lady in Red") wore a red dress and a large red hat when Marianne died.
- Lady in Red knew which areas in the building were covered by security cameras.

KNITTING DEATH

At least Arianna now had a suspect. She didn't know much about her (or him), but she had a visual representation. Yay, progress.

Arianna went to the waste management section of the cafeteria; she dropped the leftover rice from her meal into the compost hole, and the plate, utensils and napkins into the recycling one. She washed her hand at one of the sinks and went back to her place. She shoved her hand into her bag to grab her Twin Lizards project, and while doing so hit something hard: the book that Alia had given her, **VVITCHES**, was still there.

She grabbed the book with both hands and stared at its old, leathery cover. She used to read, for whole evenings in her bed, or during the weekend in the basement beside the fireplace, or during the summer in the long chair inside the mosquito tent in the backyard. Now she barely read at all; pairing knitting and reading was impractical. She had tried listening to audiobooks while knitting, but that didn't do it for her, although she suspected that she just hadn't found a good book to listen to, and that she didn't try enough because of all the podcasts she wanted to watch.

So what had Alia found into this one book that had motivated her to skip a school activity to walk to Cognit and handle it in person to Arianna?

If Arianna wanted to know, she would have to actually read it. Reading **VVITCHES** might prove to be quite enjoyable, entertaining, and educative. Lots of interesting facts about witches were most likely to be found inside this venerable copy, whose vocabulary, form, syntax, and grammar probably counted more than one occurrence of lexical archaism, title notwithstanding. Yet Alia was a nine-year-old child and, as bright and gifted as she was, still looked at the world through her nine-year-old eyes, which made her nine-year-old mouth say things like, "Marianna passed the auditions at your workplace."

"Holy shit!" uttered Arianna, quite loudly, inside the Cognit headquarters cafeteria (no one heard her, but the Cognit Total Security AI software, through one of the three hidden security cameras, was able to read it on her lips).

"She meant audit! Cognit is the firm that does the audit for Marianna's file!"

Arianna began texting Nicolas about her finding (technically it was only a hypothesis, but Arianna would have bet a month of salary it was what Alia had meant). She wrote the text but she did not press "Send"; she was, after all, on Cognit's Wi-Fi, and her phone had Cognit software installed on it. Some higher-ups would most likely meet soon to decide whether they were going to fire her or not; there was no point in giving them more reasons to lay her out than they had already by discussing work material with outsiders.

Now, it would help if I knew which company is it that we audited. I can't search the system without a company name... however... I have the victim's name to start with!

Arianna grabbed her bags and headed back toward her workstation. She nearly ran into Tom; he looked at her this time, but she went ahead without acknowledging him. If her time at Cognit was coming to an end, she would have to make it count.

She dropped her bag under her desk, sat, unlocked her computer, and selected the Organodex Cognit CRM application; she clicked inside the search box and typed "Marianna Burrow," followed by the "Enter" key. A new screen appeared on with the search results. There was just one: "Marianna Burrow, Investment Banker, RedBroom, 1114 Sixth Avenue #21, New York, NY 10036, USA."

"YES!" Arianna shouted. The vegan girl who sat across from her stared at Arianna with her wide-opened brown eyes, but her mouth remained shut—tightly shut, actually. Arianna doubted Vegan Girl would remain silent for long if she continued to talk out loud every time she had a positive search result.

She clicked on the link. The page dedicated to Marianna didn't offer much information: her office address, phone number, the one Cognit file for which she was a contact (codenamed Paragon) and her one Cognit contact: Edgar Harris, senior manager, International Tax Solutions.

She wrote everything on a piece of paper (the printout of a draft for a section of the Brome report) and clicked on the Paragon project link. "You don't have access to this file," said the computer, much unsurprisingly. She then clicked on RedBroom and accessed the client company page (the client company page contained only basic information and was accessible to all). The introduction said that RedBroom was a "Boutique financial advisory investment banking firm specialized in M&A, OTC, capital raising; it has offices in New York City, Boston, Panama City, Gibraltar, Cyprus, and Singapore." Four projects were listed under the description: Paragon, Audit Boston and...

Pharmathrice-Casavant Med M&A.

That name again. Pharmathrice. Melissa's employer.

Arianna typed the file names in her notes. There was no point in trying to access any of them; instead, she looked at the contact list further down on the page.

There was not much else Arianna would find from this search. As she stretched her arms behind her head, right before she was about to type "Marie-Louise Thompson" into the search box, she saw something familiar yet odd: Margaret, entering a closed office with Lionel Getty, a partner, along with a younger man. Margaret and Lionel obviously knew each other well: Lionel greeted her with a hug and a kiss.

What a small world it was. Even in a city that had more than eight million inhabitants, she ran into the same people all the time. Arianna knew Margaret was successful, had corporate or business career, and that successful corporate or businesswomen were greeted by partners with hugs and kisses. Still, it was weird to see someone from Ben & Jesse's Knits, the place she went to relax, at Cognit, the place she went to get stressed out.

Arianna went back to the Organodex Cognit CRM to see if there was anything on Marie-Louise. Only one project: Paragon, yet again.

This is the file I have to access.

The Paragon project was still ongoing. The partner in charge was none other than Nicky Page, who Arianna had worked with on Traphistry, the Cincinnati firm. The manager was one Richard Tally, who Arianna had never heard of. She clicked on his profile to reveal his picture: smiling, portly, with short black hair that was rather disheveled for a corporate pic. His wide smile made Arianna imagine him overenthusiastically saying, "Thank you Cognit for employing me!"

The most striking thing about the picture (the only striking thing about the picture) was that Richard looked young—very young, to be precise—for a manager. Maybe Richard looked young to Arianna only because his dark hair was neither falling out nor graying. One thing was sure: a guy with such a lack in looks and aggression was most likely very good at something, something that was useful.

That was enough research using company resources for today. The hunt for clues had been good; she had most likely nailed down Cognit's involvement in the shady business dealings that loomed heavily in the background of those deaths.

She started packing her things. The younger man who sat with Lionel and Margaret exited the office; he walked toward Arianna, looking straight at her. "You're Arianna, right? I don't think we've been introduced. I'm Brian, Heather's husband," he said, presenting his right hand.

Arianna stood up and shook his hand. "Hi, Brian! Nice to finally meet you!"

Up until that moment, she had had no idea he was Heather's husband. Now that she knew, however, she felt that she somehow did recognize him.

"This place is really nice," he said, looking around. "You guys are lucky. The last time my office floor was refurbished must have been in 1985 or something."

"It is quite an awesome place, it's true," said Arianna, with some feigned enthusiast. "Only problem is when the person sitting next to you brings a warm meal to their desk, and now you have to work with all the odors filling the air."

"I know. Go tell that to the guy who sits in the office next to mine; every time he comes back from a fishing trip, he—"

"Brian, shouldn't you stick to girls who are your own age?" interrupted a loud, nasal voice. Brian turned his head as Lionel reached Arianna's desk. "Arianna, if this guy is making you any trouble, just let me know; it will be my pleasure to escort him out so he can't bother you anymore."

Lionel now had his hand on Brian's right shoulder. Brian pointed Arianna with his left hand while looking at Lionel: "Arianna is Heather's friend, they—"

"Did he ask you to babysit his daughter?" Lionel asked Arianna, not waiting for her to answer. He then looked back at Brian and said, "How many times have I told you, Brian: stop trying to poach our employees!"

"I supposed it's written in the contract somewhere that I don't have the right to do that?" said Brian.

"You think Arianna is in the office at 7:30 for fun? Can't you see she's working hard?" What are you working on, right now, Arianna?"

Lionel did not really have the right to ask this question, not in front of an outsider; Arianna did not really have the right to answer this question, not in front of an outsider. Maybe even Lionel was testing if she'd apply the 3C (Cognit Code of Conduct), but Arianna didn't care. She had heard that Lionel disliked Bryan (Bryan the Cognit manager, not Brian, Heather's husband who he was joking with and also hugging at the moment).

Arianna thought that Lionel was jealous. Bryan-the-manager was young, smart, focused, and worked on complex files, while Lionel was a cringy, out-of-place boomer who probably spent more time playing golf than using his computer.

Which meant she couldn't let an opportunity like this pass. She put her hand besides her cheek, hiding her mouth from Brian but not Lionel, and whispered, "Broooome!" while pointing toward her screen, putting slight disgust into her facial expression and raising her eyes up their sockets.

Lionel started laughing, quite loudly: "Oh! Oh! Oh! You poor girl! Come on Brian, she's working on one of those nutty files! Oh! Oh! Oh! Some guys really prefer technicality over substance, I will tell you that, eh! Eh! Eh!" and off they went, Lionel dragging Brian as he laughed way too loud (and while criticizing the work of a colleague in front of a client and all the Cognit employees who sat around), Brian waving goodbye to Arianna, obviously embarrassed by his friend's behavior.

Just as they left, Margaret appeared next to Arianna. "Look at you, working so late. Cognit really is a demanding place."

"Hello, Margaret. It is, but... It's not as if I am the only associate in Manhattan still working at the moment."

"For sure you are not. Now, I didn't know you knew my friend, Lionel. Do you work in tax?"

"No, it was the first time I talked to him... thanks to you and Brian."

"I will see you at Ben & Jesse's Knits. You take care of yourself, sweetie. Be careful."

Margaret departed toward the elevators, where Lionel and Brian were probably waiting for her. Arianna would wait for a few minutes before going as well. An elevator ride with those three was the last thing she wanted at the moment.

She looked at the time on her screen: 8:12. She had time to go back home, take a shower, change, and also brush her teeth (what an odorous breath she must have at the moment!). Maybe she would have the time for a quick stop at Ben & Jesse's Knits... Off to Brooklyn Arianna went.

17. B&JKnits@Night

Melissa aligned velvety, purple stitches on a size 3 needle; a squarish piece, with two stumps at the lower side, hung from the needle. The stumps would soon be part of a baby sweater, one she intended to send to her niece, who had just completed her second trimester inside Aneth, Melissa's cousin who lived in Austin.

"Why is it called 3D printing when a guy and a computer do it, but only knitting when a girl like us does it?" she said.

"I can text Nicolas to ask him if you want," said Arianna. "I'm sure he'll give you a detailed answer."

"Maybe, but it will be a guy's answer that justifies the status quo of knitting being less prestigious than 3D printing."

Arianna and Melissa were the only clients inside the cafe. Yuna, the barista, was at the back of the store at the moment.

"I don't know if 3D printing is more prestigious, but I know that if this activity was called 'Sheep-Hair-Based-Analog-Garment-3D-Printing' instead of 'knitting,' I would not be doing it."

"What do you mean, 'analog'? Knitting is 90 percent Ravelry and Instagram and Etsy and online contests and, like, 10 percent actually handling the needles."

"Oh Melissa, how can you say that, this is soooo wrong! What about "digitally assisted analog sheep-hair-garment-3D-printing"?

"With a name like this, you'd be able to land funding for a start-up. We could ask your boyfriend and his buddies; I'm sure they'd fall for it."

Arianna stopped knitting and stared at Melissa without moving; Melissa had completed four stitches before she realized Arianna was fixating her. "What? Oh… sorry, I didn't realize. I will not refer to him as your boyfriend again, I promise!"

"I barely know him; I didn't even know he was doing start-ups and stuff."

"So you two have so much sex that when you're together you don't even have the time to talk about what you guys are doing in life?"

Arianna raised her eyes to the sky and expired loudly. "No, we don't have sex all the time. I'm not even sure sex is the main thing that makes us spend all those nights together."

KNITTING DEATH

Melissa interrupted her knitting. "What is it that you guys are spending all this time doing then?"

"You know what it is, Melissa."

Arianna looked down at her niece's turtle hat (the four rows that would be, in the future, a turtle hat). She had wanted to touch on the topic with Melissa for a bit. But Diana had reacted negatively when she had done so, the other time at the bar, the night she had met Nick and the rest of the boys, and she was not keen of going through a rerun.

But now it had flowed into her conversation with Melissa, naturally, seamlessly.

"Oh," Melissa said, also looking down toward her knitting.

Arianna looked at her friend; on one hand, she didn't want to appear too inquisitive, but on the other, she tried to pick non-verbal clues. The more she tried to get her way through this story, the more she found paths that led toward her friends. Both Diana's and Melissa's current jobs were, through various threads, linked to Marie-Louise, to Marianna, to their life just before they died. And this patchwork of intertwined threads brought much attention from Yuna and Alia, and many warnings from Audrey. And it seemed that the knot that held all of its elements together was a major financial fraud.

"I think it's quite hard for Diana, you know."

And so, for the first time, Melissa spoke about the issue, at least in front of Arianna. Arianna, however, had no idea what exactly Melissa was talking about. "What is quite hard for Diana?"

"She obviously knows that you are very concerned by this case… the two girls who died, the fraud inquiry. I think it weighs on her not be able to discuss it all with you."

"And why is it that she can't she discuss it with me?"

Up to that point Melissa had kept on staring at her needles as she spoke; now she looked at Arianna as her hands stopped their motion, mid-stitch.

"Because she's a lawyer? You probably know more about this whole thing than me, but if her employer, Burkett Gurewitz, is involved in this case, might she not be bound by a confidentiality agreement, or even attorney-client privilege, and so be unable to speak with us? Also, Burkett is not that big; how many corporate lawyers work there? For all we know, she might actually be working on the case."

"Your employer is also involved in the case, Meliss—"

"So is yours!" snapped Melissa. "Cognit is neck deep into it." Melissa wiped a tear from her right eye. "My ex in neck deep into it, Diana is neck deep into it—everyone is."

It was the first time Arianna had seen Melissa cry. On any other occasion, she would have tried to comfort her, but right now, the only thing that came into Arianna's mind was more questions: "Have you ever met one of the three girls who died?"

"No! Never."

Arianna felt Melissa had told the truth. She had seen her lie twice: once to a guy, over her phone, with Arianna and Diana whispering answers to respond to the guy's questions, and another time when the three of them had crashed a fundraiser (an open-bar fundraiser) and they pretended to be working for a venture capital firm. Both times she had proved to be a bad, very bad liar, her ineptitude in the matter so acute that at the fundraiser she nearly had compromised their whole open-bar-crashing operation.

KNITTING DEATH

"Look, Melissa," said Arianna, "I know my obsession with the death of these three girls is probably not the healthiest thing for me... and my surroundings."

"I think about it too, you know... but it scares me so much. These girls, they are... they were a lot like us."

"I know. Sometimes it makes me want to get out of the city. Like, not forever, but just getting away a few days would feel great right now."

"Oh! But Rhinebeck is coming soon!" Melissa wiped the tears from her cheeks with a napkin. "We'll be able to forget all about this. For a weekend, at least."

Rhinebeck was a small town in Upstate New York that hosted the Sheep and Wool Festival, the largest fiber-arts gathering in America. Arianna loved the idea of attending, but worried about the spending it involved. "Maybe... I don't know if—"

"Don't give me the 'maybes,' Arianna; you are soooo coming with us! I think Diana already found a place to stay."

Well, if lodging was included... and transportation provided... Then the only thing Arianna would have to worry about is controlling her urge to buy new wool. It was far from being a trivial issue, but at least she could contemplate accepting Melissa's invitation without bankrupting herself.

Yuna came back to the client area from the back store. "You guys need anything?" she asked, as she picked Arianna's empty cup on the coffee table.

"I'm fine," Arianna answered, rather aridly. *How dare you! Hypocrite hippie!* "I'm going, anyway."

"Oh, why so early?" said Melissa. "Are you upset that—"

"Oh no! On the contrary... Look, you're probably right about Diana." Arianna didn't want to say too much, not with Yuna around. "No, I'm leaving because I have to go back to Manhattan."

"You're not going back to work?!" Melissa said, quite loudly (which didn't matter since they were the only clients in the cafe).

"I'm not going to Cognit. I'm going to Nick's."

"Of course you guys will spend the evening discussing your various findings on—"

"I'm too tired for this shit tonight," said Arianna (who, again, really didn't want to discuss the subject with Yuna around). "It's just gonna be what it is when a girl goes to a guy's apartment at 10 p.m."

"So you're not too tired for that."

"I don't know. If I'm too tired, I'll just let him do the hard work," answered Arianna as she picked her project bag.

"Oh! How selfish of you!"

"Hey, at least I won't be thinking about the dress I will be wearing for my job's Christmas party!"

"Maybe you should. It's less than three months away," said Melissa. "Oh! I totally forgot to tell you: there's a brunch on Saturday. I thought I texted you about it, but this morning I found out that I did not."

"Diana just texted me about it."

"You have to come. If you already made plans, cancel them."

"Yes, ma'am. Have a good evening, ma'am." On this, Arianna departed. She had no time to ask Melissa more details about the brunch. If Melissa said she had "no choice" in coming, it would be good. Good food, nice place, good booze, interesting people, and no expenses whatsoever.

She walked toward her apartment; the night was cool, the sun had set for a while, there were few people in the street. Summer was nearly over. As she climbed the stairs of her building, the prospect of going back to Manhattan became less appealing; she was tired, drained, and she wanted to go to bed and sleep.

She opened the door. A cool breeze hit her. An unusual cool breeze, as she was not in the habit of leaving the one single window open. Had she been burglarized? Well, if that was the case, the joke was on the burglars: she had nothing valuable to steal, and if they'd bothered pilfering her computer, all her data was on the cloud. She wouldn't mind getting some insurance money to get a new laptop, and even renew her knitting stash, if the burglars were knowledgeable enough to recognize that her wool was indeed valuable.

But as she shut the door behind her, she heard a noise: there was something in the main room. Arianna froze. More noise. There was **someone** in the main room. Metallic noise: the emergency stairs, resonating, as the someone exited the apartment. Arianna ran to the room and threw her head outside the open window: someone ran, fast, in the alley below. Arianna couldn't see the person's face, just that it was a girl with long, blond dreads.

Yuna! Arianna shut the window, wondering how Yuna could have reached her apartment so fast. She was looking for Melissa's contact in her phone to tell her what happened, but as she pressed the screen, she understood what had just happened: Melissa had left Ben & Jesse's Knits right after Arianna. Yuna, who had heard that Arianna was heading for Manhattan, had rushed to shut the café to come over and break into her place; she had arrived first because she had biked while Arianna walked.

Arianna didn't call Melissa. Her finger scrolled down just a bit into her contacts, to the letter N.

18. Anxiety & Chill

"Knit-knit-purl; knit-knit-purl; tie the rat's right front leg to the shawl; knit-knit-purl; knit-knit- purl; tie the rat's right rear leg to the shawl- OW!"

Arianna hit Nicolas in the ribs. His ribs were rather easy to reach, as she rested her head on his naked torso.

"Okay. No more rat jokes, I promise!"

At least rat jokes meant that Nicolas believed her. It felt good to have someone to talk to who understood. It also felt good to talk to someone she could hit in the ribs. It also felt good to lay her head on that someone's torso. But then it didn't feel good anymore: her nose was itchy and stuffy and runny, which happened all the time shortly after she cried. So she sat on the edge of the bed, snapped a tissue from the box that at on the bedside table, and blew her nose.

To say that she had cried was an understatement; she erupted in tears the moment Nicolas opened his door. Again, not a behavior prescribed when in a new, casual relationship with a boy; again, Nicolas did not seem to mind and was rather empathetic with Arianna's ordeal (that is, until he thought it was fun to describe the process of knitting a dead rat onto a shawl).

"You're staring at me!" she shouted.

"Of course I'm staring at you. What am I supposed to stare at? My bed lamp? You're naked and I still have my contacts on."

"I'm blowing my nose!"

"I'm not looking at your nose."

She grunted and took back her previous position, her head on Nicolas's chest, under his arm.

"So, if I got that right, Yuna preceded you on your inquiry itinerary and warned the people you wanted to meet. Then she committed a break-in at your place, right after serving you coffee at that knitting place."

"Yep. You got that part right."

"And at that knitting place, you discussed with Diana—"

"Melissa."

"Melissa... Melissa is the Asian one?"

"That's right."

"And Melissa told you that Diana, the brunette lawyer, works on the case?"

"She thinks it's very likely."

"And you fucked up with a work assignment, which got you expelled from a project. So instead of working, you looked into the CRM and found that Cognit seems involved with two of the girls' former employers, and also that Melissa's current employer is involved in the case?"

"I thought I spouted out an incoherent rant filled with tears and sobs, but you got the main parts right."

"And that girl you met today... Charlie—"

"Charlotte."

"She wore a Bat Wing Shawl."

"She did. A superb, expertly knitted shawl with exquisite beading. And before you ask: no rat whatsoever to see on this particular Bat Wing. There was a spider, but it was made of silver or something, with some kind of gems for the eyes."

"Are you sure that what you saw in the yarn shed and what Charlotte wore are the same things?"

"I am not sure both followed identical patterns, but... they are the same thing."

"Was there any ivory in Charlotte's shawl beading?"

"I am pretty sure there was. Why do you ask?"

"It might have been polished bone."

Arianna stood up. She took a sip of water from a glass on the bedside table and sat against the headboard.

"Okay. So because both shawls are Bat Wing and one of them had a small dead animal in it, the other one must have small dead animal parts as well. I understand what you mean, although I'm not sure... Charlotte's shawl was clean and shiny. I am pretty sure no small mammal ever decayed there."

"Something else that is weird with this story: Martine. As much as I empathize with you for suddenly finding yourself with your nose a few inches of a dead rodent, I mean... it's just a dead rodent. That's the kind of stuff a bunch of ten-year-old boys would do if ten-year-olds knitted."

"Nick, what the fuck are you talking about?"

"You just told me that Martine had serious issues."

"Yes. Very serious. She's barely there."

"Exactly. Insane people do insane things. Things that don't make sense. Which is exactly what happened here."

"Nick, I know that what she did is insane... what's your point?"

"What about her parents? She lives with them, right?"

"Yes. I had the exact same thought the day after I met her. She lives with them. The knit shed is located besides the house. It probably used to be the garden shed; I don't think it was built as a knit shed on purpose. So I guess they never looked in there."

"Or they know, but they don't care because they're also insane."

"Maybe. Her mother was too proper and nice and polite to my liking. There was not a hint of sadness in her demeanor. She was not behaving like someone whose young daughter is a mental wreck."

"So she was some kind of modern-day Long Island Stepford Wife?"

"Pretty much."

Nicolas stood up from the bed and exited the bedroom; she heard him making its way into the bathroom.

She looked around. White walls, shelves, books, drawers, a snowboard hung by one of its bindings to a large hook screwed in the ceiling, a hybrid bicycle suspended in the same fashion right next to the snowboard, and a red metal toolbox, opened on the floor—the only thing that didn't look like it was resting in its proper place. There was not much in terms of decoration, but the place was clean and practical.

The toilet flushed; a few seconds later Nicolas re-entered the room, still wearing nothing. "Hey, what's that?" he said, picking up something on the floor. "VVITCHES?"

"Oh. Yes. I haven't told you about this part yet. You remember my friend, Heather? She has a daughter, Alia, who is nine. Well, Alia skipped a class visit to a museum to drop by my office, just to give me that book."

"Where did she get that?" Nicolas looked closely at the book as he turned the pages.

"Nick, you really think I asked her about the book? She's nine years old! She was all by herself in Midtown!"

"This book is old."

"Nick!"

"What?"

Arianna stared straight at him, her palms facing the ceiling, her mouth open.

"Rich nine-year-old white girls don't get killed, or even abducted, in broad daylight in Midtown Manhattan," said Nicolas. "You're worried that her mom will learn that she skipped school to talk to you and that you didn't tell her."

"I am worried by Heather's reaction, but I am more concerned by Alia's behavior. If she skipped school just to give me a book, what else is she willing to do?"

"Holy shit. This wood print is metal. This book is for real."

Arianna couldn't believe her eyes: this boy, standing naked, his head tilted forward, his eyes peering in this black book he held between his hand, who five minutes before couldn't get his eyes off her, even as she blew her nose, and who now barely answered as she talked.

KNITTING DEATH

She let herself fall onto the bed and pulled the cover over her body. She wanted to sleep, but her eyes stayed open. The day had been brutal, but somehow she was not through; what was keeping her awake was still stronger than her tiredness. Her dream was about to blow up, her life was about to crash; she was about to land back in Cincinnati, defeated and humiliated. Her current worries would be memories she would hold on to and cherish, dreams of what-could-have-been that would pop out when she would go to sleep at night, when she would get bored with her inner-American suburban life, when she'd drink and start to ramble the same old story about that time when she used to go out and party and New York—

"I wish I could tell you to stop worrying, Arianna... But, to be honest, I think this is serious," said Nicolas, as he got into the bed next to Arianna.

"You think I'll be fired?"

"Fired? I'm talking about the murders. That's what I think is serious. You're getting dragged into this story."

"If I'm fired, I'll have to go back home. I will not be a nuisance to them anymore."

"Whatever... so, this book. It's not fairy tales for kids. It's not cheap entertainment for tweens. It's a genuine historical artifact. I'll have to check online, but at first glance this is old and valuable. If you don't mind, I'll put it in my wine cellar."

"Your... wine cellar? There's a wine cellar in this apartment? And... you want to put this book there? Nick, did you... Look, if you smoked before I got here it's okay, I just—"

"I don't have a dedicated wine room, just the electric box with bottle racks inside. I want to put the book there because it's cool and dry. I'm not even sure we're supposed to manipulate this thing with our hands... and too much humidity might damage it."

Arianna threw her face in the covers. "Whatever! Put it in your freezer or dishwasher or bread machine or kombucha keg if you want."

Again, Nicolas left the bed and exited the room; he came back shortly, still naked, but instead of holding the book he held a bottle of white and two glasses. "I had to make some room," he said, smiling as he removed the twist cap.

Arianna looked at her cell: "It's 11:47. Thirteen minutes from now, I would have spent my first Thursday sober since I arrived in New York."

"It's not too late... but you'd be missing out."

She sat straight and took the cup he handed her.

"This girl Alia is onto something. She knows things we don't," he said, just before taking his first sip. He looked concerned, as if everything that had looked at before had been a game, but now things were getting real.

"I'm worried. I care about her."

"Someone around her is involved."

"Maybe Heather, her mom."

"Heather's a MILF, not a witch."

"Heather worries more about her daughter than about your pretty friends. She thinks that her karate teacher, who is also the Ben & Jesse's Knits owner, has a bad influence on her."

"The same Ben & Jesse's Knits owner who employs hippies who break into your apartment?"

KNITTING DEATH

"Yes. Audrey."

"You guys make for a strange group of friends. Most people in New York hangout with colleagues and peers and try to make connections to help them on the way up. Most social gatherings are reunions of incestuous coteries where gossip and score keeping are the norm. That's one of the reasons why dating is complicated in New York: it's either in-group pairing drama or outsiders who don't get the inside jokes and have their own social universe to cultivate anyway. In the case of your group of friends, the link is your hobby: knitting."

"Are you telling me that Josh and Mike are your colleagues? Are they...? Hey, actually I don't even know what is it that you do."

"What do you think it is?"

Arianna took a sip of the wine—it was cold, crisp, dry, mineral—she indeed would have been missing out had she opted for a (first) sober Thursday. "Something technical and complicated to explain yet relatively important in order to make some necessary part of our world work properly. It must involve a not-insignificant share of coding. Since you present yourself well, you have some non-coding responsibilities that are more social in nature but necessitate the understanding of the technical part. Your job is interesting and well remunerated, but no one understands what you do. You refrain from talking about it, not because you don't want to tell me, but because if you do I'll probably fall asleep and spill wine all over your covers."

"You're close. Quite close, actually. You're quite good at this. I'm impressed."

"And Josh and Mike are not your colleagues."

"No, they're not."

"What is it? You've been friends since high school?"

"Nope."

"Wait a minute! Martine told me about pretty boys! She told me that the Bat Wing people introduced her to very good-looking young men." Arianna's heartbeat accelerated, her eyes opened wide, and she looked straight at Nicolas: "How did you meet them? How did you meet Diana and Melissa? Have you met Marie-Louise, Marianna, or Christina before?"

"Pretty boys? Arianna, what are you talking about?"

"How did you meet Diana and Melissa?!"

"I met them the same night I met you! At that pub in Brooklyn! Well, I've seen them before, with Josh and Mike, but it was the first time I chatted with them."

"Josh and Mike—how did you meet them!?"

Nicolas sat against the bed head. He looked right in front of him, at nothing in particular, looking sad and annoyed. Afraid, even.

"I arrived in the city about two years ago—a bit more than that. I got this job, which has good pay and good working conditions. As opposed to people in finance or entertainment, I'm not expected to be in the office after six unless there's an emergency. Now, you must wonder, how is it that I live in a million-dollar apartment in Manhattan?"

Arianna had not really wondered. She had not realized she lay in bed inside a seven-figure property, although it made sense considering its size and location. "You're an early investor in a successful cryptocurrency. This investment was funded with the prize of a major fantasy sports pool, which you won when you were fourteen with the help of a program you wrote yourself."

KNITTING DEATH

"...So I got this job in the big city. My dad thought it was a shame I would sink so much money into rent, so I suggested we buy something somewhere in the boroughs or Jersey. And then my uncle insisted to join us, because he thought it was a good investment and he likes to visit New York two or three times per year but he wanted something closer to downtown. So they put a good amount of cash down and I pay the installments on the residual mortgage."

He continued. "So I'm not self-made, I'm not trust fund, either; just a white dude who gets along well enough with his old man. Now, it's all a nice setup to start my adult life, except for one thing: I'm on my own. There's no one my age at the office and I didn't know anyone who lives here. My social life consisted of tech scene events and dating apps meet-ups. It was fake, repetitive, and dry. Then, one day, I was at this bar, on my own—"

"Oh," interrupted Arianna. "You were drinking-at-the-bar-on-your-own-lonely. That much."

"I just told you!"

"You said it was "fake, repetitive, and dry." I thought the fakeness and repetitiveness were the results of your bad choice of girls. As for the dryness, it usually is the result of insufficient foreplay."

"Oh! Said the girl who's so wet, her fluids probably reached down to the mattress."

"I'm horny! It's not my fault."

Again, Nicolas looked away, the sad expression on his face.

"You're afraid. You fear they will kill you, too. This is what makes you horny. It's an instinctive reaction."

Arianna didn't expect him to say this. She did not like his explanation for her horniness. She also feared he was right. He looked back at her, with a mocking smile this time: "You said, 'I'm horny,' in the present tense—"

"Don't change the subject! Tell me how you met those guys!"

"So, as I said, just before you interrupted me: I was drinking alone at this place like an old lush, and having depleted the entertainment supply my phone had to offer, I listened to the conversations around me. Rapidly, I was caught up in a discussion by three guys who were sitting like me at the bar on the three stools perpendicular to mine. They made quite the motley crew: this magnificent male specimen, well built but with this cherub face, that mixed-race God with the big, bright, starry eyes and dark brown afro, and this ugly little roach who talked and talked and sweated and dropped pretzel bits on his shirt that was way too tight. Now, I couldn't care less about his appearance, but what he said to Josh and Mike made my ears bleed: pure bullshit. He said things about apps, development, coding, and financing that were so wrong, I barely was able to prevent myself from shouting expletives at him."

"So you confronted him and he left the bar, humiliated by your superior knowledge and wisdom."

"No! He had the decency to go away. So I jumped in. The basic idea they discussed was a cultural event schedule aggregator app—"

"Oh! The Minuit app!"

"Yes, that one. Nothing very original, but they mentioned some plugs into the industry that gave the project an interesting edge. So I start discussing it with them. I asked some questions, and at some point I showed them an app I'd made with my friends while in college—nothing fancy, it's a very simple app that indicates student rebates and discounts around campus. At that moment I didn't realize it, but later on

I learned that they were literally blown away. What I immediately caught on to, however, was that their computing knowledge was abysmal. And then I understood why they had tolerated the ignorant roach minutes before.

"And that's it. I gave Josh my business card, he paid for my drinks, and said he would contact me. We said goodbye and parted our ways. At that point, I thought of it as just a generic dive bar conversation with strangers because I was tipsy. As good-looking as they are, I was not especially impressed that they thought of making an app while having zero practical skills in app making.

"But then, Josh called me back the morning after. Which was borderline scary: why the fuck was he not texting me like a normal human being? He wanted me to come with him to an event that very night. I was caught off guard so I accepted—and anyway, I didn't have anything else interesting to do.

"I met him at the Third Avenue station downtown, we walked a few streets, and we went into this place—an anonymous door in a row house that looked like a residential place, but inside, it was an entirely different story. We passed two doors, which he unlocked by scanning his phone, and we were inside in this large venue: it was full of chairs, couches, and small tables and there was a bar at one end of the room. In the middle of it all was an outdoor terrace with a fucking swimming pool. So the sides were dark, cozy, and intimate while the middle was bright and sunny and full of bikini-clad girls.

"We sat at a table, he chatted on the phone, and at some point a waiter brought beers. I don't remember any of us ever having ordered anything; Josh later told me he'd ordered the drinks with the app on his phone. He talked to me about his project, but I barely listened. In less than five minutes, I saw two guys I'm pretty sure I'd seen on TV, the lead singer of the Turtleheads who chatted with two guys I'm positive were also playing in successful bands, as well as DJ Loth. Then, this man, who I recognized as the head of private equity at Blackstone, asked me where the washrooms are!"

"Your description reminds me of the place where I met Charlotte today. Except that I didn't recognize anyone."

"Well, maybe this whole thing will get both of us killed, but at least we'll have briefly shared the lives of the rich and famous."

"And that's it? You had a drink with Josh and you've been happy together forever after?"

"Kinda. I got hooked. I started coding for them that night when I came back home. Simple stuff, but it impressed them very much. And I got to know them: rich parents, modeling career—you'd think they had it all, but no. Something was missing from their dream life."

Arianna: "They want to be successful tech entrepreneurs, because that's the only thing that's genuinely cool nowadays."

Nicolas: "I'm not even sure about the "successful" part. To understand success, you need to understand failure; nothing ever really fails with these guys. Everyone is nice to them, all the girls want them, all the doors are wide open... No, you see, for Josh, I was a status 'good.' With me, he had his own code monkey."

Arianna: "Code monkey? That's how he sees you?"

Nicolas: "Oh no. He's quite respectful of my skills, and even a bit envious, I think. I used the consecrated expression on my own volition."

Arianna: "Still, you got into his inner circle because you played the part of something he needed."

Nicolas: "Oh yes, I did. He wanted a tech guy, so I played the tech guy."

KNITTING DEATH

Arianna: "That must have been very hard for you, being out of character all the time," Arianna said, a mocking grin on her (tired) face.

Nicolas: "Well, that's exactly the point: it was natural, but it was a bit at odds with the way I behave at my job. Behaving different if you're a tango dancer by night and an accountant by day is normal, not to say necessary, if you want to be good at both. In my case, both my night job with them and my day job at the office are similar enough that I could behave in a relatively similar way.

"When I'm with them, I'm a tech prima donna. I naturally evolved into one. They know many people, and a lot of those people proposed useless, not to say harmful, things for the app project, but Josh and Mike never provided straight, negative answers, because they don't want to hurt their contacts' feelings."

Arianna: "So you ask technical questions, and when people don't provide satisfactory answers, you explain why their proposal would not work. You're the scapegoat who takes the blame for saying no. When you realized that Josh and Mike appreciated that, you began to relish your role. So, you behaved in a way that your day-job colleagues would find ridiculous."

Nicolas: "You catch onto things fast."

Arianna: "Not enough to avoid being expelled from a project at my job. So... Josh and Mike. You've spent a lot of time with them. Was it always businesslike, with you guys only talking about that app? Did you become close? Would you call them friends? How are they? Anything weird or suspicious with them?"

Nicolas: "Mike is more aggressive and assertive. He takes his modeling career seriously and has some personal trainer gigs and a podcast. He doesn't care much about me. I think he tolerates me because Josh wants me around.

"Josh is the true basket case. I don't think he has a job or ever had one. He doesn't really do much on his own: he just reacts to events, to his surroundings. If he's called for a photo shoot, he'll show up on time; if a girl texts for sex and he's free, he'll go. He visits his extended family and some of his parents' friends when they contact him; I'm pretty sure he often comes back with a check. And as we just said, at some point he realized he was rather underachieving, so he went for the preeminent type of achievements of our era: tech entrepreneurship.

"Now, for the suspicious stuff. It never occurred to me, at any time I was with him, that there was anything that could pose a serious security or legal threat, which was all I cared about. Well, besides occasional drug consumption, but then these guys are so health-conscious, it never degenerates them. It actually happened more than once that I really wanted to get fucked with some of their friends who had good stuff, but I didn't because I didn't want to out-dope them. I didn't feel comfortable doing so.

"Now, as we know, hindsight is a wonderful thing; everything looks suspicious once you begin suspecting. First thing: I turned down Josh's offer to move into S-Loft, which is where Josh, his sister Kate, and Mike live. With them are constant rotations of visitors for which there are a number of sleeping spots that offer variable degrees of intimacy. What he was offering me was a closed room."

Arianna: "Wait... The first suspicious thing is something you did? How does that make sense?"

Nicolas: "He offered the room for free."

Arianna: "It still is a big decision. Roommates can be hell if things don't work out."

KNITTING DEATH

Nicolas: "Arianna, I own this place, right here; I could always come back. In the meantime, I would have rented it. I turned down free money."

Arianna: "But how does that make him suspicious?"

Nicolas: "Well, that's the thing. When I turned down his offer, I thought I lacked the courage to take a risk and seize this once-in-a-lifetime opportunity. But now, I'm not so sure anymore. There's a darker side to them. Most of the time, Josh is the laid-back, no-worry, happy-go-lucky type. Nothing is ever really important; everything is some kind of game for entertainment purpose, just to kill boredom. But sometimes he really looks tense and worried. With some of the people he meets, he has this air of fear and terror on his face..."

Arianna: "There's not much of substance in here, Nicolas. You got weird vibes, I understand that, but as far as we know, family members might have threatened to stop handling him free money. You did the grown-up thing. I wish I did the grown-up thing instead of playing the private eye wannabe."

Nicolas: "No you don't."

Arianna: "I know. That's the problem. Hey, that's why you came to talk to me outside, when we met, at the pub, with your friends and the girls, when I talked about the murders... everyone ignored or scoffed me, except you. Because you suspect that something is odd with your friends."

Nicolas: "OK, wait; first you say that my suspicions have no basis, but now you say that they are the reason I wanted to hear more about what you had to say..."

Arianna: "And? Am I right or not?"

Nicolas: "Well, yes. When you talked about those murders, and everyone changed the subject, I felt the same unease I've tried to describe. So I followed you."

Arianna: "So your interest on the case was not only to have a pretext to hit on me?"

Nicolas: "I used my genuine interest in your story to approach you. I can walk and chew gum at the same time, you know. Anyway, now it's your time to tell me: how did you meet these two girls, Melissa and Diana?"

"Okay, my turn... So, it was a bit more than a year ago that I graduated from Heidelberg University with a business degree, decent grades, okay contacts I made while I was there... But I'm not math proficient enough to become a finance quant, not patient enough to spend time on CPA exams, not... vacuous enough to specialize in HR. I shoot applications in all directions; I get some responses back, land a few interviews but, still, the most exciting prospect is general admin at a tire company in Saint-Louis. My lack of career prospects was weighing on me until one morning, when checking my phone as I got out of bed, I saw this new message titled, "New graduates associate program", from recruitment@cognit.com.

"I let a loud 'Oh my God!' and jolted up from my bed; I wouldn't need coffee that day. First, there was the phone interview, then the videoconference interview, then the real interview at this workshare place in Cincinnati, by which time I spent weeks dreaming about this job, even though it would have just made it harder on me if they chose someone else instead. I thought about this job all the time. I talked about the process with my mom, I talked about the company with my dad, and then I had no news for three long weeks.

"I was sure they'd choose someone else. I thought, 'This is the worst summer ever,' and then... On one bright, sunny August afternoon, as I folded laundry in the basement, my phone rang. The screen read: COGNIT. I stopped breathing, my heart was beating hard. I pressed the 'Answer' button, said hello... and this lady told me she called to make me an offer. The pay was rather low, but I didn't care: it was Cognit on the line. For them, I would have accepted a fucking unpaid internship. And, the icing on my cake: they want me at the corporate headquarters in New York City.

"Things changed with everyone, with my family, with my friends... My parents were exuberantly happy and proud. My mom wouldn't shut up about her daughter who got hired by a big firm in New York City, but I was too happy to really mind her... well, there were some cringe moments, like she would drop the news to people we barely know, or she'd be offended when someone would not know what Cognit is. My dad was more subdued, but I know he was nearly as ecstatic as she was. For him—that a major corporation hired his daughter—it was some kind of vindication for all his hard work.

"I had a month before my starting date. I thought it was a lot. That it meant I had a month of vacation, free of worries, during which I would enjoy myself: wake up late, drink wine by the pool, shop for my new wardrobe and, also, obliviously, find a place to stay in New York City. That last part didn't work out as planned, so I stayed at a youth hostel during my training week."

"A hostel? No, you didn't! You got to be fucking kidding me, Arianna!" said Nicolas.

"Nope. I swear it's the truth. Q4 Hostel in Long Island City. Tourists and backpackers and me—who wore suits for the first time in my life. After a few days, I was invited to join four colleagues who lived together in Manhattan. One of them had divided his room using discarded cardboard, duct tape, and three snowboards, so they now had a place for a new roommate—and I was the chosen one. At first—"

"Wait! What? Three snowboards?"

"Yes. Max, one of the guys, found three snowboards in the trash while walking back to the apartment drunk. He left them on the kitchen floor, which infuriated the other roommates. The kitchen is the only common room, along with the washroom, and is very, very tiny. One roommate nearly tripped on the snowboards. Anyway, they had a huge fight, but Max said he would do something practical with them, so he locked himself in his room and when he opened it back up, he said he had made a new room and that because of him, all of them could pay lower rent."

"So the next part of the story is you sharing with your co-worker Max a room that is divided with snowboards and duct tape."

"No, they put Rebecca, the only other girl, with me there.

"So four new Cognit associates together in one tiny apartment? How did it go?"

"Imagine a crossover between **The New Girl**, **The Big Bang Theory**, and **Friends**, except we're not friends and we all hate each other. I avoided the place as much as I could. I drank after work with other associates and interns at Pennsylvania 6, and Pig N Whistle, did my grocery and laundry in this cold, dark, alien world... Then one day this ad appeared on my computer for an apartment in Williamsburg. The place was old and tiny, but the rent was low—well, not in absolute terms, or even relative to my pay, but definitely below market. I sent in my application online right away and they choose me! It's tiny, dark, and lonely, but peaceful! It's also when I started knitting again.

"One Saturday afternoon I was just walking around and passed in front of this place: Ben & Jesse's Knits. There were women knitting inside! I went home, grabbed my project bag, and went back. The coffee was good, the place was cozy, and comfortable. I became a regular quite soon.

"Then one day I was at an event after work—Tax People for Cancer or something like that—and I saw these two girls who were always there at the cafe, the Asian and the brunette. We were like, 'Hey! How is your shawl going, and what do you do here?' And we drank and had fun and we all went to Melissa's apartment... and we've been together forever after. Well, up until girls in their immediate surroundings started getting killed."

Arianna and Nicolas stayed silent for a few moments. It was Nicolas who broke the silence: "Whoever did this... they know we know."

"They know we know, and they are not afraid to kill."

19. Apps & Data

One of the worse things that can happen, in firms where employees record how they spend their time to the fifteen-minute increment, is to not have anything to do. Employees who do not fill their weekly time reports with enough fifteen-minute increments devoted to billable activity typically do not remain employees for long. This situation was exactly the one in which Arianna found herself at the moment: it was Thursday, 10:56 a.m., and she had accumulated a great total of 1.5 hours of billable client work that she could fill into the CTMT (Cognit Talent Management Tool). This situation was, for Arianna, worrisome.

The great thing, when you suspect that your close friends might be involved in three murders, is that your mind doesn't have much mental space left to worry about the prospect of being fired from your job.

Also, Arianna, as she typed and searched and indexed and cross-referenced all the information and data she had gathered through her investigation, not only looked busy but also felt busy, and thus was not burdened by the shame of being idle.

Still, as busy as she felt, she did not delude herself: she brought no money in, and associates who did not bring money in were terminated. But just when she felt her name was about to pop into the wrong segment of the Monthly Talent Management Meeting, she received a message informing her that her attendance was required for the kickoff meeting of the Rudius project, a marketing analysis contract that would require approximately thirty hours of her time next week and the week after.

Arianna felt surprised, relieved, and annoyed at the same time. Surprised, as the only meeting for which she expected to be invited was the one where her employment at Cognit would be terminated. Relieved, as she was handed an opportunity to prove she could perform to her superior's expectation. Annoyed, as the "thirty-hour" project assignment did not really refer to thirty actual hours of work but was more a euphemistic Cognit-speak code for "you will work days and evening and nights and weekends on this project." Which was bound to negatively interfere with the inquiry.

After a quick, subsidized lunch at Cognit's in-house cafeteria (free-range ethical chicken sauté with bio greens) and a half-hour yoga session (Level III Advanced) provided for free at the in-house gym, Arianna went back to her desk-for-the-day.

She logged in and opened the invitation for the Rudius project launch meeting. She clicked on "Rudius" and, as expected, was led to the project's page on the Organodex. To her surprise, Rudius was not merely a marketing analysis project, but a Cognit Data marketing analysis project. Cognit Data projects were important. And prestigious.

Cognit Data. The brightest minds in artificial intelligence! The industry's leading data scientists! World-renowned algorithm designers! Working all together at the Cognit International Data Practice to find data solution for your business! The same team that, within a year of its inception, put together the world's most renowned cutting-edge Real Time Analytics service!

Cognit Data. Noise-free, spin-free core insights.

Arianna clicked the scroll-down menu of the Cognit Data section. Artificial Intelligence, Basic Queries, Big Data, Database Access, Dynamic Tables, Cognit Tables and Chart Formats, Data Mining, Database Management, Learning R, Learning SQL… Arianna stopped reading there. No one had bothered to include an "Introduction to Cognit's Data Practice" section, so she'd wait to see what this project was about before digging left and right into subjects chosen at random.

She looked at the clock on her screen: 1:28 p.m. Less than two hours before this assignment would swallow her life. She told herself she might as well work a bit on the case while she had some time. She grabbed her notebook and opened the last pages with content in it, which consisted in a single sentence:

"Everyone is a suspect. ☹"

Oh, why had she peered into this rabbit hole? Everyone who, in the new life she had made for herself in New York City, counted for her was, somehow, linked to the deceased girls.

What motivated her was not so much to catch the killer anymore: she did want to see the guilty one punished for its crimes, but even more to exonerate her friends—all of them, preferably. It might prove painful to remove the bad apple among them, but at least she would know the rest were innocent.

That is, if she didn't discover that all were involved, in one way or another, in these three deaths. This is what Arianna feared the most: all the people she loved were together involved into this vast, dark conspiracy, this entire coven tied by a sinister blood bond, which they renewed every full moon. Her fate was to end up either dead or alone. Or, worse, back in Ohio, jobless and penniless…

Arianna's phone buzzed. It was a text from Diana that read: "Patricia Jonca has a trunk show tonight in Brooklyn! We have to go!"

The message was quickly followed by another text from Melissa: "Yes! Where is it exactly? We should go to the Peruvian taco place before."

As Arianna typed her reply, to the effect that she doubted she'd escape corporate confinement on time for both the show and the meal, she whispered to herself, "Oh please, please be innocent of these murders, both of you!" She pressed the "Send" button and put her phone back on the desk.

When her eyes set again on her screen, her gaze fell right on the Cognit Data menu, the one that was devoid of an "Introduction" section. It did contain, however, a section titled "Queries & Analysis Basics." She was not sure about queries, but she liked the "Basics" part of the title. She clicked on the link. The top of the page was the tables of content: Your data set, Preparing your data, Making your data talk, Making your data tell a story, Introduction to charts and data visualization… Maybe this one was for her?

****

She reached the bottom of the page, having read all the 4,546 words of the main text, plus the various examples illustrated with tables and charts. It was… interesting? She understood most of the content—the concepts, the tools, the different steps. The page did not present data analysis as complicated calculus, statistics, and coding, but as making links between various logical elements and concepts. And it presented many tools to help find these links and illustrate them.

It was not that much interesting in itself; the interest came from the fact that data analysis was a powerful tool.

This was something she could do. But there was one thing that scared her: the prospect of spending hours staring numbers. Rows and rows and columns and tables full of numbers. That was bound to be headache-inducing.

An alarm message popped on the screen of Arianna's computer. Also, she noticed someone standing beside her deck while looking at her, a Cognit-issued laptop pressed against her chest with both arms. "Are you coming?"

And so it began, this project Rudius, which would consume all of her days and most of her nights for the next month or so. Arianna rose, fetched her laptop, shut the workstation screens, and followed the girl, who she assumed was Megan Escalante, another analyst picked for the Rudius project, according to the CTMT. She also assumed that Megan knew which room the kickoff meeting was being held in, so she followed her. Megan texted as she walked, her laptop awkwardly squeezed between her right elbow and her ribcage.

They reached the conference room, where a tall and elegant woman welcomed them. It was Germaine Steele, the manager in charge of the Rudius project. Arianna and Megan waved at her and went to sit on the opposite side of Germaine at the conference table, where another girl sat (most likely an analyst, considering she didn't look like she was old enough to drink). All three of them, the manager and the two other associates, typed and swiped, fixed to their phones in silence for a few minutes.

At last, Germaine stood up and addressed the group: "Hello, everyone. Thank you for joining me this afternoon."

She explained that Arianna and her two colleagues were tasked with training an algorithm. The whole business confused Arianna, and her two colleagues as well, by the look on their faces. As Arianna understood it, she would decide if the algorithm was right or wrong when answering subjective questions and identifying pictures.

There was much relief in the room when Germaine confirmed that the project did not involve any coding on their part; their mission was merely to agree or not with the choice the algorithm made. Yay or nay, again and again.

"This algorithm is coded to perform a rather subjective task: to decide if something is fashionable or not," said Germaine. "It is fed images and pictures, which can be anything: photographs of people wearing certain clothes, paintings, abstract drawings, or internet memes—any kind of visual file. The algorithm will judge the coolness of each picture, expressed as a number on a scale of 1 to 6, with 6 being the most fashionable and 1 the least.

"And this is where you will intervene. First, you will assign a number of your own on each picture, based on your opinion of its fashionableness. Second, after having gone through a certain number of pictures, you will write what you think that the algorithm gets wrong."

Germaine's explanation worried Arianna. Had anyone tasked her with judging the coolness of clothes and ads (and internet memes), she would have been minimally amused and enthusiast. But it was not anyone who asked; it was Cognit. Which meant there was a catch somewhere. If the only task was to write a number on a picture, then there'd be thousands of them to note.

KNITTING DEATH

Still, Arianna would have no problem going through it all if it meant her New York City adventure could go on a little longer. She would not be the first women not paid a living wage to go through a tedious, repetitive task in the history of this city.

Arianna looked at Megan and the other girl: like her, they were obviously pondering what had just been said to them and what it implied for the days to come. Like her, young women who had been tasked with a boring, unchallenging task. Like her, they were... well, pretty. And as if Germaine was reading Arianna's thoughts, and just before Arianna was about to put forward, in her mind, the hypothesis that the selection process for this project seemed rather wrong, Germaine spoke up.

"You obviously understand why you were chosen for this task. Megan: you studied fashion marketing during your undergrad at the Parsons School of Design. Nina, you have done an internship at a well-known high-end clothing company in Italy. And Arianna, you actually make clothes of your own, some of which you actually wear at work, if I am not mistaken. So, with the three of you, our programming team is in good hands, fashion-wise."

Germaine typed something on her laptop. The screen on the wall of the room lit up, displaying the picture of a middle-aged man wearing an old-school trench coat with a fedora on his head. Beside the picture were two rows of circles with the numbers 1 to 6 above them. Circle number 3 on the top row was blackened below number 3; it was the score the algorithm had assigned to the picture.

"You put your score here," said Germaine, touching the screen on the lower row of circles. "Then you press the "OK" button right here, which will bring you to the next picture—and you repeat the process. And that's it, that's the extent of your task. For now. In phase two, you will be asked to make more detailed recommendations and participate in

181

working sessions with the programmers, but at the moment we ask that you concentrate on this task only. It may seem trivial, repetitive, and un-rigorous, but you actually be building the main foundation of this mandate."

Megan raised her hand. "But what criteria do we used to assign a score? What are the guidelines?"

"There are no guidelines," answered Germaine. "Just give the score that you feel describes the coolness of the picture—with a focus on clothing. Just to be clear: we won't ask for any justification whatsoever for the score you will give to any of those images. Don't rationalize; just follow your gut feeling.

** **

A man with '80s Ray-Bans and a fluorescent bicycle cap: 4. A young teenage boy with a yellow K-Way raincoat: 4 (again?). A woman with a 1950s green checkered robe who is keying on a typewriter: 2 (something was off with her... her smile, her stare, the tone of green of her robe?). An Asian girl with a white dress in a field of sunflowers (Arianna could tooootally imagine Melissa taking the exact same pic!): 6 it would be.

** **

Arianna felt her headache already, not even an hour into an assignment whose length would be counted not in hours but in days and weeks. Despite the professed importance of her current task, it remained dumb. Check-rate-click-check-rate-click. Arianna hoped that phase two would offer more opportunities to develop some data science credentials. Cognit had powerful data tools and access to countless databases; she just had read that some projects used information from millions different cellphone users to make decisions or recommendations.

Those tools were all there, in the Cognit Data section of the Organodex, for her to use, with instructions and tutorials that explained how to use them. That would need some effort on her end. She would need to get out of her comfort zone, which she was confident she could do, if only she could dedicate herself to the task at hand.

That was a big if. Arianna was rather... distracted nowadays. If only she could use just a fraction of all these data resources to help her unstuck this whole knit-and-murder mess.

But she there was no data to look through. The Rudius project was based on data that came from a cell application, but her inquiry had no app that could supply relevant data...

Unless it did!

Peter Minuit!

There was an app that was used by many acquaintances of the three dead girls. Well, one that had been downloaded by many people, if not used.

And the person who had coded and managed that app was Nicolas.

Arianna grabbed her phone and typed frenetically: "OMG, can we meet tonight?"

There was no way to be sure Nick had access to all the data, but chances were quite good. The app would have tracked the location of its users during the few weeks before and after and, if she was lucky, during the murders.

The app's user base did not cover every suspect, but it would include data for those that Arianna wanted to exonerate. Having the location of each user for most of the time frame between the app's installation and removal might allow her to not only check who was with Marie-Louise,

Christina, and Marianna on the days they each died but also to learn who among them hung out together, when and where they met...

Her phone buzzed. "Yes, is everything okay?" Nick had replied.

"Yeah, no breaking in or anything of the kind. You still are the admin for Minuit, right?" Arianna pressed "Send," and regretted it immediately; her text made it seemed like all she cared about was his access to the app's data. She really did not want to upset him for something as silly as a rude SMS, and—

"Holy shit. I totally missed that. We'll dig into this tonight. Good catch, Cognit girl!"

Her fears were unjustified. Nicolas was nearly as obsessed as she was with this whole thing, now that his cute boy friends were in the picture. Yay, progress?

Now, digging into this, as Nick had written, would totally invade the privacy of those users. Arianna would peek into her closest friends' lives without their consent.

So be it. She way too deep into this inquiry pass on such an opportunity.

Arianna's phone buzzed again.

"Hey, we have the brunch tomorrow; don't forget to bring your things."

The brunch. With Melissa and Diana. And Nicolas's friends. And Nicolas. She would go to the brunch with Nicolas. Well, again, so be it. Her dress was ready for pickup at the dry cleaner on the Cognit building ground floor and her shoes were in her bag. The plan was logistically sound.

"Okay, everyone," said Germaine, interrupting Arianna's train of thoughts. "Our time slot in this room is coming to an end. You can continue to work on this project from your workstation, or for anywhere else for that matter. Do not hesitate to reach out if you have questions or any kind of issue."

Arianna quickly exited the meeting room without acknowledging any of her new teammates. There was so much to do, so little time that she didn't want to waste. She arrived at working space S.56, her desk for the day. But not even ten seconds after she had taken her place, a man behind Arianna called her with much uncertainty in his voice.

"Arianna?"

She turned around. There stood William Mossin, a manager to whom she never had talked to before.

"You're Arianna, right?" Could you please come with me? Someone wants to meet you."

His eyes opened wide. He looked left and right as he fidgeted with his cellphone between his hands.

"Someone wants to talk to me?" Arianna asked, with much disbelief.

"Room R-32. Can you follow me?"

The first thing that crossed Arianna's mind: was the person who wanted to talk to her someone from HR who would fire her? Probably not. This was not how Cognit got rid of employees it didn't want or need anymore. The second thing: had something happened to her parents? Again, not the Cognit way to announce such news.

Actually, everything was entirely un-Cognit-like in the way William Mossin asked Arianna to follow him. No meeting email invite, no notification through the Organodex Cognit CRM, no weaseling into small talk the notion that it would be in her best interest to join this meeting. Just this manager, who looked like he was about to piss his pants, who asked her to follow him.

Therefore, there were many avenues for Arianna to decline his request. But did she want to decline?

More than anything, Arianna was curious. So she followed William Mossin, manager at Cognit, toward meeting room R-32. As they neared the room, she saw two young men, probably analysts like her, who looked at her as she approached, their eyes big and stary, their mouths opened wide. What had hit them all?

Arianna recognized one of the two; she often ran into him at the Cognit gym. The cute-and-cut-and-aware-of-it type. More than once he had made eye contact and smiled to her. But this liftin' bro wasn't flexing at the moment; he looked as afraid and confused as William.

William stopped a few feet from the R-32 door. "Here," he said.

He didn't look like he had the intention to go in, so Arianna grabbed the door and entered. What greeted her made her stop on her track: seated at the one table, in the middle of the tiny room, was a woman, tall and serious, who stared at Arianna with wide, big brown eyes; although her skin was flawless chocolate milk and her hair curly jet black without a hint of white, something about her said she was a certain age. But what really shocked Arianna was what she wore: a black shawl with tiny, bright silver pieces knitted in its fabric. A Bat Wing.

Arianna shut the door behind her. She had used company resources to inquiry about those people, on those witches; no need for this information to get around.

"Sit," said the woman.

In any other circumstances, having this Bat Wing-wearing women appear out of nowhere would terrify Arianna. But they were in the middle of a weekday on a crowded office floor, Arianna doubted she had summoned her there to kill her.

"Sit!" said the woman, again.

Her voice carried a lot of authority. Arianna felt compelled to take the chair and sit as ordered, but didn't move. Instead, she shouted: "What do you want!?"

"Sit. Down." The women fixed her gaze on Arianna, deep, dark eyes wide open.

Arianna put her two hands on the back of the nearest chair and leaned toward: "I know that shawl you're wearing is a Bat Wing. I know the dead girls were witches in your coven. I know that this girl, Charlotte, is also a witch. I know you guys stole money and committed fraud. I know some of this fraud happened here, at Cognit. I know the murderer wore a red dress when she killed Marianna."

The women in the Bat Wing stood up and reached the door, not blinking as she fixed her eyes on Arianna. She departed through the hall, William Mossin and the two analysts following her with confused glares.

20. Hacking & Chill

"Before you ask: no other Minuit user was with Marie-Louise or Marianna on the evening when each of them died. Same thing with Christina's apartment."

This is how Nicolas greeted Arianna when he opened his door to her.

She walked inside. As he grabbed her coat off her shoulder, she said, "I was not about to ask. A witch just paid me a visit at the office."

"I knew something had happened to you!"

Arianna kissed him on the lips. "She visited me in the office. She was somehow spooky but didn't hurt me. And there were tons of people in the office when it happened."

Arianna went on and narrated her encounter to Nick, how she had been unorthodoxly summoned to a meeting by William, how everyone around the meeting room looked confused, that the witch wore a Bat Wing, how she had ordered her to sit...

And then Arianna reached the part of the story where she told Germaine everything she knew. She doubted Nick would approve. Not that she cared that much about his approval; the thing she cared about at the moment was to avoid arguing. She would not have minded lying, but there was no lie to tell, not one she could invent right now on the fly. So she opted for a strategic retreat.

"And then I did something absolutely dumb. Dumb, reckless, and dangerous. I don't know why, it seemed like the good thing to say at the moment, but—"

"Arianna, what is it that you did?"

"I told her everything I knew. The dead girls, the Bat Wing, Charlotte. The killer in the apartment building with the red dress."

"What?!"

"You heard correctly. I told her everything."

"Well, that's an... aggressive response. She probably did not expect that. That might even buy us some time before they decide to kill us both," Nicolas said with a mocking smile that did not entirely hide his fear. "So... do you think she's the one who killed the three girls?"

"No. We have a glimpse of the Lady in Red's hands in the video footage, and they are quite pale. The witch who visited me at the office had a much darker skin."

"That's even better: maybe the red one is in trouble for being lousy. But she's not lousy enough to be a Minuit user; there were no users present during Marianna and Marie-Louise's deaths."

"You mean: no phone, on which the app was installed, was present at the moment of each death."

"If you want to be precise and scientific about it, yes, that description would be indeed more accurate. That said... even if the data hasn't produced a smoking gun, it does contain a trove of intel. Besides the three victims, I've found among the users, so far: Diana, Melissa, Heather, Mike, Josh, and even your new friend Charlotte. Most of them have installed the app around the launch party in September last year and barely anyone has deemed productive to remove it despite usage stats that are rather dismal."

"And despite the app having no new content since last the New Year's Eve parties last," added Arianna.

"Correct."

Arianna felt that, on one hand, Nick was proud to show he could make a mobile app pretty much by himself, while on the other, he felt embarrassed to have contributed to a project that was rather... lame.

She sat on the couch and grabbed her laptop inside her bag. She asked Nick to hand her the dataset, but he stood there, motionless, looking at her. After a few seconds of silent non-answering, his lips started moving. She knew what he was about to say, so she cut him off.

"I know this data is very confidential. I know it would be extremely embarrassing if this data were leaked. I know it's potentially a very serious liability for you. Also. this is my personal computer, and I use it only to watch podcasts and stream movies and TV shows. And download knitting patterns."

Nick shoved his hand in the right pocked of his jeans and handed her a USB stick. "We don't even share this data through cloud services or by mail. We only use this key, okay?"

"Only this key!"

Arianna started her machine and plugged the USB stick into its port. As the operating system loaded, she grabbed her notebook from her bag. Nick disappeared toward the kitchen and started talking—to someone over the phone, Arianna assumed. He came back, earphones on, his cell in his left hand, a bowl, from which rose steam, in the other. He put the bowl on the coffee table in front of her, just as she clicked on the Microsoft Excel icon on her desktop. She opened her work notebook to the last page that was filled with her handwriting, which detailed different potential ways to query the Minuit dataset and cross-reference the information that might be found in it.

She selected the OS Finder, reached the location of the USB key, and imported the only file located there. As it loaded, a warm, sweet smell reached Arianna. Baby corn, red bell pepper, sugar snap peas, two plastic chopsticks, steam rising above it all; she took the bowl with her left hand and the chopsticks with the right.

"Thank you, Nick!" she shouted; again, he had disappeared from the living room.

Below the vegetables was some meat, which Arianna couldn't identify, and white rice. The undefined nature of the meat would have been an issue, potentially a major one, had she been in a restaurant. She shoved a bit in her mouth; it was rich, sweet, spicy - delicious. She realized the meat was duck; quite the delicacy for an informal, on-the-couch-while-looking-at-the-screen evening meal.

Christina Bain. Marianna Burrow. Marie-Louise Thompson. Diana Stanley. Melissa Chen. Heather Stuart. Charlotte Braun. All were there. All had the app on their mobile. And Minuit registered their geographical coordinates, even when the app was not in use. Which was a good thing; the data file would have been quite meager had it not been the case, considering how little time all these users had actually spent using the app.

This little fact, however, that Minuit tracked its users and registered their locations along the corresponding time and date, obviously embarrassed Nick. Yes, many apps did it anyway, but it was not supposed to be this way. It did not follow apps' creation and management best practices. But Arianna was glad it didn't. Actually, she would have been rather annoyed had it not.

Now was the time for the complicated stuff. Finding names was the matter of pressing "Find" and typing what you were looking for; cross-referencing places and times and people was more laborious. "Okay, you can do this, Arianna" she whispered to herself as she selected the PivotTable function. Her stare switched back and forth between the screen and her notebook as she followed each step she had written down, bullet after bullet.

Arianna wanted to go through the whole process by herself. Not that she had anything to prove, but rather that she wanted to be sure she covered every angle, and that she could get back into it, if she found something to query the data set about one night if she wasn't able to sleep...

She put the User variable in the filter, and restricted its value to Marianna's user number: "B000073."

"Nick, why is the naming convention restricted to fewer than a million users? Your coding betrays your lack of ambition, not to say faith in Minuit," said Arianna.

"One letter, six numbers; that's 26 million users for you," he replied.

She restricted the Time variable from August 25 at noon to August 26 at noon—roughly half a day before and after the approximate moment of Marianna's date. She then put the Longitude and Latitude variables in columns besides the Time column.

The app had registered the time/location coordinates nine times; Arianna pasted them all in Google's My Map. Nine locations indicators appeared on the map, displaying Marianna's whereabouts during the last day of her life.

Her final hours looked rather unexceptional. Four dots between her apartment and what was probably the 59th Street–Columbus Circle station, and four more between 34th Street–Penn station and the RedBroom office on Sixth Avenue. There was one lone dot in between, most likely Marianna's cell that had caught some signal from the subway train as she rode back home. It might have to be investigated later on, but for now Arianna had to focus on the big picture if she didn't want to lose herself into all the mundane, tiny details that had been captured and registered by Nick's app.

She pulled variables in, filtered them, dragged some more into the PivotTable, removed some, pasted resulting coordinates into My Maps, and stared at too many red dots spread out among too many locations in and around Manhattan.

She narrowed down her search to the phones that had used Marianna's Wi-Fi. Only three users fitted the criteria: Mike, a username RMother, and Marianna herself. She redid the same query, but with Marie-

KNITTING DEATH

Louise's username instead: Marianna, RMother, Josh, Mike, and Marie-Louise.

"Nick... Your two friends knew the girls."

"Okay..." he answered, his eyes glued to the screen of his machine. He had appeared on the couch perpendicular to the one Arianna was sitting on at some point in the last few seconds or minutes, Arianna had vaguely noticed. "Wait—what? Josh and Mike? They knew the girls?"

Now she had his attention. "Check for yourself," she said.

While this revelation was quite a catch, Arianna was not entirely surprised at this point to learn that Nick's two pretty friends were acquaintances of the deceased girls. A small world theirs was, indeed.

"So we're talking about Marianna and Marie-Louise, right? Holy shit, it looks like, on August 11, Mike spent the evening with Marie-Louise... and the rest of the night with the Marianna."

"They shared a lot, didn't they?"

Nick was obviously not amused. These murders revealed themselves to be part of his world, just as they had for Arianna. He was no longer the guy who used his detached interest in these strange death cases to get closer to her. Now they were both involved.

Nick keyed frenetically, most likely mining for clues on his buddies. There was no point for Arianna to keep digging in Nick's backyard if he was about to unearth it all by himself; she could look elsewhere.

She made a new table with only Christina's data in it. She sorted the location data, deleted repetitions, and pasted the digits in My Maps. To Arianna's stupefaction, all the dots plotted themselves tightly around one spot in Elizabeth, New Jersey. She zoomed in; unless Christina had gone out often without her phone, the poor girl had spent the last year of her life confined within a one-square mile virtual enclosure that included her apartment and the dive bar where she sang. It was sad. And frightening.

Christina had nothing in common with Marianna and Marie-Louise, except for the fact that she had been a knitter, too. And a witchcraft enthusiast, apparently.

Arianna filtered the location variable for the coordinates of Christina's apartment and unfiltered the user ID variable. Sadness again: no one else besides Christina had set foot into her place. This result represented only the Minuit app userbase—the Minuit app's rather limited userbase. Yet Arianna had the impression that this sample, as narrow as it was, painted a rather precise picture of Christina's last few months.

Arianna did the same search but with the dive bar instead of Christina's apartment. The results were quite different; the place seemed quite popular with Minuit users. Which was rather counterintuitive when considering the fact that Minuit's makers and their network seemed to be the kind of crowd that never stray too far from Manhattan and the hip spots in Brooklyn.

Marianna, Marie-Louise, RMother, Charlotte… and Diana.

Damn it, Diana… Please tell me it's not you. It cannot be you.

She sorted the data. Diana had been to the dive bar once… a month before Arianna had landed in NYC. If Arianna remembered correctly, Melissa had been away at this time, vacationing in Spain (and also breaking it off with her then-boyfriend). So maybe Diana had been, at this very moment, quite bored, bored enough to spend an evening in a Jersey dive bar. Maybe…

KNITTING DEATH

Arianna felt the urge to change the subject, to look for something else. Yes, Diana was officially on the official suspect shortlist. She actually had been for a while, but Arianna could not let the distress it caused slow her down. Not now, not when she had gone this far, not when she had gone this deep. She grabbed her notebook; its pages had filled up quickly during the past few weeks, but it contained more questions than answers.

REDBROOM*, written in large capital letters, highlighted in pink, with a large asterisk next to it. Which meant that it had to be looked into. Marianna had worked there, Charlotte worked there, and its name represented the quintessential witch's accessory.

She looked at RedBroom's location on Google Maps: 40th Street and Sixth Avenue, coordinates 40.753527, -73.985624. Again she sorted; again the same names: Marie-Louise, RMother, and Diana, along with Marianna and Charlotte.

Another name written in bold letters in the notebook: Burkett Gurewitz. Workplace of Diana and Marie-Louise but not concomitantly; Diana had started there two weeks after Marie-Louise's death, according to the data. This information also fit with Arianna's souvenirs; she remembered that Diana had switched jobs at this moment. Who else visited? Charlotte and RMother.

"Nick... Have you seen this user, 'RMother'? ID number B000033."

Nicolas looked at Arianna before going back to his screen. "Not sure..."

"I'd bet it stands for 'Reverend_Mother,' which is one of the user ID on the Bat Wing message board."

"That would make sense. I'll check the other info linked to this ID for clues."

Arianna turned the page of her notebook; "A FUCKING DEAD RAT" greeted her on her next page, written in big bold letters. She searched for Martine Cunning among the user names—and indeed it was there. There was only two weeks of activity for this account; either the app had been removed or the cell deactivated after this. At only one point during those two weeks had Martine been in the company of other users.

Arianna pasted the coordinates into Google Maps. They pinpointed to a restaurant: Per Se. The Google description included four dollar signs; a pricey venue it was. Arianna checked who was in attendance: the usual suspects (Diana, Charlotte, Marie-Louise, Marianna) plus Christine and three other users. Arianna noted the IDs in her notebook to remember to check them up later.

"Arianna... there's a large cluster downtown, near Bowling Green station. It happens three times within our sample. Do you have any idea what it is?"

Arianna answered with the negative and, again, turned the page of her notebook. "Ben & Jesse's Knits" was the largest inscription there. Arianna didn't have to read the smaller text; weird things had been said and done in this place the past few times she had been there.

Unsurprisingly, Diana and Melissa's accounts had registered the Ben & Jesse's Knits geographical coordinates quite often. There was one user, however, who was there even more often. Arianna looked it up. "Marvin McMarvski" was the name associated with the account. To say that Marvin was a regular at Ben & Jesse's Knits knit was an understatement: his phone checked in on a regular basis, sometimes many days in a row.

As if Marvin was an employee there.

"Oh my God!" screamed Arianna; "It's Yuna! Marvin McMarvski is Yuna! Yuna is a user!"

Nick left his couch to sit besides Arianna and look at her screen. "Good catch!" he said.

Hey, could you look up her locations to see if she's been around Bowling Green station? Nick said.

"What is up with this Bowling Green thing?" asked Arianna.

"They ended up there, all of them: Charlotte, Diana, RMother, the dead girls. It happened three times. The first time, even Christina and Martine Cunning."

"What are the coordinates?" asked Arianna.

"They don't have all the exact same coordinates. They did not all connect to the same Wi-Fi source, which probably means that the exact place they went to doesn't have a modem. Their phone just checked for the nearby networks."

Arianna sorted Marvin/Yuna's localization data. "Yep, Yuna was definitely around Bowling Green. Any idea what they were all doing?"

"Well, let's just say that those three dates are important days in the Babylonian calendar," said Nick, "which is used quite often in witchcraft."

21. Brunchin'

Arianna exited the bathroom, then stopped abruptly, then went back inside.

Her toothbrush. She had left her toothbrush on the counter next to the sink. In Nicolas's bathroom.

Leaving her toothbrush at Nicolas' was a big nope. Especially on the day of their first official date.

She grabbed the buccal hygiene instrument and resumed her course toward the bedroom, where she shoved the toothbrush inside her bag. She then grabbed her phone and sat on the edge of the bed. Arianna didn't especially want to look at her phone right now, but she also didn't want to make it look like she was waiting after Nicolas, who was staring at, and typing on, his laptop.

"There's coffee in the kitchen. I'll be with you in five. I have to take care of this first."

"Coffee! Yay!" exclaimed Arianna as she bolted up from the bed toward the kitchen. That was unexpected; so far, every morning she had woken up there, she had left in a hurry for the office, with him also heading out to work.

An empty cup waited for her beside the coffee maker, which a freshly brewed coffee pot was sitting in—its fresh aroma filled the kitchen, but somehow had not reached into the bedroom. She poured the hot, dark liquid into the cup and sat on a bench next to the counter, holding her coffee between both her hands, just under her nose.

Arianna sat straight across the mirror that was hung the wall next to the apartment's entrance door. As she caught her reflection in it, she was surprised herself by her own smile. Oh, the power of an unexpected caffeine fix. She saw herself from head to toe, from a different distance, and with different light than in the bathroom. The cream sweater dress fitted nicely, the gray flat shoes matched with the dress, and her hair was good. She was overly satisfied with her look.

Preoccupation with her look was a full glitch above its normal level and not because it was her first official date with Nicolas. The additional-preoccupation-factor stemmed from the fact that she was about to attend a private event with a bunch of people she didn't know, most of whom could be described as something between "rich" and "wealthy" with a varied dose of "influential" added to the mix.

The event was in a private house in Westchester, a place that was, as far as Arianna knew, like a regular suburb but filled with mansions and palaces and domains and castles.

Nicolas walked into the kitchen, dressed in a pastel cashmere shirt over a pink polo, pale khakis, and white loafers. On one hand, he was slightly overdoing the brunch dress thing. On the other, he looked great in it, and his model friends were the kind of guys who showed up to brunches in ripped-out T-shirts and old jeans filled with holes—so he would stand out.

Ideally, Arianna would have preferred not to arrive at this event with him. But she didn't want to go there by herself, and Melissa was heading there from her parents' place in Boston, and Diana was also arriving from somewhere else than NYC—so she was quite glad that Nick was okay with going with her.

"Nick? Why are you staring at your coffee maker?" she said, after he spent at least ten seconds looking at the machine, still and expressionless.

"I want coffee. But I'm already nervous and sweaty and feeling a tight knot in my guts. I'm not sure coffee is a good idea right now."

His nervousness was understandable, as they suspected that among the friends they would meet this morning was a person who had recently killed three young knitters. Arianna did not think her own relative calmness in the same situation was a product of her exceptional courage; it was just that Nicolas had, well, things to lose. She did not. Her job was going down the drain, soon she would have to leave New York in shame and lose the great friends she had made there, a fate worse than getting on the wrong side of a fanatic killer, as far as she was concerned.

"When you hesitate between coffee and not coffee, the answer is always coffee."

"I'll grab a reusable cup then. We should go now."

Nick looked ready but had not mentioned how he intended to get them to Westchester. Why wasn't he calling an Uber?

Arianna could ask, but she had no intention to contribute to the ride fare whatsoever, so she shut up. Maybe she was an exploitive date but she wasn't an ungrateful one. A bit like the Founding Fathers in reverse: she would not ask for representation without taxation.

Still, Arianna didn't like the uncertainty of the situation. She had told Diana and Melissa she'd be there by 11a.m. and it was already nearing ten. She wanted to be there early, when only a few people had arrived, to get introduced quietly before the place was full of people chit-chatting in small groups. Fashionably late was not an interesting option; managing her anxiety was higher on her list of priorities.

"Give yourself a fucking break."

"What?" Arianna turned toward Nicolas, surprised, a bit shocked. What had he just said… to her?

"So what if you don't wear a designer dress? You made it, so far, all by yourself."

"What are you talking about?" said Arianna, even if what she meant to say was more in the line of, "Yes, I'm self-conscious about the clothes I wear, and while I'm somehow positively surprised that you noticed, I'm not sure I really, really value your opinion on the whole matter." Instead, all she said was, "But—"

"That's more than most chicks who wear designer dresses can brag about."

"We're going into a huge mansion full of rich and successful people. I'd be stressed and self-conscious even if I had ten million in my bank account."

Nick stood there just in front of her as she sat on the bench; she grabbed his legs with her heel and pulled him close to her. He kissed her on the lips. He smiled. He was most likely happy she had, at long last, showed some sign of vulnerability; she had admitted she was stressed out by what people would think of her.

He liked her. She knew it, she felt it. She enjoyed it. Was it reciprocal? Well, she did like him, too, for sure.

She liked him beyond the utilitarian aspects of their relationship.

She liked that he was into her.

She liked that… she could get a decent, proper male to be into her, and to have him, for all intents and purposes, exclusively.

She liked that she worried about breaking his heart.

He let her go, she stood up, they put on their coats (a beige raincoat for her; a blue bomber jacket for him) and they left the apartment. As he locked the door she summoned the elevator, then checked her phone: 10:31. Maybe had he had arranged for a ride during her shower? She was pretty sure he had spent all the time she had taken her shower in post-coital slumber. Maybe he would call an old-school NYC yellow cab?

This uncertainty irritated Arianna. There was a lot a stake; all of those she thought had decent chances of being involved in the murders would be there. She wanted to be there early. Now was not the time to fool around.

Maybe he was scared. Maybe he was trying to delay their arrival there, hoping something would ultimately prevent them from reaching the sinister Westchester mansion where they would be in harm's way, at the mercy of the killer… That, she could have understood—but not forgive. It would be entirely reasonable for Nick to recuse himself from this crazy murder story but not to hinder her own inquiry.

The elevator door rang, and they moved inside. She pressed the ground floor button, but he then pressed the basement button. She turned her head toward him: "Why are we going to the basement?"

"Because that's where my car is."

* * * *

"So, you're not too embarrassed to show up there in a ten-year-old Civic?" Nick said, as the car rolled down the Henry Hudson Parkway.

"A ten-year-old Civic is an obsequious status good when you live in Manhattan," said Arianna. The vehicle was clean, did not make any strange noise, and had no visible parts broken. It obviously was not used often and was most likely well maintained. Also, they would be on time—that is, early. The car was more than fine to her.

"We're going to Westchester. We'll look like we're cleaning staff or yoga instructors or dog walkers."

Arianna did not feel like explaining to Nicolas the difference between inadequate clothes and an inadequate car. He knew he had scored big by providing not only convenient and comfortable transportation but, more importantly, a way to get out fast.

KNITTING DEATH

She stared at him; behind his head was the Hudson River, its shore dotted with high-rises, its water scattered with boats of different kinds—her first car-bound trip in NYC.

"So, let me guess," Arianna said. This had been your ride since you turned sixteen. You saved money to buy some used car, but your mom was worried that it would not be safe, so for your birthday your dad paid the difference between the crappy used car and the new Civic. Every time you came back from college for recess, your dad and you performed basic maintenance like an oil change and clean-up. One time, your dorm buddy offered you this funny bumper sticker; you said you didn't put it on because you thought the joke was lame, but you knew your dad would not—"

"My aunt Jeanine died of cancer when I was eighteen. Her only son was in jail, so just before she passed away, she gave me the car on condition I would visit her son from time to time. I went there on the first Saturday of each month. It was really hard on him and really hard on me seeing him deteriorate between each visit. One time I did not go, during midterms. I called him and he said there was no problem. A week later, I received a call—they had found him dead, hung inside his cell."

"Oh! I'm so sorry…" whispered Arianna.

She felt so bad. She had assumed Nicolas's life had been easy—easier than hers. She had assumed everything, even though she barely knew him.

She stared at the road ahead, in silence. She knew he would not be mad at her. She knew he would say it was no big deal, but still she felt bad. She felt… cheap. She…

Arianna realized that Nick was looking at her. And that he was smiling.

"It's not true! Your story is a lie! You caught me! You fucker; you caught me! If you were not driving right now, I'd punch you in the ribs!"

"I know. That's why I only make this kind of joke when I'm driving, baby."

"And I fell for it! I can't believe I felt for it!"

Arianna nearly had said, "Don't 'baby' me!" but had stopped herself before the words had exited her mouth. He was probing the field, cautiously, displaying affection and possession while maintaining deniability. He was totally joking when he 'babied' her, wasn't he?

**

Arianna and Nick remained silent for most of the rest of the ride. At some point, Arianna realized they were not on the highway anymore but on a narrow two-way road in the middle of the forest. She was surprised to be in such a dense wooded area less than an hour's drive from Manhattan.

Sometimes she could catch a glimpse of the homes hidden behind the trees. They were large.

They reached an intersection where were located a few businesses—well, there was a Shell gas station, a liquor store, and a post office.

"Nick…"

"Yes, Arianna?"

"Are we really turning on North Salem Street?"

"We are. North Salem Street, Cross River, New York."

"Jesus Christ. They take this witch thing seriously."

They did not stay on North Salem Road for too long; Nick's phone made them turn on School House Road, which was straight, narrow and gravel. The screen on the dashboard indicated they were about to reach their destination. They reached the last turn. The massive cast-iron doors indicated to Arianna that they had not reached the destination's street but its entrance.

Oaks lined the narrow entrance path; at the end of it was a grey stone façade, which appeared to grow as they neared it. Arianna distinguished three rows of windows.

To their right was a small parking area with three cars. Nick steered the Civic into an empty spot. They exited and headed toward the main door. She took his right arm with her hand. He brought his forearm higher and forward. His fist was clenched, tightly; he was nervous about the whole thing.

She was not. She wanted to get over with it. Maybe a part of her wanted to die, right here in this mansion if her New York venture was about to fail. Another part of her didn't really believe there was any significant danger to begin with. And another part thought it was weird to think so many different, more or less mutually exclusive things at the same time.

They climbed the steps that led toward the main door, which opened before they reached it. "Welcome to Devonore", said a young woman clad in a black-and-white service dress. She smiled, which reassured Arianna; a formal, robot-like maid who did not show any emotion would only have heightened Arianna's anxiety about the event. The servant's demeanor let Arianna hope that people inside would be… humans.

The interior of the mansion was as impressive as its exterior: woodwork walls, massive chandeliers hung from a ceiling that looked two stories high, ancient furniture, and a young man dressed in a white-and-black formal attire who asked Arianna for her jacket. She handed him her coat and bag and followed his colleague, identically dressed, who invited Arianna and Nicolas to move toward the next room, a spacious living area with couches, divans, and chairs, all of which looked as if they belong in a European castle.

Within all this vastness stood only two men, still young but older than Arianna and Nicolas. One wore a pale blue suit over a green V-neck T-shirt, the other a dark gray cashmere shirt and dark jeans. The one with the blue suit waved and smiled, which Arianna interpreted as an invitation to join them. As she approached, Nick walking besides her, she noticed their clothes (and shoes) were all high-end brand items.

"Hi! I'm Paul," said the one in the pale suit, presenting his right hand. "And this is Allen. You must be the Cognit girl?"

Arianna took Paul's hand. "I... Well, I do work there."

"Are you the hosts?" asked Nicolas after shaking both men's hands and introducing himself.

"Oh no, we are just unfashionably early. Allen hates being late," said Paul.

Allen was all dark, with what looked like a permanent five-o'clock shadow and hair coming out from the edge of his sleeves and collar; Paul, who had short light-brown hair and big green eyes, was all skinny and nervous and gesticulated much.

"At last!" interjected Paul, looking beyond Arianna's shoulder.

She turned around. A waiter walked toward them, carrying a tray with four flutes filled with a pale, bubbly liquid. They each grabbed a glass.

"To new friends," said Paul as they all raised their glasses.

A rather ambitious toast, thought Arianna, as they literally had just met.

"And you, Nicolas," Paul continued, "you must be... wait," he paused, looking at Nicolas, his right hand on his chin, as if he was asking time to guess or remember who Nicolas was.

"The computer guy," said Allen. "Am I right, Nicolas?"

"I... guess you are."

"Well, you two seem quite informed regarding our respective professions. I can't say I am aware of what it is that you are doing—if you don't mind me asking," said Arianna, taking a sip of her glass (was it champagne? Whatever the appellation, it was a sparkling delight in her mouth).

"We're the art department," answered Paul. "Allen does the counting, I just do the talking."

"Oh, that's interesting!" said Arianna, genuinely curious. "What kind of art?"

A large smiled illuminated Paul's face. "Oh, my dear. The art of conjuring value out of thin air."

"Paul!" said Allen, obviously not at ease with his partner's comment.

"Please, Allen," replied Paul, putting his fingers on Paul's forearm, "we're family here! We're here to celebrate and have fun!"

"Well, you're right," conceded Allen, looking away. "Maggie will be dancing on a table before the sunset, won't she?"

"Oh, you bet she will. She dodged a hot one, the old witch!"

"We all did," replied Allen, again looking away before raising his voice. "Hey, Stan! How is it going?"

A man, middle-aged, rather short but who looked well built under his white linen suit, approached fast, a wide grin on his face, both his arms up in the air. "Allen, my man!" he said, hugging Allen and slapping his back.

"Stan, you know very well that Allen is my man," protested Paul with an over-effeminate voice and tone.

Stan then grabbed Paul, who seemed rather unenthusiastic about the embrace. "Don't be greedy, Pauly. And who's the beautiful young lady?"

"The young lady is Arianna. Who, as you can see, is with Nicolas, so will you please refrain from your usual predatory manners?"

"Hello, Arianna; hello Nicolas. Wait—are you Nick who is Josh's friend? The one who coded the app?"

"Well—I guess?"

"That's him!" interrupted Arianna, reaching closer and grabbing Nicolas's arm, "He's the one who did the Peter Minuit app. And by "did," I mean "singlehandedly coded.""

Nicolas obviously did not expect Arianna's intervention; he looked at her with big eyes, a deer caught in headlights.

"Oh come on!" she said to him, rather loudly. "This is not a place for false modesty." She then turned toward Paul. "Do you agree with me, Paul?"

"I could not agree more!" he said, raising his glass toward Arianna.

"Nicolas, everyone here knows the app sucks because pretty-boy-Josh didn't feed anything into it. But the coding is solid."

Arianna's mouth was on automatic pilot. It was now a machine that transformed intel from her dilettante inquiry into gossip. Paul's silent "O" face told her he was amused, not to say impressed with her bitching. Allen's subtle grin told her she had scored with him as well. As for Stan, he grabbed Nicolas's arm and led him away. "Hey come with me," he said. "I'll introduce you to my friend Kevin; he just arrived. I'm sure you already had more than enough with those two fags."

Arianna stared at them as they departed, her mouth open, shocked by the disgustingly homophobic slur, and somehow annoyed Nick would follow him without protesting.

"Oh, don't mind him, dear. Would you believe Stan was the one who introduced me and Allen to each other?"

Also, Arianna remembered they were here to uncover information on what looked like three related murders, not admonish bigots. She had all sorts of questions to ask Paul (Who lives here? What is it that Stan does? How do you know him?) but as she was about to open her mouth, he shouted.

"Oh, Brian's missing a morning on the green to brunch with us! This MUST be a special occasion!"

"It's not worth it without Al", said Brian. It was Heather's Brian, who just had materialized behind Arianna and stepped forward to shake Paul's hand. He then shook Allen's hand: "It's on for tomorrow morning, Al!" and then he turned toward Arianna and kissed her on the cheek. "Hey, Arianna," he said, which prompted Paul to ask why they knew each other.

"I'm knitting buddies with Heather. Which is great, because not only do I get great knitting tips from her, but I also get drunk on Brian's booze," said Arianna, after which she raised her glass toward Brian.

"The single malts are safe and my Thursday nights free. So, I saw you guys were chatting with Stan; any idea where he was heading? Something I need to check with him."

"Oh, please, Brian. You know about the rule about not bringing up work here," complained Paul.

"Yes, and also the other half-dozen rules made up by you," Brian said.

"As you can see, Arianna," said Paul, "Brian, and also Allen, are totally in awe with Stan, the magic accountant at Gaba. You should be careful; he'll get in the head of your Nicolas as well."

"Don't listen to him," said Brian to Arianna. "I just worked with Stan on the Pharmathrice deal. We've been through the grind together."

That name again: Pharmathrice. It was Melissa's employer; it was an element of the fraudulent transaction that made the background, if not the motive, of two of the three murders; and now Brian, who was Heather's husband and Alia's father, had just mentioned that he had worked a deal with this company—the Pharmathrice deal.

She looked at Paul. She had imagined this brunch to make her coy and intimidated and shy; somehow Paul had inspired her to get all gossipy and bitchy. Being gossipy and bitchy gave her enough fake confidence to forget, for some moments, that the murderer (or murderers) she was trying to unmask was likely among the guests present in the mansion at the moment and that this person might be onto her plans to catch her (or him).

"Well, that's one file I'm happy didn't land on my desk. Don't you agree with me, Paul? Unless there was an art side to this shitshow which, at this point, would not even surprise me, to be honest."

Paul nearly choked on his champagne. Arianna was pretty sure he had made a significant effort not to spill his sip. Did he think her comment was funny or inappropriate?

As Paul caught his breath, Brian answered, "The art was in the accounting. Or that's what we thought, until this Fed guy showed up to piss in the punch. For a while, I was sure we were toast. I'll tell you one thing: Brian and Stan, and the girls at Burkett; they're good. In more than twenty years, I haven't seen many people pry themselves off from the Fed's mandibles."

Arianna had a hard time following Brian. Who were "these guys"? Why didn't Brian include himself among "these guys," especially since he'd been "through the grind" with his buddy Stan?

Paul excused himself and let the group. Arianna realized Allen had also left. She was now one-on-one with Brian.

"So I've heard you worked Nicky Page," he said. "You liked it?"

Nicky Page, the Cognit partner. The one who had brought Arianna to a meeting with Silvia Prescott, chief operating officer of Cincinnati-based Traphistry. That project had gone well, which was enough for Arianna to say she had "liked it, "considering how precarious her situation felt with her employer at the moment.

"I know Nicky well," he continued. "Silvia really enjoyed working with you. A big fan of yours—maybe not as much as Alia, but a fan nonetheless."

Arianna didn't like where this conversation was heading. She and Brian's daughter Alia got along fine, sure, but characterizing her as a fan made Arianna uneasy. Was he aware that Alia had momentarily skipped school to meet her at her office building in Midtown Manhattan?

"Oh, that's Stan there! Look, I'm supposed to be at your office in the next few weeks; we should have lunch, you and I."

"Sure," Arianna said as Brian departed toward Stan, and by "sure" she meant "not in a million years will I have lunch with you, Brian: this is so awkward; please stop; you are the husband of my friend Heather for the love of God!"

More people had filled the vast room while Arianna had been chatting—at least twenty-five, split in five or six groups. The tall windows let bright sunrays in; people smiled and laughed in their expensive clothes when they were not taking sips from their glasses. The other end of the room, opposite from where they had arrived, led onto a hall that was also fitted with large windows, where there was what seemed to be a buffet with glasses and silverware that reflected the sun and plates full of bright colors (fruit?) and coffee pots.

Arianna's heart, again, raced into her ribcage. All of them! They're all involved in it! All the guests in the mansion, all her friends and their surroundings, the dead knitters—they were all involved with the SEC case. And the way Brian and Stan and Paul and Allen had talked and acted, she was increasingly under the impression that this little brunch had been organized to celebrate the SEC dropping the case.

She grabbed a fresh glass of champagne from the table and chugged half of it.

"Arianna!" shouted a familiar voice as she swallowed the bubbly wine.

It was Melissa, radiant, smiling, perfectly fitted into a flower-patterned Ted Baker summer dress, with silver earrings and a necklace that glittered under the sunrays.

KNITTING DEATH

"I'm so glad you made it!" Melissa grabbed a flute and, lowering her voice, approached Arianna. "You know, I think you're right. There is something fucked up going on."

Melissa very infrequently swore, which told Arianna that it had all begun to distress her. Arianna felt like saying, "Well, at long last, I've been telling you guys for nearly three weeks now." But that would have been rude toward Melissa. And also, un-empathic toward her friend.

But before Arianna could utter a word, Melissa shouted: "Vince!" Then she looked at Arianna and whispered, "We have to chat later, in a spot that is private and quiet!" and then ran (well, walked fast) toward a tall, athletic man with a square jaw and linen jacket maybe a tiny bit too small for his muscular chest and arms.

Arianna was alone. On any similar occasion, it would have been a cause for worry, not to say anxiety, while at the moment she rather enjoyed the occasion to reflect on exactly what had just happened, since Nick and she had stepped into this Westchester mansion and especially after what had been said. Also, she could take a plate and fill up on the delicious-looking buffet that lay right beside her, and all of it would be guilt-free, as loading up on food had become, after two glasses of champagne before eleven, not gluttony but necessity.

She ignored the left side of the table, which contained the cottage cheese and fruits for the health-conscious crowd, and focused on the center, awash with bacon and sausages and scrambled eggs and smoked brisket, and the right side, with croissants and Danishes (real ones, freshly made with real butter) piled upon superposed silver trays.

Arianna picked a croissant, sliced it open across its length with her fingers, and stuffed it with eggs and bacon. The croissant was light and fluffy, the egg and bacon not so much —although both were perfectly cooked and unctuous and delicious, which she realized as she took a bit of her improvised breakfast sandwich. Yes, this meal would probably do wonders to slow down the alcohol on its way between her belly and her brain.

As Arianna ate on her own, she moved a bit toward the huge living room to see what was happening there. Even more people had arrived since she had checked last; the place was not crowded but getting quite lively.

Melissa stood right next to the burgundy curtain that flanked one of the windows, laughing and gesticulating and often touching the great male specimen that she was so happy to meet here. He was more subdued, although Arianna wouldn't have said he lacked interest; he most likely was the unexpressive athlete type.

A few yards to Melissa's right, on one of the embroiled couches, sat Heather, elaborately coifed with locks and bangs, all mangled yet harmoniously so all above her head. She had on the nicest cocktail dress: pale green, perfectly fitted, with just the right amount of cleavage to show off her generous breasts. Arianna was nearly sure the item was a Marchesa of the most recent collection, the kind that would require many of Arianna's paychecks to acquire, especially when considering the predations her salary suffered from the rapacious New York taxmen.

Her egg-and-bacon croissant finished, Arianna fetched a slice of green melon and one of cantaloupe, and also one strawberry, which she dropped into her glass. As she shoved the melon in her mouth, she intended to resume her quiet observation of the crowd, but the moment her gaze left her plate, she found herself staring straight into Josh's big green eyes.

There was nothing wrong, per se, in making eye contact, especially in a private event with an acquaintance you actually expected to meet there.

Especially when the acquaintance was hot. Yet, as attractive as Josh was, he gave Arianna a nervous, uneasy, shifty look. And he turned his gaze without waving or smiling. And then he looked back to the man he was conversing with, then glanced back at her for a second as he talked, close to his companion's face.

That was wrong. Well, it was worrisome, considering her presence at this event was mostly motivated by her suspicion that the people responsible for three murders might be among the guests.

Stan appeared next to Arianna and grabbed a glass of champagne. He smiled warmly and said, "Oh Arianna, how I wish I was thin like you; I too would spend all the time at the buffet!"

The remark made her smirk. It came across as sincere. She followed him with her eyes as he walked toward a tall, lanky, bony man who was entirely bald and whose eyes looked dark and shadowy, so deep where they located in their sockets. Then it hit her: this man was known, well known; she had seen him in ads, videos, and show icons on Netflix. She didn't know who he was, but he was a well-known actor.

She put her plate, now empty, on the buffet table, when she heard, "Hello, Arianna!" behind her. She turned around. It was Charlotte, the girl she had met in the mystery café/bar/villain's lair only two days before. "How are you doing?!"

"I'm good," said Arianna. "You look... great."

Arianna's greeting was unusual but sincere. Charlotte's white cotton dress, all embroiled in peach, seemed to float in the air, enveloping her perfect figure along the sun rays that still illuminated the buffet area.

"I didn't know you would be here this morning," Arianna said. "I wouldn't have wasted your daytime office time with a coffee if I had known I'd run into you here." Charlotte was all smile and radiance, but was not the giggle-ish type; there was quietness and composure about her. More reasons to be suspicious, as far as Arianna was concerned.

"I can't say that I'm entirely surprised by your presence, but those cupcakes were worthy of skipping an hour of work."

If she had been honest, Arianna would have said that those cupcakes were nearly as worthy as finally laying her eyes on the mysterious Bat Wing, which Charlotte had shown her on that occasion.

"Arianna, let me introduce you to Professor Hamilton," said Charlotte, looking past Arianna. As she turned around to meet the academic who stood behind her, Arianna imagined a boorish, unkempt, older man overdressed with an ill-fitting and un-matching suit, or a dry and serious middle-aged woman. And then Charlotte, after using her as bait to avoid an acquaintance she did not want to talk to, would disappear toward more interesting people.

But as she completed her 180-degree turn, Arianna realized she had guessed wrong. Professor Hamilton was, on the contrary, lean, tall, and young, with chiseled features and a bright smile.

"Hello, Arianna. Please call me Sal. Charlotte, would you please cease this 'Professor Hamilton' nonsense, for the love of God"?

"Oh, sorry Sal. Sal is the head of PeniAnte SFH," continued Charlotte, "one of the hottest start-ups in town."

"That's not what I meant—" Sal looked genuinely embarrassed. Mildly embarrassed, but embarrassed nonetheless.

Charlotte went on. "So when Sal is not directing his graduate students at NYU, he leads advanced research to develop new micro-sensors and recharging devices that use body heat."

KNITTING DEATH

"Body heat?" said Arianna to Sal, before turning toward Charlotte. "How very so interesting."

"Isn't it?" added Charlotte.

"I don't recall having ever hired you for marketing," said Sal, while stretching to grab a cinnamon bun off the tray on the buffet table. "So, enough about me. Tell me, Arianna, what is it that made you end up in Westchester this morning?"

"Oh, it's rather simple: I met Melissa and Diana at this knitting cafe in Brooklyn, and we've been hanging out ever since."

"The knitting mafia—why do I even ask?" said Sal, before ripping a bit of cinnamon bun with his fingers and shoving it in down his mouth.

"Arianna works at Cognit," said Charlotte. "She works on mandates with Nicky Page."

"Oh, for real? Wow. At first, when Cognit did its launch campaign, I thought the whole thing was just a generous icing of branding and marketing over a shallow, generic consulting practice. But you guys are actually quite ahead of the pack in artificial intelligence."

Again, Sal's enthusiasm seemed sincere. Also, she suspected that Charlotte knew Sal's opinion about Cognit, and that it was the reason she had mentioned her employer.

"I can confirm the shallow, the generic, the branding, and the marketing. As for the AI, the closest I've been is a mandate on consumer data project."

"Oh, I can confirm to you: there are real brains working at Cognit. Even among the human staff. This firm will continue to grab market share and push the competition around. You're at the right place at the right moment."

"I'm sure you are right, although it doesn't always seem this way..."

Arianna felt too much annoyance, frustration—outright anger, even—toward her employer not to poke some derogatory comments at it. Yet it was not the game she had come to play; this morning, she had to act as if she belonged to this crowd of high-achieving, successful, rich people. Sal had given her a golden opportunity to brag about her job—she'd have to take it.

"...but you're right; this week I had the chance to work on a consumer data project that used AI. So I guess you're right about being in the right place at the right moment— although working in boutique investment banking firms seems to have quite interesting perks," she concluded, peeking at Charlotte as she took another sip from her glass.

"I brought Arianna to Jeanine's," said Charlotte to explain Arianna's remark to Sal. "I think she really liked the cupcakes."

"Did you know that Jeanine goes to Colombia herself to pick the coffee beans?" Sal went on, detailing Jeanine's coffee-bean-picking trips to South America and the people she met there. He barely looked at Charlotte, staring most of the time at Arianna, speaking with great enthusiasm. Arianna was flattered, as Charlotte was very pretty and exquisitely dressed, while she was outfitted with a discounted, off-the-rack, generic business attire.

Charlotte didn't seem to mind, and actually seemed quite happy of having introduced Sal and Arianna. Martine Cunning's words resonated in Arianna's head: "They will come for you, too. They will invite you to nice events in beautiful places with impressive people, with delicious food, they will offer you well-paying jobs, you will meet pretty boys... rich women... rich, gorgeous men..."

A ruckus arose from the main room. Sal stopped his coffee bean storytelling to see what was going on, as did Charlotte and Arianna.

They stepped over to the edge of the buffet area to have the full view of the room: everyone had turned toward the entrance hall and they cheered and applauded and shouted.

"Looks like she has arrived," said Sal, and he left, passing the buffet toward the other part of the house, the one that Arianna hadn't seen (yet).

"Excuse me," said Charlotte as she also departed toward the same direction.

Arianna looked back toward the main room. The person who received this acclaim was now visible to her: it was Margaret, who glowed and smiled at the people who greeted her with many kisses and hugs.

Arianna recognized the person she was kissing and hugging at the moment. He was a tall man, pale, bony and balding, rather large but with no significant belly to speak of, whose plaid pants and polo had obviously been chosen more with golf in mind than brunch. And this man was a partner at Cognit. Arianna had no idea what his name was, but she was sure he was one of her superiors. Right beside them was another one of her superiors: Lionel Getty, the partner she had seen at the office with Margaret, and whom she had made laugh by trash-talking Bryan.

On one hand, Lionel being here would be an extra source of stress on an already quite stressful morning. On the other, that gave her the opportunity to look like an employee who got around and met people. Like an analyst who brunched in Westchester, less than a year after having been plucked out Cincinnati after graduating from a no-name college.

And then, right behind the partner and Margaret, Charlotte materialized. And she chatted with Diana, to Arianna's worry. They knew each other, Arianna knew, but knowing and witnessing was not the same thing.

Everywhere she looked it was luxury and murder suspects—a beautiful nightmare it was.

Arianna's cell buzzed. It was a text from Nick: "I need a smoke. I got 2, main exit, walk to the right Ill b there."

Smoking had not crossed her mind before that moment, but oh! How nicotine would mix just perfectly with the caffeine, alcohol, and adrenaline that filled her blood at the moment. She crossed the grand salon toward the main entrance, back from where she came from, exchanging polite smiles as she passed other guests. She refrained herself from running, but her quick pace brought her rapidly outside where, after a few yards hopping to the right of the main entrance, she saw Nick. He sat on the low branch of a massive oak, his cell in his right hand, his thumb hitting the screen.

As she approached him, he pulled two cigarettes from the breast pocket of his polo shirt. Up to that very moment, Nick had always looked glad to see her. As hard as he tried to appear cool and detached, Arianna always felt how happy he was to see her. It was not the case at the moment. He was preoccupied, too preoccupied to appreciate her. As she neared him, he put one cigarette directly in her mouth, the other in his, and lit both in succession—without leaving his oak branch.

Arianna inhaled deeply and kept the smoke in her lungs for a bit, making sure her brain would translate enough of the nicotine intake into a much-needed endorphin release.

The scenery around—the lush green lawn, the massive trees, the flowers beds—was beautiful and soothing and hitting her brain with the message, "There is no danger." A couple walked in front of them, most likely going on for a stroll in the beautiful front yard to enjoy the sunny but fresh late-summer morning. They passed by, they smiled and waved, they continued their walk. He wore a navy blazer over a white shirt and beige trousers; her, a pink cotton dress. Both were slightly older than Arianna and Nicolas, but their smiles and stares and waves were warm and complicit; they saluted them as insiders to their group. As everyone had, so far.

Nicolas threw his cigarette butt in the grass. "I have to admit you're better than me at this thing. I stuttered and choked while you got on the gossip beat with the very first two guys we met."

"You're the computer guy; I'm the Cognit girl. If you're the insufferable tech prima donna, then I have to be the gossipy biatch." She gave him a quick kiss on the lips; "That would look suspicious if you were too socially confident in this particular context." Before he could argue or protest, she added, "I need to pee."

Nicolas jumped down from his branch and they walked toward the main entrance. They went back inside and inquired about the location of the washrooms to the servant/maid/butler who staffed the entrance. He pointed to the right, into a hall, opposite to the one leading to the main reception room. There, two signs hanging on gold chains from the ceiling bore the standard gender pictograms, indicating distinct male and female bathrooms.

So far, the building, as large and luxurious and grandiose as it was, had looked entirely residential; the bathrooms signs, however, gave it a somewhat commercial vibe, yet still within the high-end hospitality sector, as far as Arianna's knowledge on the matter went. Behind the large wooden door below the female sign was indeed a multi-stalled installation—still all gilded and embroidered enlightened with classical glitter. As Arianna emptied her bladder, overfilled after drinking much coffee and champagne, she heard steps on the granite floor. Someone else had entered the bathroom.

The rhythm of those steps, the way that person exhaled as she checked herself in the mirror, the noise her bag made when it was dropped on the marble counter—all were quite familiar. As Arianna exited her stall, she was not surprised to see Diana performing routine maintenance on her makeup. Arianna was rather anxious to face her friend, but when Diana saw her in the mirror, she turned around and exclaimed, loudly, "Arianna!"

Diana hugged and kissed Arianna; she looked genuinely happy to see her.

"I'm so happy you made it! Is this your first time in Westchester?"

"Not at all; I used to come here all the time. I spent two summer camps here when I was in junior high."

"Well, maybe you'll meet some of your old camp mates today," said Diana, entirely aware of Arianna's sarcasm.

As Arianna pulled away from Diana's hug, she noticed her necklace: a silver medallion engraved with a pentacle and symbols and letters. There was nothing wrong with the esthetics of the piece, but it made it hard to forget that Diana was suspected of being an evil witch.

The bathroom door opened; it was Alia. She would have looked entirely adorable, with her flushed red cheeks, perfect curled locks that fell around her head, and white laced dress, had she not shouted, "Why are you helping them?! They are evil! You know they are!"

Arianna was shocked by the anger and aggressiveness in Alia's voice. She was also shocked that a nine-year-old had to ask the questions she didn't dare asking to one of her best friends. Diana, however, did not look disturbed by this sudden attack.

"Alia, I do not help anyone doing anything evil. I do work in a highly competitive environment with a lot of moral ambiguity, but I'm hardly the only one around", said Diana.

"That's not what I'm talking about and you know it!" shouted Alia.

"Alia, you're right, but only about half of the whole story. The other half: you got it all upside down."

The argument was interrupted by another intrusion; a uniformed servant informed the trio that their conversation would have to continue elsewhere as there was some maintenance and cleaning to be performed in the bathroom. Alia stormed out; Diana followed through the exit; Arianna was determined to follow up with Diana but someone grabbed her left arm from behind as she exited the washroom.

She turned around; it was Nick, who whispered in her ear: "The Reverend Mother's red laptop is in the building."

Arianna's first reaction was to be annoyed. Nick had prevented her from following Diana and continuing their bathroom conversation. Her second reaction was to say, "Oh shit!" as the red laptop belonged to the killer, most likely. She then felt her belly tying up in a knot and her heartbeat accelerating. If the killer's laptop was in the building, so was the killer, who at this point might very well be aware that she was onto her or his heels.

As Arianna went through this succession of reactions, she realized Alia was still there, standing next to Nick.

"We know where the computer is," said Alia. "We have to grab it! When we have it in our possession, your boyfriend will hack the password."

There was so much information for Arianna to process at the moment: how had Alia and Nick, who have never met before, ended up talking about the red laptop of the lady dressed in red, the one shown on the security camera footage at Marie-Louise's apartment the morning of her death? How did they know this item was in this building at the moment?

"Alia," asked Arianna, quietly, "how did you find the laptop? What do you know about its owner?"

"It's the Spider Queen's computer! It must be full of incriminating information! Yuna and I, we—"

"Yuna!" Arianna cut in. "What does Yuna have to do with this?"

"She's with me. We located the computer together. She saw the Queen get in her room—"

"Wait—Yuna is here? In this house? Alia, what are you doing with her? Yuna burglarized my apartment!"

"I know she did. It's for your protect—Damn, here comes my mom. I'll talk to you guys later. Arianna, take this!"

Alia grabbed Arianna's hand and put something in it (again). She then hopped away toward the main ballroom. She passed right next to Heather, her mother, who started talking to her, but Alia continued on her way, entirely ignoring her. Heather then continued on her way toward the ladies' restroom but hit a locked door. She went back toward the main hall, either not noticing Arianna or ignoring her. Arianna was pretty sure Heather was on the verge of bursting into tears. Because of her daughter's behavior? Or because of something related to the murders?

"Dammit, you have to go after her!" said Nicolas, close to Arianna's ear.

"Are you crazy? Her mom just ignored me. I'm not throwing gasoline on this fire. You go after her!"

"No, I won't! I don't know her, I don't know her parents, and she's nine. I can't run after her!"

"What do you mean, you don't know her? She just told you about the red laptop!"

"And that's the extent of the only conversation we've had, ever."

Arianna looked to her right, toward the main hall; a group of people was coming over. She grabbed Nick and dragged him further down away from the bathroom area. They reached an open double door that led onto a room; while much smaller than the main ballroom, it still was large, elaborately furnished. The furniture and tapestry, dark and classic, were brightly lit by the sun that peered through the numerous, tall windows; together it gave an overall warm and comfortable feeling. No one else was there, so Arianna and Nick could resume their conversation.

Before Arianna could say anything, Nick started: "Not even five minutes ago, just as I exited the bathroom, she came to me and told me she had located the Queen's laptop. My first reaction was to ask its color. Since she answered red and that's not too common for laptops, I jumped to the conclusion that we were talking about the laptop we saw on the camera footage. She told me where it's located—it's in a room on the floor above us."

"But who's the Spider Queen?"

"I don't know!"

"Why didn't you ask her?"

"I did! But instead of answering, she burst toward the women's room. She must have realized you were likely there. That's why we need to get hold of her!"

"What we need to do now is to grab the computer! And we need to do it fast because Yuna is also after it. We need to get hold of it before she does. Let's go upstairs."

"Arianna! It's dangerous! Even if you get hold of it, what will you do? Stoll down the hall with a red laptop in your hands, hoping no one will notice?"

"You're totally right! I need something to hide the computer. I'll get my bag from the cloakroom. It's right there in front of the washrooms."

Nick protested but followed her—to the cloakroom, then down the hall, away from the washroom, the main entrance, and away from the other guests, she hoped. As they paced the hardwood floor, she realized that she held something (again) in her right hand. She looked at it: it was a pencil sharpener. Alia had given her a large, very large, white pencil sharpener.

"There, a staircase. Stay here, I'll go. Where is it?" said Arianna.

"Alia told me all the guest bedrooms are in one hall; there is a painting with tigers in it, hanging on the wall right next to the door of the room with the laptop in it."

"Tigers?"

"Yes. Tigers. The red laptop is beyond the door that is next to the painting with tigers."

"Let's go then," said Arianna as she stormed upstairs.

Blood ran fast through Arianna's head, over-pumped by her overexcited heart. She wanted to remain unheard, a challenging task when wearing high heels and walking on a hardwood floor.

Someone was coming her way in the hall! Quickly, she fetched her iPhone from her purse and keyed in her access code. If she couldn't be discreet, she would at least try to show that she didn't care, that she belonged in the hall, that her presence there was legitimate.

"Hi, there!" said the stranger in a beige linen suit as his path crossed her. Arianna lifted her eyes briefly, smiled a bit, and lowered her eyes back on her cell. Was the stranger suspicious? He looked tipsier and flirtatious than suspicious—but what if he was a putting on a show? What if he was onto her?

Arianna reached the end of the hall. Tall windows let the sun flood the house. To her right, the hall led toward one of the multiple staircases within the mansion; to her left was one of its multiple massive rooms.

Arianna looked back. The strangers looked at her, waved, and disappeared toward the balcony where the guests chatted and laughed and drank mimosas.

Quickly, Arianna came back on her steps and approached the second-to-last door to her right. She pushed down on the massive brass handle. It was unlocked. She glanced right and left: no one was in the hall.

Arianna pushed the door forward, just a tiny bit. "Hello? Hi?"

No answer.

She slipped inside and silently shut the door behind her.

Something caught her attention—something that moved. She looked right, froze, and held her breath. It was a young woman in her mid-twenties with auburn hair neatly held on top of her head, wearing a silver necklace and a cream sweater dress, and holding a brown fabric bag: Arianna's own reflection. The mirror was so gigantic, it appeared as if there was someone standing at the other end of the room.

Arianna looked around. The bedroom was at least twice the size of her Brooklyn flat; searching through would take some time, time she did not have. She tried to calm herself and look at the room methodically. Then she saw it: the laptop. The Spider Queen's laptop.

Arianna grabbed the computer and shoved it in her bag.

She looked around for some clues, like clothes, handbag, document, but the room was entirely devoid of personal effects of any kind. One big bed, one big couch, one big secretary with one big lamp—and one less computer—and mirrors, mirrors, and more mirrors. Time to get out if she didn't want to get caught and end up as Murder Victim No. 4.

She stormed out of the bedroom, her bag on her shoulder. Back toward the stairs, walking fast, praying no one would notice her, her belly tied into a painful knot. She reached the staircase. Nick was downstairs, fidgeting with his phone. He threw a quick glance toward her and saw that there was something in the bag.

"Let's get out of here," she said when her right foot hit the ground floor next to Nick.

"Right now? But Arianna; that would be super suspicious!" he said, whispering, following her in the hall toward the main entrance.

"I don't care!" she replied, not whispering at all.

"Arianna! Damn it—are you insane? You'll get both of us killed!"

They reached the cloakroom. Arianna unslung her bag and brusquely shoved it on Nick's torso; he grabbed the bag with both hands and much surprise and horror on his face.

"Arianna! For the love of God!"

"We're leaving! I want to go home! I don't—"

And for the second time in less than two weeks, Arianna expelled the content of her stomach on the floor. While the incident was embarrassing, it did provide a convenient and convincing excuse for leaving.

22. Prying Open

Nick and Arianna were in her apartment. This unexpected situation was due to Nick's uncle being at his place. This was rather problematic, as Arianna and Nick wanted to freely discuss the murder suspects and accessing a stolen computer's data. So, after stopping at Nick's place to drop the car, change clothes, and pick up a laptop and hardware items, they had taken the subway to Arianna's place.

The presence of Nick's uncle had not been part of the plan. If it had, Arianna had not been informed. That bothered Arianna as she had not cleaned her place. There were clothes all over her bedroom and dirty dishes in the sink. Not that she was an especially messy person, but she never had any visitors and was very busy. Sleep was more important than cleaning (and so was knitting).

Nick sat at the tiny table in the kitchen, his black laptop and the Spider Queen's red one taking all the available space. He held his phone against his right ear, talking to a guy name Jack, asking many computer-related questions.

There was not much Arianna could do to help. Anyway, she had much Rudius work to do if she didn't want to fall behind and have to spend whole nights to complete the assignment on time. She went to sit in her living room with her work laptop, ready to handle coolness scores, picture after picture.

Another man with a fedora hat: 2. A young boy in a brown jumpsuit with a dog: 3. A young woman with a gray suit and fishnets: 1.

Arianna was not in the mood. Everything annoyed her. The brunch had been nerve-racking, her head ached, her belly hurt. She had stolen the laptop of someone who was very likely to have killed three young women. That someone would probably put Arianna at the top of her list of suspects for this burglary. That someone probably knew where Arianna lived and worked.

Well, bad mood or not, Arianna had work to do. Germaine had clearly said that the project consisted in indicating her opinion on each picture. But right now, her opinion was that she hated all of them. Cognit's super AI algorithm would most likely perceive her mood switch, which couldn't bring anything good. Maybe if she boosted her score by on—

"GOT IT! I'M IN! YES! YEEES!"

Nick's enthusiastic shouts pulled Arianna from her inner rambling. She jumped off the couch and hopped into the kitchen. Nick was slouched over the red laptop, his nose just a few inches from its screen. "Here we go. Let's have a look at the content of this red machine."

Arianna, leaning above Nick's shoulder, stared attentively to the screen. The desktop's wallpaper picture was spooky: red and white signs and sigils on a black background. The software icons, however, were familiar, belonging to the Microsoft Office Suite. Nick double-clicked on the Outlook icon and soon the screen shown an inbox full of emails. "Grab a seat," said Nick. "You'll take the red laptop, and I'll access them with my machine. Let's dig!"

** ** **

Arianna frantically clicked and scrolled, her face glued to the screen of the red laptop; her eyes zigzagged down emails, scanning for keywords and clues inside the account of reverend.mother@MahicantuckCoven.org.

KNITTING DEATH

There were twenty-six different email windows opened on the screen, but none gave any indication on the identity of the Reverend Mother, none contained anything looking like a smoking gun or like a confession. "Hi, Reverend Mother"; "Thank you, Reverend Mother"; "Well understood, Reverend Mother"; Reverend Mother this, Reverend Mother that, an inbox that contained 103 messages, yet nothing that indicated that this Reverend Mother had a real identity, a real name—nothing. The more Arianna clicked and scrolled, the more she felt she wouldn't find any ID on this machine.

And what those emails actually contained was not making her feel better about those witches. "That witchcraft thing... it's not LARPing," Nick had said, again letting loose with his geek nomenclature in front of her.

> Macerate ashwagandha, ginger, and duck livers in liquid hen fat for two nights, add powdered lingzhi, and heat gently—do not boil. Drink a full cup during new moons—

No time for this, Arianna thought, until her eye grabbed a reply by Diana:

> The potion has a musky and rancid taste, but it has an overall enjoyable tonic effect.

Reading the unappealing recipe is one thing, reading that Diana (SISTER Diana) drank such a mixture is on another lever altogether. How could she? There was an attached document that supposedly contained more recipes. **No time for this!**

The witches had a well-defined hierarchy: one Reverend Mother, a few sisters, and some acolytes. And it appeared, so far, that the email account on the red laptop was only used to communicate within this group, within the coven. Sister Diana, Sister Charlotte, Sister Marie-Louise, Sister Marianna, Sister Heather, Acolyte Christina, and Acolyte

Martine. There were also other acolytes who Arianna did not know: Acolyte Carrie, Acolyte Sylvia, and Acolyte Alessandra.

While nothing so far gave any formal clue as to the identity of the Reverend Mother, glancing at her emails gave Arianna a real bad vibe. A vile personality transpired— generous and charming with the few sisters, abusive with acolytes.

Reverend Mother to Acolyte Christina:

> What a pity. You have the voice, but do you have the guts to power it? This wailing on the scene was pathetic.

Reverend Mother to Acolyte Martine:

> I need someone close to Randy. You volunteered. Now is not the time to stop seeing him. Furthermore, you can learn a lot from spending time with him.

Sickening, yet again not illegal. Stay focused, Arianna! Arianna sorted the emails chronologically and scrolled to late August, around the time the girls died.

> Dear coven-mates,
>
> What happened to our sisters is tragic. We grieve their loss and what they could have been within this coven. They made enemies, they strayed from our path. Let it be remembered then even the best and brightest among us most follow our code and practice the discipline, least await oblivion and countless efforts wasted into the abyss.
>
> We will remember. We will not forget.
>
> Your Reverend Mother

Well, that was interesting. The email was grieving, yet the tone was also somehow passive-aggressive toward the dead sisters. The content of the inbox brought nearly as many questions as it answered.

Some more searching: all sisters continued to exchange emails after this message, but many acolytes went dark. Acolyte Carrie, Acolyte Alessandra… and Acolytes Christina and Martine, the last one who sent one final "LEAVE ME ALONE! GET OUT OF MY HEAD!" before her name ceased to appear as a sender, a recipient, or a subject of discussion.

Not so much for Christina:

> "She was failing her apprenticeship, even before this tragedy hit us. She lacks both the wits and the willpower to develop her potential. Let her rot in her own self-pity; she will not bother us anymore."

Ditto the Reverend Mother, in an email to… Heather. At the end of the conversation, she replied:

> "I was never a fan, but I worry about her. She is not going well."

It was also, pretty much, the extent of the emails that contained reaction to the death of the three coven-mates, although Arianna suspected that some emails must have been permanently deleted. Maybe Nick would be able to retrieve such deletions? He looked busy at the moment—Arianna would ask later.

Arianna took her notebook and flipped through the first pages. One sentence, scribbled in bold gray marker, caught her attention: "Weekend with Stacey ☹." As annoying as it had been, this is when her inquiry had really begun. She read bellow: "Meetings with Aline Li, Jane Desmond, and Linda Rossi." The names of the three women she had met during the Craftfest at the Brooklyn Convention Center. Arianna searched through the emails: no results for Aline Li or Jane Desmond. But there was one for Linda Rossi. Arianna clicked on the highlighted item:

> Hello, Reverend Mother:
>
> Thank you for welcoming me in your coven. I look forward to meeting you and the other sisters. The next meeting with Gayle is already scheduled with Charlotte. However, considering Jason's position, I would rather make the introduction directly to you. Please let me know if this suits you.
>
> Best,
>
> Acolyte Linda Rossi

Well, well. How interesting; Linda, the snobby, haughty, artsy girl who didn't have time to chat to people who visited her stand at the fair, was a witch. Or had been a witch; there was no sign of her elsewhere in the inbox. Yet, something interesting in the next message: Re: Bat Wing.

> Charlotte,
>
> Not all good knitters make good witches; not all good witches are also good knitters. Yet the bond is strong between both crafts—always has. Completing one's unique Bat Wing requires Focus, Finesse & Fortitude, and as such this knit-along will reveal good prospects as much as poor ones.
>
> The message board is a laudable initiative, but please don't cast the net too wide. Ours is an exclusive group that only accepts the best.
>
> Your Reverend Mother

That email answered one important question—what this Bat Wing thing was about. But it let another mystery unresolved: what about the luxury? Charlotte was all about designer clothes, exclusive venues, and luxurious expeditions, while Diana was not. Yet they seemed to be on an equal footing, both within the coven and in their professional lives.

Arianna's body pressed against the back of her chair. She exhaled, loudly.

Nick raised his eyes from his screen. "Come on, Arianna. We're getting really close. It's either Margaret or Melissa; all the others are sisters and have their own Mahicantuck Coven addresses."

"It's not them," said Arianna. "I've just seen their names… Wait." Arianna selected one of the first emails she had read and read it aloud: 'Good work, Sister Marianna. Please share this document with Margaret.' And I've run into Melissa elsewhere, and she is also referred to in the third person."

"That would mean," said Nicolas, "that the Reverend Mother is someone who is not usually found in their immediate social circle. Maybe even the sisters do not know her real identity."

"Nick… That Diana got dragged down into a weird cult where she eats magic mushrooms macerated into rancid hen fat is one thing, but her following the orders of an anonymous leader is entirely different—and entirely unlikely."

The duo continued its inquiry in silence. Again, Arianna added opened email boxes.

Reverend Mother:

> Diana, you do well with this Fed guy. Keep it up.

The Fed guy. Was he part of the team who had dropped the case? What had Diana done for him to drop it? Lots of references to "the Fed guy," most of which implied Diana in a way on another.

The next message in the email thread was from Charlotte:

> I've seen you holding hands with the Fed guy. You ARE dedicated, Diana.

Ah, was he the mysterious older man that Melissa and Alia had caught on about indeed holding hands with Diana? Diana's answer:

> He's coming out to his family. It's very hard for him these days. I mostly listen a lot, to be honest.

"Well, so much for Diana seeing an older man," said Arianna, out loud. Yet as reassuring as it was to know that Diana being a witch didn't mean she slept with disgusting older men, it still didn't bring much light onto the identity of the Reverend Mother.

Frustrated, Arianna violently swiped up on the laptop's touchpad. When the inbox content stopped scrolling, one line caught Arianna's attention—and cut her breath short:

> The Cognit Girl.

Arianna clicked on the item, carefully, as if doing so would make the computer explode.

Only two emails were part of the conversation: Reverend Mother and Diana.

> Diana, about the Cognit girl. Stay close. She's curious. And since you like her so much—please remember what happened to the curious cat.

Diana's answer:

> Reverend Mother, I still play dumb when Arianna mentions the death of our coven-mates, but her curiosity actually might help us find the killer.

Well, that was interesting. Diana thought someone other than the Reverend Mother was the killer. It was reassuring, as it lowered the chance of her being complicit with the murders. But what was she supposed to make out of this? Diana protected her, but was the Reverend Mother onto her? A dark thought ran through Arianna's mind. If Diana covered her, had Arianna endangered her by stealing the laptop? Would Diana be the fourth victim because of Arianna's action?

Arianna continued reading the thread:

> Cognit is the result of warfare at the top. Old structures are crumbling. If some rents and sinecures are being destroyed, others are being created.
>
> You see Cognit as a wide opening, I see a likely trap. What is too good to be true often is.
>
> Yet this doesn't mean you can't harvest the fruits that grow around the trap. Tread carefully.

The Reverend Mother's comment about Cognit was rather cryptic, but at least it was unthreatening. And also out of scope if she wanted to stick on finding the Reverend Mother's identity or a proof of her involvement in the deaths of her coven-mates.

Arianna closed that window. The next email subject was another one named "Bat Wing."

> Sister Charlotte,
>
> This specific knitting project is indeed one of the best ways to identify promising prospective members.

> Clothes and housing are what separate humans from animals. Men are builders, women are weavers; this is why knitting is a sacred practice, for the same reasons that the ranks of the initiated were once filled by so many masons.
>
> Your time is precious; the time you devote to the Bat Wing message board is well invested and has brought us interesting prospects—and as you know, interesting business opportunities.
>
> Your Reverend Mother

Again, Arianna closed the window; the next one had the most generic subject line ("Next Thursday") but had been flagged because it contained the expression "Peter Minuit"—the mobile application that Nick had coded for his friends Josh and Mike.

> Marianna,
>
> I am aware that this mobile gadget is useless. I am not asking you to transmute this pig into a racing horse, just to put enough glitter on it (around it) to make it shine. Technology does not have to be sound to make so-called investors open their purses. The past twenty years have made this very clear.
>
> Your Reverend Mother

Nicolas's app had been used to defraud investors—ouch! He looked tense enough at the moment without adding to his burden; Arianna decided that she would let him discover about this all by himself.

Arianna stood up, grabbed a glass from a kitchen cabinet, and filled it with water. She leaned against the counter as she drank, looking at Nick, who was so entranced by what he had read that had not noticed she was now looking at him.

KNITTING DEATH

What a mess, thought Arianna. They had no name nor smoking gun, but a murderer who very likely knew Arianna and Nick were on her heels. How crushing it would be if her parents found Arianna dead in her tiny flat. Especially if the murderer made it look like a suicide… that would be even worse. At least if it was oblivious that she had been killed, her parents would not blame her—they'd blame the violent, impersonal, cosmopolitan big city.

Arianna went into the tiny living room and grabbed the one item she would need, if she wanted to spend her time well while peering through numerous email threads: her notebook. She sat back in her place in front of the red machine and opened the notebook to the beginning. Yet just as she intended to follow methodically her notes, one thought derailed her plan: she had only looked in the computer's mailbox and had not searched for other documents.

She pressed on the Windows Explorer icon. The application opened on the "Frequent folders" and "Recent files" list. Two items attracted Arianna's attention: a PDF file entitled "***539 Amsterdam Ave" and a Word file named "Pharmathrice Casavant M&A." The first was the address of Marianna's apartment, and the other was the transaction that had been scrutinized by the federal prosecutor.

Arianna clicked on "539 Amsterdam Ave." It was a floorplan plan—the apartment building's plan. Onto which there were handwritten notes in blue pen. "Camera 3"; "Camera 5"—nine cameras in all, each with their capture zone angle, also drawn in blue pen.

"Bingo!"

At last, something that looked like a tangible element of proof. The document that the Lady in Red had used to devise a way to kill Marianna without being caught.

She opened the next document: "Pharmathrice Casavant M&A."

Surprise! On the cover page was a large Cognit logo.

Also, the document was 143 pages.

* * * *

Arianna and Nick sat outside on the fire escape, her back against the door, his against the railing; each had an opened bottle of Dos Equis in their left hand. She looked at cars and pedestrians on the street below while he stared at the red bricks. His shirt's sleeves were rolled up. She wore a white top. It was a balmy evening, quite warm for October.

"They drink blood and cat piss. They ate raw guts and bugs. Diana ate raw guts and bugs. They mixed herbs and mud and chopped-up lizards and they fucking ate it. They subjected themselves to sleep deprivation, hunger, and cold. They intoxicated themselves with roots and mushrooms. Diana intoxicated herself with roots and mushrooms."

"Arianna… Diana protected you. She might do all these things, but she went to great lengths to avoid getting your name on the hit list."

"Diana lied to me. She told me she was going to her parents' place in the Adirondacks, when in fact she went on a trip to pick mushrooms." A trip to pick mushrooms with Charlotte.

"She also lied to the Reverend Mother to say that your father was a high-level officer in the Ohio Bureau of Criminal Investigation. Most likely to deter any hostile action against you."

"I know that she protected me. I also know that she did fucked-up things while pretending to be a normal girl. She's supposed to be a lawyer who loves knitting, not a drugged-up freak who eviscerates cats."

"They don't eviscerate cats. What they do isn't so different from your latest diet fad or microdosing trend. I can't believe that this is what bothers you when the girls are running a straight-up financial racket."

Arianna expected Nick's reaction, his focus on the money shenanigans, and his dismissal of the blood-drinking part. Expected or not, his reaction was annoying nonetheless. "There's nothing illegal there, either, Nick."

"Not illegal but borderline… and reckless; no wonder they got into trouble with the Feds. You should read the thread with this guy, Rodney Wilkens. Rodney is the chief operating officer and one of the owners of a small but successful business, Traviskuls. Traviskuls makes parts for medical devices and machines. It's nothing shiny or glamorous, but they make money. So Rodney has money. And the witches wanted to get their hands on some of this money. So they approached Rodney to invite him to sink money into an 'investment fund'—that's what they made it look like when they reached out to him. But that's not how they treated the whole thing when they discussed the matter between them: they described Rodney as a prey. They even had an expression to describe the process… I forgot—"

"Spot-Track-Tame-Awe-Bleed," said Arianna. "I've run into this expression as well. I'm sure there's nothing illegal there—it's bad taste to describe sales and investment targets that you court in such a way, but bad taste has never been illegal in this country."

"Arianna, what I've read described plain extortion!"

"I'm sure that's what the U.S. Attorney said just before he dropped the case," said Arianna before taking a sip of her bottle. Her own words tasted bitter on her lips: extortion.

"We don't know when we'll run into Alia next… And Yuna will think we're with the bad guys."

Arianna stood up. "Alia will be at Rhinebeck next week, I'm sure of it. But we can talk to her before that."

"Rhinebeck?"

Arianna grabbed her phone. "Let's call her."

"You have her phone number? She… she has her own phone?"

"Yes and yes. Heather gave me her number a few months ago. I was heading to her place to knit and chill with the girls and there was an issue with the intercom in her building's entrance and Heather had to step out to do some errands. Anyway, I have Alia's phone number." Arianna keyed the call button on her device.

"But Arianna, it's past nine; won't this sound suspicious?"

"I should have done this week ago. I know th—Alia? Is that you? It's Arianna. Can I speak to you? Is this a good time?"

Nicolas stared at Arianna as she listened, her device pressed against her right ear. "Alia, I'm with Nick; I'll put you on speakerphone, okay?"

"Hi, Nick," said the tiny voice through the phone's speaker. "I'm in my room. No one can hear me speak, but the witches might have tapped our lines."

"We'll take the risk," said Arianna. "We need to. Nick and I are stuck. We need your help."

"I'm stuck, too. My mom wants me to stop the martial arts lessons with Audrey."

"I'll try to help you, Alia. But first, I have a simple, yet crucial question for you: who is the Reverend Mother?"

"I don't know."

"Alia, please tell me you're kidding me…" said Arianna, hiding her eyes in her left hand. "There must be at least one person that you suspect is the Spider Queen? I mean, the Reverend Mother?"

"The Reverend Mother hides! She makes her moves from the shadow, cowardly, from behind the sisters she manipulates into doing her evil biddings," said the tiny voice through the phone's microphone.

"Alia… Is this something that Audrey or Yuna has told you?"

"No. I've asked Audrey and Yuna many times who the Reverend Mother is, but they say I should not bother myself with this question. Their answer is that it's not important, or that it's dangerous to get involved. Which is totally a contradict—" Alia became silent.

"Is everything okay?" asked Arianna.

"Yes. I think my mom is coming upstairs. I'll have to hang up. You guys will be in Rhinebeck next weekend?"

"I will," said Arianna.

"They plan a big ceremony there, in some sort of sacred grove nearby. I need to hang up now."

23. Hudson Valley Ride

The DaimlerKia Jupiter flew at high speed on the Taconic State Parkway, cutting through the dense forest. The road was narrow; the foliage's bright yellows and reds blurred together with the remaining dark greens on both sides of the car as it followed the road, cutting through the forest. Arianna's laptop rested on her lap, idle. She had aimed to work but stared through the window instead. She enjoyed the speed; she also enjoyed that she wouldn't have to pay any ticket if they ever got caught speeding by the New York State Police.

Alia broke the silence. "Can I go to Marlene's place after school next Thursday? We need to work on a project together."

"I don't see why there should be a problem," said Heather.

"Her place is in Alphabet City. I'll need a ride back home after dinner."

"I'm in Manhattan all day on Thursday," said Brian, who was driving. "Just call me when you are ready to go."

And that was it. The passengers continued to ride in silence. This pleased Arianna much. She felt tired and drained, with a hint of fear always hovering in the back of her mind. Work and witches had made the past week gruesome and nerve-racking. Endless hours spent staring at the screen of her work laptop to grind through the data assignment and at the red laptop looking for clues pointing at the Reverend Mother's identity. And to make things worse, she'd had a fight with Nick and they had not talked since the previous Monday.

The origin of the conflict was that Nick wanted to flee. Leave New York City. Bail out. And that Arianna refused this solution. The conflict itself had erupted when Nick had made it known that he strongly resented Arianna's refusal. And had decided to tell her, once again, that the reason she didn't want to leave was because, deep inside, she wanted to be killed. Once again, she shouted but this time with expletives.

"Your death wish is ridiculous! You will ruin your life for three girls you didn't even know! And you don't even do it for them: your reasoning is that Cognit can't fire you if you're dead or recovering after they try offing you! You are fucking pathetic!"

Nick had not chosen his moment well for shouting at her, not with all the tension, stress and danger that she'd recently gone through.

So Arianna had left his place. And they had not talked since. For all she knew, he might have left for his parents' place. On the other hand, he was entirely capable of showing up in Rhinebeck, under the pretext of tagging along with his cute friends.

Anyway, she had found a way to get there without him: Heather had texted three days before to offer a ride. She had not mentioned where she had learned Arianna was in need for such a ride, although Arianna strongly suspected the whole thing was Alia's doing.

Heather was a member of the Mahicantuck Coven—she was one of the witches. She was not an especially active one, at least according to the conversations intercepted on the red laptop. She abstained from most weekend activities, did not seem especially interested in mushrooms, herbs, and charms, and her participation in the coven's financial transactions appeared mostly limited to leveraging her numerous contacts.

Brian, however, was an ever-present character in the red laptop's emails; the witches never conversed directly with him through their coven addresses but shared many conversations in which he participated. He often worked with Margaret; "Forward to Brian and Margaret" was a sentence she must have read a hundred times since gaining access to the Reverend Mother's mailbox.

An electronic signal resonated in the car, coming from its speakers, pulling Arianna out of her daydreaming.

"Hey, Arianna! It's your best friend and colleague, Lionel Getty, who's calling me!" said Brian, while pressing the answer button on the dashboard screen. "Hey, Lionel, how are you? I'm in the car with my family, heading upstate. Can I call you back in forty-five minutes?"

"Oh, hello everyone. Hello, Heather. No worries, Brian; just call me when you have a moment. You have a safe trip. Goodbye everyone."

"We'll talk later. Bye, Lionel." Brian hung up. "Sorry I didn't mention your presence, Arianna, but knowing Lionel, he would have added your time here with us on my next bill!"

"No worries at all, Brian. You guys are generous enough to bring me along without having to get invoiced for it. Anyway, he sounded way less exuberant than last time." Arianna tried not to be entirely closed off toward Brian and Heather despite her gloomy mood.

"Oh, Lionel. He's that kind of guy: he's either jolly and loud or just morose."

"So basically, you're saying he's bipolar?" said Alia, who sat in the backseat besides Arianna.

For a moment, Arianna feared that Alia's comment would trigger another fight with her mother. But instead, it made Heather smile.

"I don't know about that," said Brian. "Maybe he is… So, Arianna, last time, you were telling him that you worked on one of Bryan's projects?" Brian was asking about the senior manager at Cognit.

"I was. For the past two weeks, I've been twenty-four-seven on a Cognit Data file."

"Cognit data? I didn't know you had a background in data science. They are well reputed, even with tech-sector people."

"I don't. The assignment is actually a fashion analysis. They brought in two girls who have experience and studies in this field plus me, because I, quote, "make my own clothes," unquote."

"Good for you!"

Arianna was not entirely sure it was "good for her." Staring at spreadsheets for hours gave her headaches. After spending days staring at pictures and rating them, she now had to write a three-page document explaining the process and her insight on the coolness-measuring process. This was not a follow-up task she had expected. To be more precise: she struggled to write sentences that did not sound entirely idiotic. And she increasingly felt this was her final make-or-break assignment.

But still, as much as she doubted how much time was left for her at Cognit, for a whole bunch of people (that is, witches), she was known as "the Cognit girl." Only Diana referred to her as "Arianna" in the email threads she had read. One of the sisters she didn't know, Ashley, had even suggested that Charlotte contact her, the Cognit girl, for help on the PharmaThrice file: "Why don't you ask the Cognit girl?" the email said. No one had replied. Maybe Charlotte had texted or called Ashley to say, "We don't ask Arianna for help because she thinks one of us killed Marianna, Marie-Louise, and Christina."

Even Heather, who sat in the passenger seat just across from Arianna, had used the expression: "The Cognit girl was at my place last night; she is indeed interested by our sisters' murders, but she is definitely not the one who killed them." Well, thank you Heather... but using "the Cognit girl" still felt, somehow, dehumanizing.

The car exited the highway, rolled just a few hundred yards onto NY Road 52, and stopped at a Sunoco gas station. Brian got out to fill the tank; Heather opened her door. "You guys need anything? I'm going inside to buy a bottle of water."

"Same thing for me, please," said Alia, while Arianna answered that she didn't need anything. Heather exited the car; as soon as she had shut the door and left toward the convenience store, Arianna turned toward Alia. There was a lot to ask and very little time before Brian or Heather would be back.

Arianna's mouth opened, but no sound came out. In Alia's hand was a white piece of paper. Written on it, in sparkling gray marker: "Say nothing. They are listening."

24. A Luxurious (but Comfy) Country House

Large but intimate, rustic yet luxurious, full of warmth and comfort; the house where Arianna and the girls lodged was just perfect. There was more space and amenities than in most single houses, yet it felt natural to just hang around in leggings or sweatpants or pajamas. It was cozy.

The house was an actual log cabin. And the interior was full of animal skins, antique skis and sledges; there was even an ancient musket on the wall. Across the spacious living room, behind the large floor-to-ceiling windows was a massive balcony, where a more modern piece of furniture sat—a Jacuzzi.

Everyone was there: Diana, Melissa, Charlotte, and Sylvia, whom Diana had introduced to Arianna, even though she already knew quite much about her. She was a chartered accountant, specialized in business valuation, and was also an astrologer with expertise in Babylonian astrology. Heather and Alia also were in the living room at the moment, although they were staying in a neighboring cabin (where Brian was at the moment most likely conversing with Lionel). There was also Margaret, who was about to leave, a dark raincoat over her shoulders; she chatted with Melissa near the entryway.

In the center of the room was a large, low-polished hardwood coffee table that sat on a white bearskin carpet; on the table were multiple skeins of yarn, needles, printed patterns, project bags, cellphones, and wine glasses.

There were three couches around the table, all with different yet matching plaid patterns. Diana and Sylvia sat on one couch, chatting about a knitting podcast Arianna didn't know. On another couch was Charlotte, concentrating on a yellow, short-sleeved shirt with elaborated motifs. And on the third were Heather and Alia, who sorted skeins and dye bottles they would sell at their stand the next day at the fair. They seemed to be getting along very well and having fun together—it was heartwarming yet puzzling, since Alia had just told Arianna that she thought her mom was spying on her.

Unless, of course, Alia was careful about being on her best behavior to lower her mom's suspicions.

Arianna grabbed her glass of wine and went to sit beside Charlotte. She opened her bag and pulled her White Tiger socks project.

Ah! If her past self could see her, standing in this magnificent cabin with the friends she had made in New York City, attending Rhinebeck for the first time. Oh, the beautiful, but oh-so-thin veil that hid a terrible nightmare, in which a bloodthirsty witch would disembowel her, dry her internal organs, and pulverize them into a fine powder she would use for concocting potions and poisons…

"Disney princesses are the worst, Melissa. The damage they have caused is massive."

Arianna was pulled from her daydreaming by Diana's voice.

"Diana, what are you talking about?" asked Melissa.

"Their only redeeming quality is that many of them were taken from old folklore stories and legends that carry hidden truth and wisdom, and that their popularity in the modern age keeps these stories in the general subconscious mind. But as models, they are terrible!"

"These are stories for little girls—for kids. What are you talking about?"

"The princesses have no agency. They don't make many decisions; things happen to them. And when they act, it's while mimicking toxic male aggression."

"Diana being scholarly again," commented Sylvia.

"I know there is some truth in what you say," said Alia. She then turned toward Heather, smiling, "but Belle remains my favorite."

The pattern! Arianna had forgotten the pattern printout in her backpack, which was upstairs in her room. She jumped from her couch and climbed the stairs; at their upper end was a mezzanine hallway. On one side were the four bedrooms doors, while the other sides opened onto the living room and its giant windows. She stopped to stare down. Although worried, she did not feel in danger—immediate danger. Arianna just couldn't imagine any of these girls waking up in the middle of the night to slash her throat while she slept, or pouring poison in her coffee during breakfast. Maybe she was wrong. Maybe she would wake up in the middle of the night, tied up to her bed, all of them surrounding her, their faces hidden under heavy black hoods as they chanted incantations in a long-dead language…

Arianna entered her room. In the middle of it was a rustic wooden single bed with an orange-and-cream quilt. On top was her bag, her jacket, her shawl, and… a stuffed unicorn?

Arianna had not brought any stuffed unicorn. Arianna did not own a stuffed unicorn. There had been no stuffed unicorn on the bed, or anywhere in the room, when she had put her luggage there, not half an hour before.

Arianna grabbed the unicorn. Under it was a piece of paper, onto which was written, in shiny gray marker: "The ceremony is tomorrow at midnight. I'll stay here and cover for you. 41.961581, -73.909888. Don't forget my sharpener."

25. Sheep & Wool (& Angry People)

It was already 2 p.m. when Arianna passed the gate of the New York State Sheep and Wool Festival. She had intended to attend the exhibits in the morning, but Melissa had invited her to the spa: she had free passes. It would have been hard to decline. Arianna was tired, all the stress had worn her out, she was sore, her back hurt in multiple different spots... So now, instead of being sore from the stress, Arianna was sore from her massage. Yay, progress!

The fair was crowded. She headed straight for one of the site's buildings, where some of the vendors she wanted to meet would be located. As she walked toward the building, she passed enclosures full of sheep and also one with alpacas.

She reached the building and entered. Skeins, so many skeins! Skeins of all colors, hanging from displays, stacked high on counters, filling bins and boxes. People all over the place! (Women all over the place.)

One sign attracted her stare—one familiar sign: "Ben & Jesse's Knits."

Audrey was there, placing needles packs on a white wooden tray table. There were at least thirty yards separating Arianna from Audrey, all of them filled with festival-goers. Yet, Audrey lifted her eyes and stared straight at Arianna. And smiled.

Arianna reached the stand and waved at Audrey.

"Hello, Arianna. This is the first time you attend the festival if I remember correctly."

"It is."

"Are you enjoying it?"

"I have enjoyed the entire fifteen minutes that have transpired since I've passed the admission gate. Melissa offered me a free massage at the spa this morning, which I was not able to decline."

"I can understand."

"On another subject... Is Yuna here?"

"She is. At the moment she is shopping for raw wool. Do you want to talk to her?"

"Audrey... Yuna broke in my apartment the other day."

"Yuna entered your apartment without your consent?"

"Yes."

"And I suppose you had a security camera inside that caught her?"

"No. I saw her. I heard her going down the emergency stairs and I saw her run into the alley. She was facing the opposite direction as she ran but, as you know, she has distinctive hair and—"

"When did it happen?"

"Last week."

"And you did not call the police? And you waited a week to tell me, her employer?"

"Audrey... I don't have any proof that she did it."

"No, but I believe you. And if I ask Yuna she will admit the truth. Did she take anything from you?"

"No. I'm pretty sure she did not."

"You mean she did not find what she was looking for. Arianna, Yuna is my student and my employee. There will be consequences for her

KNITTING DEATH

actions. Now, I will ask you a question: if you had the opportunity to look into Yuna's room with only a very low chance of getting caught, would you do it?"

"Well, the fact is that I did not break into her place. Your question is very hypothetical!"

"Yet the right answer to my hypothetical question is very simple: a firm 'no!' Yuna and you are caught with the same obsession. I will repeat what I have, more than once, told both of you: this is dangerous.

"Arianna, I don't know which specific video you are referring to, but your description of it sounds like it is indeed me that is in it. What is it that bothers you? You already knew that I practiced martial arts."

"In this vid, you break a large brick by hitting it with your bare hands."

"This comes with proper training, discipline, and concentration. If you are curious, you should come to the dojo."

"Maybe I should do that!"

Arianna left, annoyed. Why had she talked about Yuna's break-in? It had not been her plan. She walked fast, passing much slower visitors, with no destination in mind. She then noticed a familiar figure. Margaret. She was heading in her direction. Arianna slowed down and said "Hi," but Margaret passed and continued on her way, without acknowledging her presence.

Arianna was shocked. It was virtually impossible that Margaret had not noticed her; there were many people, but the crowd was not dense, and they had been nearly face to face, with only a few feet between them.

"Well, fuck you, old cunt!" said Arianna, not especially loud, but enough that an old lady nearby looked at her, a disapproving frown on her wrinkled face.

It's at this moment that Arianna decided to head back for the house to load up on free food and relax. This would be a long night: she might as well sleep.

26. Maze, Fire, Blood

"Text me if you change your mind! Bye!"

Melissa had tried to convince Arianna to visit a local pub with her. All the "sisters" had disappeared toward various destinations.

"My parents came over and we're having dinner in Kingston," said Diana.

"This lady will show me how to use a waving mill," Sylvia had said.

As for Charlotte, Arianna had not seen her since the previous day. It looked like Alia might be right about the ceremony.

Arianna had told Melissa she had to work. It was a plausible lie. And the echoes she heard from the big living room downstairs indicated that Melissa still was going out, despite not having anyone to go with her.

The main door shut. Arianna was now alone in the log cabin; it was time to go. She already had on her sports cargo pants and a dark wool sweater; she put on her thermal vest, laced her hiking boots, grabbed her backpack, and headed out.

The location corresponding to the coordinates that Alia had supplied was located 2.5 miles away, according to Google Maps. While most of the journey would be on country roads, the destination point was located right in the middle of the forest. She would have to find her way there, in the dark…

** **

...well, not so dark. The moon was full, probably not a coincidence considering the witches' appetite for the Babylonian lunar calendar. If the sky remained clear, maybe Arianna would make her way through the forest without having to use her flashlight, which was more likely to notify the witches about her presence than help her find her way in the woods.

The air was chilly yet dry; it did not feel too cold. No cars drove past as Arianna walked on Old Post Road, a narrow country road mostly flanked by open fields. After a bit longer than half an hour, she reached a wooded area. Arianna looked at her phone; it would soon be time to charge headfirst into the forest.

Looking around, she saw that the ditch beside the road forked, with one branch going in the general direction of her objective. She jumped in with both feet, expecting to land in a foot of water or, worse, break her ankle on a rock. Instead, her feet dug a little in the mud; it appeared the ditch would be practical.

She followed the ditch as it climbed toward the forest in a nearly straight line. Something seemed to block the ditch. Approaching the object, Arianna recognized the circular concrete end of a culvert. She climbed out of the ditch; there was a trail, with two tire tracks. The location would be to her right, not too far. From now on she would have to be careful. Indeed, after a few yards, she heard noises. Was there a party nearby? She looked at her phone: it was coming from the coordinates' location.

While careful and alert, Arianna maintained a good pace. The voices were still far enough that no one would hear her if she rustled some dead leaves or crunched on a dry twig.

The trail was coming into a clearing. Arianna could distinguish the light was from a bonfire, and the voices became louder.

They were singing. Female voices, singing in unison. Arianna could not distinguish any lyrics. While not joyous, it wasn't creepy either. It did, however, made Arianna's heartbeat accelerate greatly.

She still could go back... But went forward instead. She now distinguished the fire, with silhouettes dancing around. The song lyrics still did not make sense. It was not English, not German, not Spanish... Okay, it WAS starting to creep out Arianna a little. And the dance. It looked wild, with many gestures and jumps and long hair flying...

"Ai! Ai! Aaaaiaaaa!"

Diana. That was Diana's voice.

There was something beside the fire... Well, not beside, but in the clearing, much closer to Arianna than the fire. A building? A barn? A shack?

Arianna veered to her right and walked until the building was between her and the fire. She then bolted forward. She stopped a few yards from the building; it was, indeed, an old wooden shed. With an old wooden door. Arianna approached as silently as she could and pressed her ear on the wall. Nothing. No noise, but many smells: smoke and... something nasty. Something that stunk.

Arianna grabbed the door's handle and pulled. It opened without much noise. A fire in a rock fire pit, with a large cast-iron cauldron suspended above. Arianna was at the right place, no doubt about it.

She approached the cauldron. The rancid smell became much more intense.

A noise! Behind! Arianna was sure there was absolutely no one—but here was Margaret. With a Bat Wing.

KNITTING DEATH

It was not the sophisticated lady Arianna knew. Instead of makeup, Margaret's face was covered with fingerpainted lines in red and black.

"You and that hippie girl!" Margaret shouted.

In her right hand, next to her hip, a knife. A very long knife.

"Didn't your parents tell you it was impolite to rub your nose in other people's business?"

Margaret approached, slowly, while shaking the knife. It was not an ordinary knife; the blade had many curves, like a snake slithering on the ground.

"Don't you have enough work at your job as it is? Not only are you after me, but you do it for free! Oh, I know you don't work for anyone! No one pushed your CV on top of the file. It's the Cognit AI that chose you! Well, they should adjust the code to reject nosy, sneaky, stupid girls like you! What do you think—that I'd let you ruin all my plans?"

Arianna was boxed in; to her left was the table, to her right the cabin's wall, and behind was the boiling cauldron and fire. In front of her: a mad, angry woman who wielded a strange, but obviously well-sharpened dagger.

"Haven't you understood by now that I'm quite powerful and that just with the snap of a finger I can end your miserable and irrelevant life? Well, it's too late now! You will die!"

Margaret lifted the dagger high above her head, with both hands, the tip pointed forward, toward Arianna.

And then she froze. Margaret looked down. In her abdomen was a US size 50 knitting needle. Arianna let go of the needle and recoiled. Margaret tilted to her left, knocked the cauldron over, and fell into the fire pit.

27. Sabbath & Beyond

Diana rubbed Arianna's right hand with a wet towel, removing the last traces of Margaret's blood. The flow of tears from her eyes had dried up, but she still sobbed. There was lots of red and black (mixed with dried tears) in Diana's face—was it dirt or random paint? Arianna couldn't tell.

"I'm okay, Diana. I'm not hurt," said Arianna, who was sitting on the bathroom counter.

"You nearly got killed. I knew she was dangerous. I knew she was dangerous *for you*." Diana's voice was on the edge of breaking again.

"You protected me, Diana. I'm not sure about the Photoshop you made of my dad as a state police chief, but it did the job."

Diana dropped Arianna's hand and stared at her, her eyes wide with surprise. "Wait, you know about the false profile I made of your dad? Who told you?"

Arianna smiled. "No one. I stole Margaret's computer."

"Oh my God. No wonder she wanted to kill you. Where did—" Diana paused mid-sentence, kept silent for a few seconds, and shouted: "Westchester!"

"Yep."

"And Nick cracked her password."

"Yes. It's Alia who told us the location of her room in the mansion. We had to strike fast before Yuna could get hold of it."

Again, joy left Diana's face. "That was reckless and dangerous."

KNITTING DEATH

Arianna got down from the bathroom counter and looked straight at Diana. "Yes, but that's how I was able to peek into her emails, which is where I learned, among other things, that you were covering me. Still, I don't understand why you just didn't tell me it was her who had killed Marie-Louise and Marianna. And maybe Christina, too. That would have been easier for everyone."

"At first, I just didn't know. It never occurred to me that the Rev... Margaret could even consider killing anyone, let alone two sisters. She definitely had turned bitter, angry, and mean, but murderous is not something I would have added to the list. As you probably grasped while reading through her emails, she made those two horrible murders she'd committed look like an outside attack on our coven. And I believed her... at first. At some point, her paranoia got the best of her... she couldn't help herself but to allude that a similar fate to those of Mariana and Marie-Louise awaited us if she suspected our loyalties. Charlotte and I trod carefully to—

Screams and shouts interrupted Diana. They came from the living room. Diana opened the bathroom door and exited, followed by Arianna. Everyone was there: Heather, Charlotte, Audrey, and Yuna.

And a woman, tall and serious, with wide, big brown eyes, a flawless chocolate milk skin and curly jet-black hair.

The Mother Superior.

To whom Yuna shouted, "You really think we'll believe that you tried to prevent Margaret from hurting Arianna? You're her boss; you must be at least as bad as she is—"

"Stop it, Yuna," interrupted Audrey. "The Mother Superior obviously doesn't condone Margaret's behavior. I'd even say the only reason Mother Superior appeared among us tonight was to prevent her from causing more mayhem and suffering that she already has done."

"Mother Margaret steered away from the path," said the Mother Superior. "Sister Diana and Sister Charlotte informed me that they suspected she was behind the death of two coven-mates. It does appear they were right. I also found that this coven committed many other transgressions to our code under her guidance."

"Well, what do you intend to do about it?" shouted Yuna.

The Mother Superior eyes opened up slightly more. She stared directly into Yuna—in a rather frightening way, Arianna thought. "You mean, what will you do? This is Audrey's coven now."

For a moment, Yuna looked as if she would recoil in fear. But suddenly, anger filled her face. "Audrey is not a witch!"

A faint smile appeared on the Mother Superior's face and her eyes disengaged from Yuna; she looked at Audrey instead. "Mother Audrey has not used our nomenclature, nor has she followed our traditions—until now. Oh, she is very reluctant to take over the plundering machine this coven has been turned into. And this is exactly why it has to be her that does it. Which, I'm afraid, was the sisters' plan all along," she said, glancing first at Charlotte, then at Diana.

Audrey intervened. "Diana, that you brought this whole ordeal to me by frequenting my cafe and bringing Margaret there, I can accept—I am equipped for such a face-off and you obviously needed help from the outside. But the risk you put upon Arianna is unacceptable!"

"Ah," said Charlotte as she rose from her couch. "Unacceptable to you but not to her. The pressure Arianna put upon Margaret was just a big enough distraction to help us secure most assets controlled by the coven away from her. Also, we did make precautions to protect Arianna. We made a false profile of Arianna's dad. Margaret thought he was a high-level officer in the Ohio state police."

"Oh please!" shouted Yuna, "That false profile of yours was so persuasive that Margaret came inches from slicing Arianna's throat with that snake knife! And all that so that your coven could... control assets? Or whatever that means."

"My coven? You mean, our coven, Sister Yuna. A coven whose wealth lies in the determination, dedication, skill, and talent of its coven-mates. And which also happens to control $180.1 million in assets of various types."

Charlotte paused, but Yuna did not say anything. The expression on her face said that she had a hard time processing all the new information thrown at her. Arianna was pretty sure her own faced looked exactly the same as Yuna's.

Charlotte went on. "Well, Sister Yuna, I was told that you had shown some curiosity for our range of professional occupations, so why don't you take a shot at managing the coven's war chest? You see, Diana and I have had our dose of balancing numbers, and we'd rather focus our energy on learning from our new..."

Charlotte's voice trailed off and she suddenly looked down toward the floor. Arianna did not understand why, until she realized that the Reverend Mother was staring at Charlotte with (again) wide, frightening eyes. She then turned toward Audrey. "A plundering machine, as I said. I will go now."

The Mother Superior silently moved toward the main door. Yuna looked at Audrey, and while no words left her mouth, her expression clearly said, "Is all of this real"? Audrey's resigned expression made Arianna think it mostly was.

Charlotte still stared at the ground. She looked like a regretful child who had been scolded. That made quite the contrast with her usual attitude, she who was always teasing and mocking and above everything. This Mother Superior definitely had an effect on people...

"Mother Superior!" Arianna suddenly shouted.

Everyone in the room turned their gaze toward Arianna, included the Mother Superior, who was about to exit through the main door.

"You came to my office. You did not have a visitor's pass. You used a room that was reserved. The people who were supposed to be in this room stood in the hallway, looking idle, confused, and scared. What happened there?"

"I wanted to talk to you in a quiet place. So I told them to get out of the room—and to call you."

Before Arianna could say that her response was in no way an answer to her question, Yuna said, "She used the Voice! That's another witch trick! This is what Margaret used to drive all these girls crazy!"

The Mother Superior said: "Margaret's misuse of this ancient art, especially against her own coven-mates, has more to do with my presence here than her wild banditry in the financial realm. Again, Mother Audrey has significant resources to help those lost sisters heal, resources which I am sure will prove to be much more potent than what passes for medicine nowadays. I suggest that you assist her in this endeavor; it would help you regain focus and self-control, which the misadventures of the past months seem to have strained."

Yuna sent a quick glance to Audrey—and then nothing. She kept silent. It looked like the Mother Superior had touched upon a subject that had been already discussed between them.

Still, Arianna still was waiting for an answer to her question. It seemed quite clear for everyone in the room, but not to her.

"Mother Superior. This... Voice thing. Is this what you did when you tried to make me sit in this conference room? I mean, I felt a strong urge to sit, but—"

Diana interrupted Arianna. "Tried to make you sit? Arianna, are you saying that you resisted the Mother Superior's voice?"

"She did," answered the Mother Superior. "This was rather impressive of... Sister Arianna."

Epilogue

Arianna practiced breakfalls on a bare, cold concrete floor while in the middle of a four-day fast. Arianna drank potions made with mandrake and henbane and mushrooms. Arianna saw things after drinking potions made with mandrake and henbane and mushrooms. While spending the night more or less alone in a dense forest.

Those experiences, practices, intoxications—that is, her initiation to witchcraft—were brutal and harrying. Yet she was doing well, quite well according to Mother Audrey and the more senior sisters.

There was one branch of witchcraft, however, where Arianna didn't do so well.

Money Magic.

As far as Arianna was concerned, Money Magic was just accounting and management and tax, all things that Arianna already had already touched upon (as opposed to kicking stuffed dummies hung by a rope to a tree branch while fasting and ingesting hallucinogens).

She had, after all, a degree in business and a job in business consulting. So she had notions about accounting and management and tax.

She also had an upper-five-figure pile of college and credit cart debt to manage while living in New York City on the salary of a Cognit associate. That was her first challenge. Her first problem to solve before she would be allowed anywhere near the coven's fabulous war chest.

"Melissa will be good at this. I think she's good with money", said Arianna.

"Her family is from Hong Kong. Maybe money is natural. Spending the night outside in a cold forest might be less so. Hopefully, we'll see soon."

"Why not now?"

"She is being vetted."

"And I'm not?"

"You have been. It takes longer with Melissa – Hong Kong has a lot of witches. We just are careful about infiltrations. But we've looked extensively into her background and it appears she's in the clear. By the end of the month, we should be good to have a conversation with her."

"Diana," said Arianna, "the two other girls, Marianna and Marie-Louise… they lived a life of luxury. Apartments in the Upper West End, sailing trips down the coast to Florida, brand-name clothes. You don't. Why?"

"I… I thought…" Diana quickly shoved a tear under her left eye with her right index finger. "I felt it was dangerous to burn through the coven's funds. The Rev… Margaret said that luxury items, activities, and apartments were investments worth considering for some projects, some approaches to business. Marianna and Marie-Louise went for it, but I tread much more carefully… Somehow, I always knew she could be dangerous. I've always tried to keep my net contribution to the coven in the green."

KNITTING DEATH

"One last thing... where is your Bat Wing?"

Diana smiled.

"Oh! Arianna. I'll start knitting my Bat Wing with you. As soon as Melissa is with us!"

JEAN K. TAMER

Printed in Dunstable, United Kingdom